Born

Joe Cannon

YELLOW BRICK PUBLISHERS

Second Edition 1993

Published by :

YELLOW BRICK PUBLISHERS
2 LONSDALE ROAD
QUEENS PARK
LONDON
NW6 6RD

IBSN 0 9520560 1 1

Cover printed and bound by Lonsdale Press Ltd, London NW6

For Ellen, whose love and devotion made this book possible.

Foreword

This book tells the story of Joey Bello, a hard man and a criminal with twenty years of porridge under his belt.

Jailbreaks, gangland feuds, armed robbery, sex and murder are the ingredients of a tale which pulls no punches. The brutality and violence of the underworld, both at home and abroad, are depicted in stark realism.

Though this novel is founded on fact, certain characters and episodes are fictitious. Only when reference is made to actual happenings are real names and places mentioned.

The Author
London 1988

Contents

1. Born Rotten

He was 'dangerous', a hard man with a ready pair of fists and a shooter tucked into his belt, born and brought up in Notting Dale which has more villains to the square mile than any other manor in London.

Among his schoolmates were some famous names in the sports field who rose from their slum beginnings to carve out respectable lives. So where did Joey Bello go wrong?

People who knew him say he was simply born rotten, just as surely as if he had been given a stocking mask and a sawn-off shotgun as a christening present.

His early environment did not mould his character. Had he lived in the posh district of Holland Park he would have turned out to be a cad and a bounder. As it was, Notting Dale supplied the accent and the education (or lack of it) and he was on his way to becoming a thief and a villain.

Notting Dale lies adjacent to Notting Hill, which is at the arsehole end of the Bayswater Road. The council flat where he lived with his parents plus six brothers and four sisters was part of an old house which had gone to rack and ruin. The family daily risked life and limb as they trod the decaying stairway and rotten floorboards. He was only a babe-in-arms and his Ma had to watch her step when she was carrying him around.

He was three years old when the Second World War broke out. It coincided with his family removing to a new home in Avondale Park Gardens, which was altogether more suitable for a large family. There was a yard at the rear and a large open space at the front where the kids could play in fine weather. At a later stage in the war the Council provided them with a bonus in the shape of a large iron-framed cage, which was erected in the front room and was designed to protect them in case the house fell down. The younger end of the family made full use of it as an Aladdin's cave, a pirate den or a refuge from some parental anger. An area which attracted their childish curiosity was the underground shelter which had been constructed in the middle of the large open space in front of the houses. It was intended to provide an alternative to being flattened inside a metal cage. His mother didn't go a lot on either of these safeguards, vowing that no bleeding Hitler was going to send her down holes in the ground when she had her washing and mending and God knows what else to do. Yet every time the air-raid warning sounded she would gather her kids around her and shepherd them down to the shelter.

The war had been going on for a couple of years when the time came for Joey to begin his schooling. He didn't go a bundle on the State's efforts to prepare him for a useful life as a responsible member of society. In his childish eyes the teachers were a terrifying bunch of ogres, handing out clips round the earhole and sketchy instruction in the three R's (Reading, Riting and Rithmetic) in approximately equal proportions. He didn't care much for the discipline either, and as a result spent more time roaming the streets with his mates than he spent in the classroom. It was called 'playing the wag', going to school in the morning, getting marked in, then disappearing for the rest of the day. There was plenty to occupy their time. High on the list of out-of-school activities was dodging the School Board inspector, who roamed the streets looking for truants. He had no chance really. Hunting a mob of fleet-footed kids who knew every alley and side-street like the palms of their hands was no job for a middle-aged geezer with a C3 Army medical rating.

Some afternoons were spent at the local cinema. They clubbed together for one of them to pay for admission. The lucky one would choose a suitable moment, usually the fortissimo part of a cowboy picture, to open one of the emergency exits and let the rest in. Once they were inside the ushers were no problem, since they were elderly men or women who had no wish to tangle with a gang of tough kids. On hot summer days the temptation to go swimming was almost irresistible, but it was out of the question. The baths in Lancaster Road also housed the public washing facilities which were regularly used by their mothers. Apart from this, a further deterrent was the daily presence of a female dragon known as Nitty Norah, the champion de-louser of Notting Dale.

This lady had the most unappetising job you could imagine. Groups of kids, about twenty or thirty at a time, were marched to the baths from the local schools. The not-too-tender hands of Nitty Norah rubbed a foul-smelling fluid into their scalps, after which a fine-toothed metal comb was painfully raked through the wet locks. Norah would collect a fine haul of lice which she surveyed with the same sort of pride as a Scottish laird would regard the bag after a good shoot.

There were compensations in Joey's life at school which went a long way towards making it tolerable. On days when physical training was on the curriculum, Joey was always among those present. The reason was that boxing instruction was part of the programme, and he had discovered in himself a talent in, and a liking for, the noble art of self-defence. This was not surprising. His father had been a well-known bare-knuckle fighter, his brother Bill was a promising amateur who was later to turn pro and had had over two hundred fights. His uncle Jim was a boxing referee and his other brothers were very handy with their dukes. At St Francis', his first school, he began to learn the rudiments with a little help from his Dad, who used the backyard as a training ground.

It was in the nature of things that he should be expelled from St Francis', whose Headmaster expressed the opinion that a zoo would be a more fitting place for his further education. He didn't go to a zoo but to another school on the manor. The law insisted, his parents had to agree or be prosecuted, so he enrolled at St Johns'. This place was very similar to St Francis', and he hated it just as much. His life became a constant battle against authority, a situation which was not made any better by the fact that his home was within a stone's throw of the nick in Sirdar Road, one of the two stations in B Division of the Metropolitan Police. The other station was a Victorian building at the corner of Ladbroke Road and Ladbroke Grove, not far from Holland Park tube. He was to become intimately acquainted with the interiors of both these places, but that lay in the future. At the time he was aware of the proximity of the Old Bill, which hampered his activities to some extent.

Shortly after his ninth birthday the war in Europe ended. He was now an accomplished little tea-leaf, a pint-sized terror who couldn't be left alone with anything of value unless it was nailed down. Even then he would find some way of capturing it. He had been at it for a long time, nicking lead from bombed buildings, for which there was a ready sale and no questions asked, and either alone or mob-handed making raids on the local shops.

He was only caught once, when he teamed up with a kid called Hooker to do some shops in the area. The way they worked was that one of them would distract the attention of the shopkeeper while the other crept in below counter level and nicked whatever was handy. They would then share out the loot in a nearby air-raid shelter which they used as headquarters. The scheme was a huge success until one day as they sat in the shelter gorging themselves on sherbet dips and toffees, they were surprised by one of their shopkeeper victims along with their respective fathers.

There was no chance of putting in a decent plea as their mouths were full of evidence, nor did the situation lend itself to peaceful discussion. Joey's old man took off his belt and gave him a good thrashing, Hooker's father performed likewise with his son, and there the matter ended. The hidings didn't deter them. They were back in business the next day.

It was round about that time that he collected his first black eye. He was very much king of the kids on the manor with a reputation as a battler, so he didn't take kindly to anyone who questioned his authority. He got into an argument with one of the local girls, a right tomboy who ran around with the boys, played football with them and was the first Woman's Libber in his experience. She slung Joey a right-hander which made him see stars. He was so shocked that he forgot to hit her back. By the evening, when he arrived home, the eye had developed into a real beauty, a classic shiner which spread the colours of the rainbow over half his face. Naturally his old man wanted to know how he had come by this spectacular disfigurement, so he went into a song-and-dance about an attack by a gang of kids from the Portobello Road. His sister Doreen put the kybosh on that little romance.

'It was Joanie Farmer did it, Dad,' she said. 'I saw her.'

Joey had to take a lot of stick from the family over that caper.

His brother Bill was very scornful. 'Fancy letting yourself get belted by a Judy,' he said, and carted Joey off to the Rugby Club in Walmer Road, where he handed him over to the warden with instructions to give Joey some special coaching in self-defence 'in case he was attacked by any more girls'.

*

The Rugby Club was a new experience for Joey. Its full title was the Rugby School Club. It had been started some years previously by the boys of Rugby public school as part of their social service work. The idea behind the project was to get poor kids off the streets and into an environment where they could be given every encouragement to become useful citizens. The warden was a chap called Jim Lane, a dedicated youth worker.

Joey enrolled as a member of the club and turned up more or less regularly for three years. The main attraction of the place for Joey was the excellent boxing instruction, of which he took full advantage. In the inter-club contests in the London Federation of Boys' Clubs he picked up a few cups and medals in his weight class which was, believe it or not, five stones and one and a half pounds.

His boxing skills improved as a result of his association with the club, but one couldn't say the same for his character. St Johns' school saw less and less of Joey Bello which didn't seem to bother them unduly, and he spent a lot of time at the local markets helping the barrow boys and earning a few bob. Yet the most fruitful source of income lay in the derelict buildings and their rich store of lead and zinc.

Unfortunately there's always a fly in the ointment. Joey's particular fly was the Old Bill who, now that the war was over, were able to devote more time to the prevention of felony which was a way of life for most of the population of Notting Dale. He missed many a good tickle because of their increased watchfulness. Their suspicions were quite naturally aroused by the sight of a ragged-arsed nipper carrying a heavy sack through the streets en route to the nearest scrapyard. As a consequence he was obliged to find other targets for his thieving. Such targets were not hard to discover. Notting Dale was a poor area where the residents showed no great eagerness to pay their bills. On the other side of the picture were the gas and electricity undertakings whose public services did not include the provision of free lighting and heating. Hence, every house in the district was equipped with pre-payment meters whose coin-boxes yielded a rich harvest of bobs and pennies to the enterprising thief.

The modus operandum was simple. The front doors of the houses were furnished with Yale locks, but the majority of the inhabitants saw no reason to spend good money on duplicate keys when a single key suspended from a length of string through the letter box served the same purpose. So it was just a matter of fishing out the key, nipping inside, forcing the fragile locks on the coin-boxes and clearing out the contents.

Another caper which paid dividends was the sell-back. Joey would climb over the fence at the rear of a scrapyard, sort out some portable gear and then take it round the front and sell it to the dealer, who had no idea that he was buying his own property. After all, one piece of lead pipe looks very much like another. Percy Horn, the largest scrap metal dealer on the manor, was a frequent victim. He still managed to make a fortune.

The end result of Joey's thieving was that he always had ample supplies of cash money. His greatest problem was concealing it from the family, for in his home there was little privacy. Luckily his old man was out all day on his job as a meter inspector, which he had held for thirty years, and his Mum worked mornings as an office cleaner. His brothers and sisters, however, were in and out of the house at all hours. To lessen the risk of discovery he used more than one hiding place for his ill-gotten gains.

The bedroom which he shared with his brothers was his first choice as a safe deposit. He levered up a floorboard in one corner of the room and slipped a roll of notes into the cavity. His second choice was the loft at the top of the house, which was full of old furniture and the discarded bric-a-brac of a large family. There were so many hidey-holes that he could take his pick, which he did, varying the locations from time to time. The bulk of the money he stuffed into a cocoa tin with a close-fitting lid, which he buried in the back garden.

It was just as well that he took the precaution of dividing the loot, because one day his Mum decided to give the bedroom a turn-out. She noticed the loose floorboard, took a look under it and found the wages. When Joey came in that evening his father was sitting in the living room with the evidence spread out on the table in front of him.

'What's this, Joey,' he said as his son walked in the door.

'Dunno, Dad,' Joey said. His confession of ignorance earned him a clip round the ear.

'It's money, you thieving little bleeder,' said Dad. 'Where did you get it?'

Joey turned on the waterworks. There's nothing like a few tears for softening a parent's heart.

'I don't know nothing about it, Dad,' Joey sobbed. 'It don't belong to me.'

He stuck to his story. Dad questioned Joey's brother Peter, who also knew nothing. Joey learned then his first lesson in law, that suspicion is one thing but proof is another. Joey didn't know what happened to the money but he reckoned that Mum copped for the lot, because the table was that much richer for a few days. In a way Joey was rather proud to contribute to the family budget even in a roundabout way. As for the loss of the cash, it didn't mean a thing. There was plenty more in the loft and the garden, so he didn't go short.

Looking back over his life, Joey could honestly say that he had never been really concerned over money, principally because he had always had enough of the comodity, and neither greed nor penury drove him to crime. As to his violent tendencies, when he was boxing as a kid he was not content to obey the rules. When the bell went he was conscious only of a desire to destroy the other fellow, to beat him into the ground. It was a feeling in him over which he had no control, and it was the same when he grew up. If it was him or the other chap for it, then the other had to lose.

He was hooked on boxing at a very early age, influenced to a large extent by his elder brothers, but brother Bill was his hero. He did his training in a makeshift gym behind a barber's shop in Princedale Road. Joey often went along to see him work out. It was magic. He could still smell the sharp odour of embrocation and stale sweat which contrasted oddly with the perfumes drifting in from the barber's shop, and retained vivid mental pictures of the gloved gladiators knocking hell out of each other, grunting and groaning and scuffling their feet on the resined canvas.

He watched points carefully, because he had his eyes set on a career as a professional fighter. He soon caught on to the fact that a pro is not inhibited by sticking too close to the Queensberry rules. His brother Bill fought in boxing booths and local venues where the refereeing was not too strict and the audience bayed for blood. He knew all the tricks of the business, pulling an opponent on to the punch, treading on the toes, going in with the head down and the shoulder under the chin, popping the thumb in the eye and so on. He began to use these tricks at the Rugby Club, and soon became known as a dirty fighter, which didn't bother him at all so long as he came out on top.

On one occasion he came across a kid who knew as much about the dirty trick end of the business as he did. They mauled each other for a couple of rounds, but in the third Joey got fed up and steamed in with his head down, butting the other kid in the face. The instructor stopped the bout on the spot and gave him a rucking, which did no damage to Joey's pride. It didn't mend his opponent's broken hooter either.

Sometimes he would go along with Bill to Lime Grove, a well-known venue which had seen the debut of many a budding champion. Alf Mancini, of the famous boxing family, handled most of the promotions there. Joey's uncle was on the panel of referees. Lime Grove was only a couple of miles down the road from Notting Dale, and whenever Bill was performing he pulled a good crowd from the fight fans on the manor.

The events at Lime Grove were conducted according to the rules of the British Boxing Board of Control and all the fighters and their managers were licenced, so Joey had no chance of slipping into Bill's corner as sponge man, a job he had often done in less proper surroundings. All the same he got as close to the ring as possible and shouted and yelled advice to the fighters. At times like these Joey felt he was really living.

There were some odd characters knocking round the Dale when Joey was a kid, old lags who remembered the days when the Old Bill never ventured into Bangor Street after dark, eccentrics of all shapes, sizes and sexes who found the lure of the Portobello Road irresistible and many others who lent colour to the surroundings.

Father George was a character who came to the Dale just after the end of the war. He was anything but the conventional Roman Catholic priest, in fact in his biography he confessed that he was not cut out for the job. He was a great sportsman, mad keen on cricket and boxing, and one of his first acts was to start a boy's club, using the premises of St Francis' school in the evenings.

He was very friendly with Joey's brother Nobby and they often came back home together for a bite to eat after an evening at one of the local pubs. All the family liked him, probably because he didn't put on any airs and graces. On one of his visits he had a few words with young Joey, asking him what he wanted to be when he grew up. It shook him when Joey said he was going to be the toughest of the tough in London.

One of the reasons he found favour with the residents of the Dale was because he had plenty of bottle. When it came to it he wasn't afraid of having a go, as was proved when a certain firm connected with Billy Hill came to the Warwick Castle looking for Big Ginger. There had been some aggro at Sandown Park races and Ginger was marked down for a bit of treatment.

The Warwick Castle was owned by Ruby, a notorious ex-jewel thief who had once made a well-publicised escape from Dartmoor. The pub was patronised almost exclusively by the villains of the Dale, and Ginger had considerable support among them. On this particular night some of the hounds were all tooled-up in readiness for a full-scale battle.

Someone had tipped off the Reverend Father and, when the firm came on the scene, he was standing at the bar waiting for them. What he said nobody knew, though many garbled reports were circulated later, but it ended with the firm marching out of the pub without seeing to Ginger or anyone else. It transpired that the whole thing would have fizzled out in any event, but Father George was not to know that when he fronted the gang.

Joey was on his third school, Addison Road Secondary Modern which, unlike St Francis' and St Johns', was co-educational. He wasn't much into the girl scene, regarding them as inferior beings fit only for an occasional groping in some quiet doorway or fumbling attacks on their virtue in the dark privacy of a bombed building. Not that the female presence at Addison drove him to play the wag increasingly. He was a natural-born truant.

From the academic point of view he wasn't all that bright. Indeed at the age of fourteen his handwriting was deplorable, he could do simple addition and subtraction and the sum total of his knowledge in other subjects could be written in large letters on the back of a postage stamp. Nevertheless, he could estimated to a penny the value of a lump of lead piping and he knew at any time the exact value of the sums hidden in his various safe deposits.

In spite of what was an excellent cash flow situation, a source of constant irritation was that he could not spend his money on such obvious adornments as clothes and jewellery. While some of his older mates strutted about in the latest fashions, he had to be content with cast-offs from his brothers, jerseys with holes in the elbows, ragged trousers with patches in the arse and shoes which had been cobbled so often that very little of the original leather was left. He only had one consolation. He was able to indulge his appetite for sweets and purchase the loyalty of other kids with showers of bullseyes, peppermint chocs, hundreds and thousands, gob-stoppers, jelly babies and the like.

Inevitably the day came when he was caught bang to rights on a bomb site with a pile of lead neatly packed and ready to be carried away. He appeared before a juvenile court by way of the nick in Sirdar Road and copped for twelve months probation, which didn't hurt as much as the belting his old man gave him. Probation was a bind. He had to report to the probation officer once a week, who kept in close touch with his school, which limited Joey's activities to a great extent. He didn't feel any social stigma, because most of the other kids on the manor were in the same boat.

The most important by-product of Joey's trouble with the Old Bill was the effect on his finances. His card was marked at the local nick and the copper on the beat knew him by sight, so he had to be extra careful. With no money coming in and quite a bit going out to support his life-style, it wasn't long before he was down to his last couple of pounds. He decided to try his luck on the neighbouring manor of Paddington where he wasn't known.

Opening up new fields may work in some businesses. It didn't work in Joey's. In the Dale he was among friends. Paddington was alien territory where he was on his own against some tough competition. It wasn't long before he was nicked, and this time the juvenile court wasn't so lenient. They decided that what was needed to bring Joey back on the straight and narrow was a spell at an attendance centre, which was how he came to be introduced to Peel House.

The attendance centre scheme for young offenders was a Home Office idea designed in theory to rehabilitate teenage criminals through work and discipline. What happened in practice was that Joey reported to Peel House every week and spent a couple of hours scrubbing floors under the casual supervision of a staff who couldn't have cared less what he did so long as they collected their wages.

Joey was now a fully paid up member of the Juvenile Crime Club and as such had a certain status in the Dale. The young kids looked up to him as a professional while his equals, fellow floor-scrubbers, tried to rope him in on any villainy that was afoot. In the result Joey was as surely a candidate for Borstal as if he had his name put down at birth.

It was a relief when he was able to opt out of the State educational system and leave Addison Road Secondary Modern. He was given a written reference by the headmaster, in which he did his best to conceal his opinion of Joey under a mass of flowery prose. With a fixed determinaton to avoid any form of work which did not return high wages for the least possible effort, he fell into screwing (not the sexual variety) and, under the expert tuition of his seniors, soon became highly skilled in the art of breaking and entering.

For a time everything in the garden was lovely. He kidded his Mum and Dad that he was working on the barrows, made regular contributions to the family budget and was thus in a position to indulge in the luxury of new clothes in place of the hand-me-downs that he had been obliged to wear. He went screwing practically every night, either alone or with one of his pals, and was so successful that he began to believe that he had a charmed life. He swaggered around the Dale in his new gear, spending money as though it came out of a tap and, as he now sees clearly, attracting the attention of the Old Bill, who had him marked down for treatment when the opportunity arose.

They had their chance before long. He set out one night to do a snouter's in Shepherd's Bush, wearing the proper gear of dark sweater and trousers, rubber-soled shoes and black gloves. What he didn't know as he flitted through the back streets was that he was being followed by a pair of CID men.

He went in about eleven o'clock. The door was a doddle and, since he had cased the joint thoroughly, he knew exactly where to put his hands on the cash. He had it in his pocket, about a couple of hundred notes, when the Old Bill jumped him and he was caught bang to rights.

This would have been an ordinary nicking but for one important difference. He was carrying a .22 Browning automatic tucked into the waistband of his trousers, a foolish touch of bravado which was totally unnecessary. He had bought the weapon for a few quid from a kid who had nicked it from his elder brother. There had been a full clip in the gun when he got it, but he had fired off four rounds in a quiet part of the Wormwood Scrubs.

When the Old Bill came across the shooter in the course of giving him a rub-down, it was like a scene from the Sweeney. The detective constable extracted the gun and held it out for inspection by the detective sergeant.

'We've got a real desperate villain here, Sarge,' he said.

The DS took the shooter and slipped out the clip. He had handled guns before and he made that obvious.

'One up the spout, eh? All ready to shoot some poor innocent citizen. This should get you about ten years, chummy,' he said.

Joey kept his mouth shut. There wasn't much point in saying anything. When they got him into the nick they gave him a lot of verbal, suggesting that he made things easier for himself by confessing to various unsolved burglaries. Joey didn't fall for that one. He knew he was for the high jump, so the least said soonest mended.

In due course he appeared before Stamford House Juvenile Court, where they were beginning to know his face. They didn't exactly welcome him with open arms as a member of the club. He was committed to an Approved School where, so the authorities thought, he would see the error of his ways and have his feet set in the paths of righteousness. It was the 16th of October 1962. Joey was sixteen years old.

There were a lot kids to whom home was just another four letter word, whose parents didn't give a monkey's for them and who didn't feel deprived when they were taken into care or otherwise disposed of. It wasn't like that in Joey's family, for they were very close to each other with strong emotional ties, and if one of them got kicked they all limped. Now for the first time in Joey's life he couldn't go home to Mum and Dad and the rest of the family because he was locked up and likely to be in that situation for sometime.

That wasn't the worst of it. For a couple of years he had been going steady with a girl of his own age. Her name was Ellen and they used to spend as much time as they could in each other's company. Now all that was finished and the romantic side of his future looked bleak. He made up his mind there and then that he would have it away at the first opportunity.

He was detained at Stamford House overnight. On the following morning he was told that he would be held for classification before being sent to the grade of Approved School which could be entrusted with the person of one Joey Bello, youthful desperado and menace to society. Having been nicked in possession of a loaded shooter, it was a safe bet that he wasn't down for transfer to a convalescent home. His destination would be a place where they would be long on discipline and security and short on home comforts.

The authorities didn't seem to be in much of a hurry to decide his fate. On the other hand he was determined to be out of Stamford House as soon as possible. To an expert, which was how he thought of himself, breaking out of a gaff presents roughly the same problem as breaking in. He gathered a half-dozen kids together and led a mass escape to freedom over the back gate. There's not only safety in numbers but helpful confusion as well. Needless to say they were all recaptured pretty quickly, but Joey did get as far as the Dale and a meeting with Ellen before he was picked up. The rest of his stay at Stamford House was short, but he didn't lack attention. To judge by the way the staff kept watch on him they must have considered him a valuable commodity, and when Mum and Dad came to visit they didn't relax their vigilance. Father George made an appearance and did his best to convince Joey that what had happened wasn't the end of the world. Joey couldn't agree with him but at least he tried.

The authorities finally made up their minds that St Christopher's Approved School in Hayes was a suitable place for Joey's further education, a prospect which was as welcome to the boy as a third nostril. Having spent years playing the wag from St Francis and St John he was now to be locked in the bosom of St Christopher, the patron saint of travellers. Maybe it was an omen, for he definitely intended to travel as far as he could in a direction away from that seat of learning.

St Christopher's was a large country house standing in its own grounds in the suburb of Hayes about ten miles from the centre of London. From the outside it looked like a public school, but there the similarity ended. All the windows were securely screwed up and there were locks and bolts everywhere. The inmates wore a uniform of sorts, short cord trousers and a battledress-style jacket, which gave no sense of pride to the wearer and was definitely no joy to behold.

The kids were accommodated in dormitories, each containing as many as could be crammed into the available space.

During the night hours attempted buggery and other forms of sexual assault were common, but Joey was not one of the victims. He knocked seven shades of shit out of the first lad to try it on with him.

His reputation as an escapee had followed him from Stamford House, so he had to watch points for a few weeks. He was a good boy, went quietly about his work and caused no trouble; then one night he took the screws out of one of the dormitory windows, using a screwdriver he had nicked from the metalwork class, and had it away. One of the kids put the screws back and his absence was not discovered until the following morning, by which time Joey was enjoying the hospitality of one of his married sisters in the Dale.

His period of liberty lasted ten days, which he put to good use. He screwed a few gaffs and blued the proceeds on evenings out with Ellen, but in due course he was nicked and it was back to St Christopher's. They were a forgiving lot. He got a touch of the cane which only acted as a spur, for he was out again the same day. The festive season was only a few days away, and he was set on enjoying Christmas in his own way.

He was more careful this time. He stayed away from his usual haunts, had a good Christmas, a riotous New Year and was in fact free until the middle of April when he was picked up in Paddington by an eagle-eyed PC. Back at St Christopher's they offered to waive the caning routine if he gave his word that he wouldn't try another escape. He chose to take the punishment without mortgaging his future and sure enough he was away again within a couple of days.

His unofficial leave lasted almost two months and might have lasted longer had he resisted the temptation to make one in a storebreak which was a non-starter from the off. He should have known better than to go to work with a couple of right amateurs with a lot of rabbit and no bottle. They got into the gaff with no trouble, which wasn't surprising because as soon as they were inside the lights went on and the Old Bill was waiting for them mob-handed. That episode marked the end of Joey's on-off relationship with St Christopher. He had chanced his arm once too often. On the 9th June 1953, at the County of London Sessions, he was sentenced to Borstal.

2. Borstal Boy

Joey's first step on the road to Borstal was a few weeks in the young prisoners' wing at Wormwood Scrubs. This was his first taste of bird and he didn't go for it all that much. The screws put themselves about and went in for a lot of shouting and hollering, which scared the living daylights out of most of the kids. It didn't frighten Joey.

He had his first introduction to the system of 'slopping out', a degrading and disgusting experience which took place in the early hours of the morning when they were unlocked. It consisted of a line of kids carrying their pisspots to be emptied in the single recess on each landing. These pots contained the filth accumulated during the night, urine, spew, turds of shit and spittle, all to be disposed of in double quick time. The last in line waded ankle deep in piss and shit. Joey thought to himself then, as he often thought to himself later, that even animals are not subject to such horrifying treatment. If the RSPCA ever got into the Scrubs they'd close the place down.

He had just about had a bellyful when he was told that he had been allocated to Portland Borstal, near Weymouth. There was a dozen of them all told and they went by coach under the watchful eyes of a couple of screws. It was a fine August day, the sun was shining brilliantly and, as the coach bowled along at the start of the four hour journey, they were all in fairly good spirits. A few kids burst into song, but the screws soon put a stop to that.

Joey had never in his life been farther away from London than the hopfields of Kent, where most of the poorer families from the Dale spent the month of September each year. They travelled by horse and cart or packed into a lorry laden with bedding, chairs, tables and household goods. Their homes were a collection of corrugated iron huts, their beds straw palliasses laid on wooden frames. Starting at seven o'clock in the morning the families picked hops all day and in the evenings, while the parents went on the piss in the local pubs, the kids would play games round the shanties. Some of the older ones paired off and went into the fields for sex sessions, whch led to the usual crop of shotgun weddings the following Spring.

Portland, when they finally arrived, turned out to be a grim, semi-fortified group of buildings perched on a rocky island site which was joined to the mainland by a long causeway. Joey kept his eyes open when he got there and reckoned that the chances of escape from this drum would be nil. It must have been the windiest part of the British Isles. There was a rope strung permanently between the kitchen quarters and the main building, but even with the aid of this device the crossing was a struggle against the elements. That they got their food on time was a daily miracle.

The Borstal was divided into 'houses', a sort of public school idea which was intended to encourage good-natured rivalry. The rivalry was there alright, but it wasn't very friendly. There was Drake House, Benbow House and there must have been other naval heroes whose names were commemorated. Joey found himself in Raleigh, a name that meant nothing to him except that he had often nicked bicycles of that description.

He soon settled into the routine. They were made to work hard but there were some compensations. One of the screws was a former professional boxer by the name of

Vince Hawkins, who spotted that Joey had the makings of a fighter and gave him some personal coaching. It was a funny thing that there were no classes in safe-cracking or breaking and entering but plenty of opportunity to learn how to punch peoples' heads in. Nothing ensures respect and a trouble-free passage through Borstal more than the ability to hammer a fellow inmate into insensibility.

It was quite by accident that Joey became the Borstal barber. He had never handled a pair of scissors before, but that didn't seem to matter. After a ten minute course of instruction from one of the screw he was let loose to do his worst, and some of it was pretty horrible. However he soon got the hang of it. Some of the lads were quite proud of their barnets and a bit of care on the barber's part was rewarded with a gift of snout which could be exchanged for sweets or other goodies. Just the same, though he made a few friends he also made some enemies. That was where his fighting ability came in useful.

They were a mixed bunch at Portland, drawn from all parts of the British Isles. There were the Cockneys from London, the Jocks from Scotland and the Taffs from Wales. The Irish were known as Paddies, the Liverpool lot as Scouses. Then there were the Brummies from Birmingham with accents so thick it was hard to understand them. It was natural for cliques to form. Each little mob though it was the business and the others were idiots. The Scouses were the worst. They were an evil bunch who never missed an opportunity to cause a row. One day they picked on a Cockney kid and gave him a proper seeing-to, which led to a punch-up between Scouses and Cockneys. Joey was in the thick of it from the start and copped for one of the hard cases who opened proceedings by grabbing Joey by the lapels of his jacket and butting him in the face. The bone cracked, the claret flowed and for a moment Joey was blinded by the pain. Then he went berserk. Putting a knee into his opponent's cobblers he gave him a couple of hooks as he went down and then kicked the shit out of him.

The fight was broken up by the screws and the injured carted off to hospital. Nothing could be done about Joey's nose which remains bent and deformed to this day, but he never forgot the lesson he learned. Hit first, hit hard and keep at it until the other bloke goes down and stays down.

Joey said goodbye to Portland early in 1955 when he was called up for compulsory military service. He couldn't figure out why the Army needed ex-Borstal boys, perhaps they were running out of Generals. Whatever the reason, Joey found himself in Cattrick Camp in Yorkshire, Signalman Number 23104525, Bello, J., 7th Training Regiment, Royal Corps of Signals. He had already spent almost a couple of years in a semi-military environment so he should have slotted into the Army without too much trouble. Unfortunately he fell foul of the second lowest form of animal life in HM Forces, namely the Lance Corporal in charge of his section who had obviously seen Joey's record and knew that he came from Borstal. Also Joey's broken nose and general air of tough cockiness weren't to his liking as he never tired of telling him. He was forever making snide remarks about 'decent lads being forced to associate with criminals'. Joey swallowed all this for some time, but it couldn't go on indefinitely.

Matters came to a head one day on the rifle range. They were at target practice and Joey was lying on his stomach facing the targets when the Corporal started rucking him. He was standing behind Joey and to his left. Joey rolled over and brought his rifle round until it was pointing directly at his tormentor.

'Shut your fucking mouth,' said Joey. 'Stop digging me out or I'll let you have it in the guts.'

The Corporal went white and started to twitch. Joey almost laughed at the spectacle, although inside he was seething with rage. His finger trembled on the trigger. At that moment he was capable of murder. Then, because he had either to carry out his threat or put the gun down, Joey lowered the rifle. The second he did so the scream went up and NCOs ran in from all directions. He was dragged to the guardhouse and, in the ensuing punch-up, a lot of military furniture was wrecked. In the end he was overwhelmed by sheer weight of numbers.

The episode marked the end of Joey's military career, which had lasted precisely six weeks. He had, according to his discharge papers, 'failed to fulfil Army requirements', which was a polite way of describing his behaviour. Luckily, he wasn't charged with attempted murder. On the 1st March 1955 Joey was back in Civvy Street among his old mates in the Dale, where he was welcomed with open arms.

Things hadn't changed much during the time he had been away, but there was a lot of buzz over a bloke called Christie who had gone in for murder in quite a big way. He lived in a shabby house in a shabby cul-de-sac called Rillington Place, just by Lancaster Road, and he was up to all kinds of shabby tricks, luring women to the house, screwing them then killing them, hiding the bodies in shallow graves in the backyard and behind false walls in the house.

Three of Joey's old mates lived in the house next door to Christie's place for years. Some of the stories they had to tell were frightening, strange noises and screams in the night, hysterical female voices crying out for mercy.

'We didn't do nothing about it,' said one of them. 'Wasn't any of our business anyway. He was just a funny little guy with a bald head and glasses. To look at him you wouldn't think he'd hurt a fly.'

'He wasn't hurting flies,' said Joey. 'He was bloody killing human beings.'

Joey found himself fascinated by the strange and ghastly doings of this creature. In the local library he turned up back copies of the papers carrying reports of the murders and the proceedings at Christie's trial. He found it almost unbelievable that the man had carried on doing a job of work during the ten years over which the crimes had been committed. He had actually been in the employ of the police at Harrow Road nick before taking on a job as a road haulage clerk. What a nerve, thought Joey, working for the law during the day and bumping women off at night.

'He knocked off seven women,' said one of Joey's uncles, a man who knew everything and everybody on the manor. 'What a cunning sod. I used to play cards with him down the Kensington Park Hotel nearly every night. He'd sit there cool as you like, butter wouldn't melt in his mouth and all the time he was thinking about the last murder he'd done and how he was going to do the next one.'

'Makes you think, don't it,' said Joey. 'A killer like that on the loose for ten years and behaving as normal as you and me.'

Talking to people here and there, looking up the facts in the library, Joey began to piece together the segments of the life-style of the mass murderer, trying to understand what compulsion had driven this outwardly respectable man into the fantasy world where he could give free rein to his sexual perversions, regard murder as part and parcel of the daily round and hide his dark secrets behind a mask of conformity. As damning fact piled on damning fact Joey became obsessed with his search for the truth.

According to the reports, Christie's first victim was an Austrian women called Ruth Fuerst. The manner of her death was not revealed, but her body lay buried in the backyard of the house in Rillington Place for ten years, as did the body of the second victim, Muriel Eady. The women were respectively twenty-one and thirty years of age. Joey wondered what power Christie possessed that enabled him to persuade these comparatively young women to enter his house and submit to his sexual advances. They probably thought, Joey concluded, that Christie looked too quiet and ordinary to be dangerous.

Six years later Christie claimed his third victim. It was a bizarre feature of the case that Beryl Evans' husband Timothy was convicted of the murder of the couple's baby and executed, and it was only at his trial that Christie confessed to killing the mother.

In his statement to the court he described how he killed Beryl Evans.

'She brought the quilt from the front room and put it down in front of the fireplace,' he said. 'She lay on the quilt. She was fully dressed. I got on my knees but found I was not physically capable of having intercourse with her owing to the fact that I had fibrositis in my back and enteritis. I turned the gas tap on and as near as I can make out I held it close to her face. When she became unconscious I turned the tap off. I was going to try again to have intercourse with her but it was impossible – I couldn't bend over. I think that's when I strangled her.'

As he read the words Joey shivered. What a bloody monster, he thought, whining about his ailments preventing him from screwing a woman who was dead or dying. Another thought occurred to him. Why, after having committed two murders and successfully hidden the bodies, did Christie wait six years before claiming a third victim? Or had he waited?

Joey turned to the report of the fourth killing. In this case the victim was Christie's wife who, according to the killer's statement, woke him during the night when she had an attack of convulsions.

'She was choking,' the statement went on. 'I did what I could to try and restore her breathing, but it was hopeless. It appeared too late to call for assistance. I could not bear to see her so. I got a stocking and put it round her neck to put her to sleep.'

Joey studied the report more closely. After 'putting his wife to sleep', Christie had buried the body under the floorboards in the sitting room of the house. The murder had been committed on 14th December. What a way to wish the wife a Merry Christmas, thought Joey.

To usher in the New Year Christie embarked on an orgy of killing. In January and February he put an end to three women in their mid-twenties. Kathleen Maloney, Rita Nelson and Hectorina McLennan were the flies who came into the spider's parlour. They were strangled, trussed up and stuffed into an alcove in the kitchen, which Christie then boarded over.

The balloon went up when, after Christie had moved from the house, the incoming tenant discovered the bodies of the three women in the boarded-up kitchen alcove. The police went into action, the four other bodies were dug up and, a week later, Christie was arrested in Putney.

At his trial Christie confessed to the murder of seven women and, in reply to a question from prosecuting counsel, he said that there might have been more victims but he had forgotten. Evidence of sexual aberration was produced in the shape of cuttings of pubic hair from the bodies of some of the victims which were in Christie's possession. There was also evidence to the effect that the killer had had sexual relations with the dead.

In his summing up Mr Justice Finnemore said, 'This is a man who remembers what he wants to remember and forgets what it is convenient to forget.'

The jury of nine men and three women took one hour and twenty four minutes to find Christie guilty of murder.

Reading the final words of the report, Joey shook his head. He realised that he was no nearer understanding the truth about this monster than he had been at the beginning of his enquiries, and the thought bothered him.

Never mind, he thought, maybe one day it will all be clear to me.

3. Thugs

It was a warm summer evening just after midnight. Joey, Danny and Boysie were standing on the flat roof at the rear of the tobacconist's shop, taking a careful look at the fanlight beneath which lay the storeroom and about three grand's worth of snout.

They weren't interested in the tobacco. The information was that the two old birds who owned the shop were right at it fiddling the Income Tax, and that somewhere hidden on the premises was upward of fifteen thousand pounds in readies.

The area was undergoing re-development and right opposite the shop stood a new block of high-rise flats. The old girls lived in the flat above the shop and the trio were standing only a few yards from their kitchen window.

Danny got out the case-opener which he carried down the leg of his trousers, bent over the fanlight, there was a sharp crack and they were half way home. Joey pulled the stocking mask down over his face and shifted the .45 revolver which was stuck in the waistband of his trousers. His palms were sweating. He took off his gloves, wiped his hand on his jacket and put the gloves on again. Danny and Boysie were masked and gloved up. They were ready to go in.

They stood very quiet for a few moments in case the noise of the fanlight being forced had been heard, but all was silent. According to plan Joey was the first to go, followed by Boysie with Danny bringing up the rear. Joey slid over the transom, hung there for a second with arms at full stretch, then let go. He was so intent on speed that he simply dropped straight into the darkened room without first having a butchers. Directly below the fanlight ws a big wooden chair, the old-fashioned sort with knobs on which he didn't see but certainly felt, for one of the knobs stuck right up his arse. It was bloody murder. Joey felt as if his spine had been pushed through the top of his head. He couldn't move, and he let out a yell as the other two dropped on top of him. They ended up in a heap on the floor amidst a racket that sounded like the crack of doom.

They hardly dared to breathe, but lay there waiting for the scream to go up. It did. The two old dears weren't interested in coming downstairs to find out what was wrong. They stuck their ancient heads out of the window and yelled.

There was no going back now. Anyway they didn't intend to leave the gaff without what they had come for. They sorted themselves out and rushed up the stairs with Joey in the lead waving the shooter. The two old birds were dragged away from the window and Joey waggled the gun under their noses, which shut them up a bit sharpish. They tied them up with the sheets off the bed and began the search for the money.

They turned the drum over and found readies in the most surprising places. Hidden under a pile of clothes in the bottom of the wardrobe were a couple of large square biscuit tins crammed with notes. Under the mattress they found a stout envelope full of fivers. There was more loot under the carpet. Joey was thinking about pulling up the floorboards when Boysie called him over to the window.

There was a small crowd in the street below, standing around and staring up at the front of the building. They weren't being very active, but that meant nothing. Some body would have been on the blower to the Old Bill who were certain to appear on the scene shortly, so there wasn't much time for the trio to have it away.

Joey stuck his head out of the window, let out a tremendous roar and fired off a couple of shots with the .45. He must have looked and sounded terrifying, what with the stocking mask and the rest, but it worked. The crowd scattered and shot off for cover in all directions as the three vaulted through the open window and dropped on to the pavement. Joey fired another shot in the air as they ran for the car.

Billy, the fourth member of Joey's little team, had been waiting down the street in the motor. As soon as he saw them on the move he started the engine, slammed in the gear lever and accelerated away as they scrambled in. It wasn't a bad motor – Billy had nicked it the previous day in the West End – but since they didn't intent to keep it there was no reason to treat it gently. Billy threw the heap through the first corner and then put his foot down. They were away.

Joey began to look around for fresh fields. What should he tackle next? The tempting window displays of jewellers and furriers provided the answer. Joey teamed up with a pair of characters who were supposed to be experts at the smash and grab.

Their first job was a fiasco. They had marked down an ideal target, a jewellers' shop with a valuable collection of tom on trays behind the glass. It was a simple matter of smashing the window, grabbing the trays and having it away. Or at least that's what they thought.

In a stolen van, from which Joey had removed the rear doors, they descended on the scene in the middle of the afternoon. One of Joey's mates was at the wheel, the other in the back. They were gloved up and wearing stocking masks.

A smash and grab operation has to be carried out at speed and every second counts. The driver swung the van across the front of the shop and then reversed so that the open back was right against the window. Using a pickaxe, Joey smashed in the window but in his enthusiasm he knocked the trays back into the shop, where they were beyond his reach. By this time the driver had counted up to five, rammed the car into gear and was off down the street, bouncing off other vehicles and scaring the hell out of the pedestrians. The job was a dead loss.

They didn't give up. A few days later they repeated the process, but this time Joey used a club hammer to break the glass. He came unstuck again. When he had cased the shop he hadn't noticed that there was a sort of second window suspended on chains, which was designed to sweep the trays of tom back into the shop in case of a smash and grab. Once more they had to flee empty-handed. They were clearing the windows alright, but in the wrong direction.

After that little lot they decided to give jewellery a miss and concentrate on furs. Joey sorted out a suitable shop where there was a really smashing mink stuck on a dummy right in the centre of the window. They had nicked a large Humber Snipe saloon for this job. They pulled up outside the furriers' and Joey's mate, swinging a pickaxe, sprinted across the pavement. Within a few seconds the window was a heap of broken glass. As the mate stood guard to discourage any have-a-go merchants who might be about, Joey dived into the window to claim the pussy. The bloody thing was fastened to the dummy with what seemed like hundreds of pins. As Joey tugged at the coat, one of the sleeves came away in his hands. By this time the furrier had come to the conclusion that there was a maniac in his window tearing his stock to pieces, and was coming forward to do something about it. Joey wasn't going to lose out on this caper. Grabbing the dummy, coat and all, he jumped out of the window and shot across to the car, followed by his mate swinging the pickaxe. There was a lot of screaming and shouting from the crowd which had gathered. They probably thought it was a kidnapping, seeing what looked like a bird in a fur coat being stuffed into a car by a couple of masked thugs. They made their getaway, but it was a pretty shabby mink which they delivered to the buyer, with whom Joey had already agreed a price. He knocked off a bit for the damage, but the trio came out on the right side.

They eventually got it together as a team and earned a nice few quid. Their early experiences taught them to be prepared for the unexpected, and they were lucky on several occasions when a bit of quick thinking got them out of bother. There was one job, however, where luck deserted them altogether.

They had been put on to a warehouse job, a wholesale snouters, which they planned to hit in the early hours of the morning. It was in a deserted area and looked like a doddle. They nicked a large van with a roll-up shutter at the back, copped for a stout plank from a building site and went to work.

The technique of warehouse-breaking is to back the van up against the entrance doors, put one end of the plank against the lock, reverse the van at full throttle and smash the doors in. What happened in this case was that the plank splintered and the bloke who was holding it got the sharp end through the thigh. It was a terrible wound. Joey didn't dare pull out the massive splinter for fear of doing more damage. With the poor sod lying in the back of the van yelling his head off, they made for the nearest hospital.

When they got there they carried him inside the casualty entrance, made a commotion and scarpered. It all came out right in the end and the fellow survived, but he was to carry a monstrous scar for the rest of his life. Sixty stitches were needed to put his leg together again.

Another caper that didn't produce the expected result

was a warehouse job when Joey made one with his old pals Yocker and Jack the Hat, a man who was to be the victim of a brutal murder for which Regie Kray was sentenced to life. They had reliable information that this warehouse was full of first-class woollen gear, sweaters and suchlike, which would have a ready sale among the market traders who were always happy to pick up a bargain and no questions asked. They decided to have a lorry load of this merchandise and, since they were dead skint, the sooner they claimed it the better.

Yocker was given the job of nicking a covered lorry, and the three of them set out in the early morning. The lorry was parked in a side street near the warehouse and, while Yocker and Jack kept a look-out, Joey crept round the back to find a way in. He came across a handy window which gave way to some coaxing with a crowbar and quickly nipped inside.

The place was packed from floor to ceiling with large cartons. He put his hand inside one of them and felt soft, woolly material. This was the goods alright. He opened the wide doors of the warehouse, Yocker backed in the lorry and, while Jack kept an eye on the street outside, the two of them crammed the gear in until the vehicle was packed to capacity. They had it away without any trouble, dumped the load in Yocker's garage and got rid of the lorry.

They had already made arrangements with a chap called Gentle Bobby to shift the loot so, while Yocker went off to fetch him, Jack and Joey had a wash and brush up and a much-needed cuppa. When Bobby turned up they bowled along to the garage.

'Right. Let's have a look at the gear,' said Bobby.

Joey opened one of the cartons and Bobby pulled out some of the contents. They were not woollen sweaters but socks, multi-coloured, diamond-patterned socks, thousands of them.

'Christ,' said Bobby. 'What do I do with this lot? 'There's enough socks here to kit out a bloody army.'

To give him his due, Bobby was a grafter. He knocked out the whole load, but at a fraction of the price they would have got for sweaters. For months afterwards it was easy to recognise Bobby's friends and acquaintances. They all wore multi-coloured, diamond-patterned socks.

Joey did a few more jobs in the smash and grab and warehouse line, but the game wasn't worth the candle. As he mooched around the West End he saw that there was good money to be earned without too much risk. Illegal gambling flourished in the many clubs and spielers and plenty of cash money was floating around, which had to be protected. The club owner couldn't call in he law. He could, however, use hired help as an expensive but necessary part of his operation. Joey decided to have some of that, which was how he became a minder.

4. Fight for Control

In the mid-fifties London was the scene of terrible outbreaks of violence with rival gangs of Greeks, Maltese and local villains fighting for control of gambling and prostitution. Everybody carried a knife or a gun. Some carried both, and shootings and stabbings were regular events in the clubs and spielers which had sprung up in Soho and the East End. Even in the plush nightspots of Mayfair the rival mobs fought out their bloody battles.

Among the notorious faces were Billy Hill, the governor of the West End, and Jack 'Spot' Comer, another contender for the top jolly's position. George Caruana was top man among the Maltese. He was laying the ground for the takeover from the Messina brothers, whose careers as ponces were drawing to a close under the threats of repeated nickings by the Old Bill. They had had a good run for their money and made themselves vast fortunes in the vice rackets.

There were many other assorted villains about, but there was no doubt as to who was the boss. Billy Hill who had, like Joey, done a stint in Portland (Class of '27 as the Yanks would say) was at the top of the heap. He had come up the hard way but, although he had served several sentences including a stetch in Dartmoor, he had really made crime pay. Among the jobs that were down to him were a bullion robbery at London Airport in 1947, the Eastcastle Street Post Office blag in 1952 and the KLM gold robbery in 1954. The rewards from these jobs alone must have run into six figures. He wasn't nicked for any of them.

*

A favourite meeting place for villains at this time was Lyons' Corner House in the Strand, not far from Charing Cross station. It was open day and night, but the mobs gathered in the early morning hours. Joey was there once with a couple of mates when a firm from South London began to take liberties. It looked as though Joey was on a hiding to nothing; but three fellows at a nearby table came to the rescue. They were Tommy Smithson and two of his pals.

Joey had known Tommy for some time. He had a good-looking blonde girl-friend called Fay Richardson and owned a spieler in Berwick Street in the heart of Soho. He was a great favourite with the local brasses, who used to take their troubles to him. He was always ready with a shoulder to cry on or a handy tool to give them another sort of consolation. It was his habit of holding out the helping hand that led to his death.

What happened was that his girl friend Fay, later to become notorious as Fay 'Kiss of Death' Sadler in the Pen Club murder in 1960, was banged up in Holloway on a charge of 'kiting' or passing dud cheques. Tommy put the bite on George Caruana for funds for her defence but the wily George wasn't having any. On a fine afternoon in June 1956 Tommy called at Caruana's house in Carlton Vale with the intention of collecting.

Caruana was not at home, but Tommy came face-to-face with a pair of Maltese, Philip Ellul and Victor Spampinato, both associates of Caruana. Ellul was carrying, and two shots put an end to the career of Tommy Smithson. One hit him in the shoulder, the other struck him in the neck, severing the carotid artery.

Tommy died in the gutter. His funeral was a splendid affair attended by a host of villains and about three-quarters of Soho's prostitutes.

*

Joey's career as a minder was doing quite nicely. He flitted from one club to another in the Lancaster Gate and Queensway areas. The money was good and he didn't have too much aggravation. All the villains knew him and his connections, so they took care not to step out of line. The ordinary punters were no trouble. If they misbehaved a couple of sharp slaps would put them right. Joey soon earned a reputation as a reliable man and his services were in demand. He settled on two clubs in the Paddington district as the best paying propositions. One of them was the Conduit, owned by Ronnie Costello, a run-of-the-mill drinker open from three to eleven. The other was the Miramar, a late night supper club, well furnished, with cabaret and a good class of member.

A good minder is essential to the proper running of a club or nightspot. He is not just a heavy, though he must be handy with his fists in case of serious trouble. His real function is to smell out aggravation and put a stop to it before it develops into a battle. The owner of the club should not be involved in this. For instance, one club owner Joey knew would wade in with fists flying at the first hint of bother, which was definitely the wrong way to go about things. Since the geezer was about six feet four and built like a brick shithouse, his appearance alone was sufficient to frighten most people.

This fellow's name was Tiny Evans, and he visited the Miramar quite regularly. Joey dropped into his club one evening for a quiet drink and noticed that one of the clients had trouble written all over him. When the balloon went up, Tiny performed as usual, but the punter was a rough handful and Tiny had difficulty chucking him out. Coming back into the club and looking worse for wear, Tiny sorted Joey out and gave him a rucking in front of all the customers.

'Why didn't you give me a hand?' he said. 'You could see I was in bother.'

'Leave it out, Tiny,' Joey replied. 'I don't work here. You should get yourself a good minder.'

This remark seemed to get up Tiny's nose. He went on a bit, poking Joey in the chest with his finger. Such liberties Joey didn't allow. He gave the big man a right-hander, Tiny went down and Joey left the premises. The following day he had Joey nicked for assault, which cost him fifteen quid in fines and compensation at Marylebone Magistrates' Court.

There are certain people who should never be in the club business. They are fond of putting themselves about but when the crunch comes they run screaming to the law. This maybe does something to restore a bruised ego, but it does nothing at all for a man's reputation.

Jack Spot was one of the clients at the clubs which Joey frequented. He lived nearby in Hyde Park Mansions at the corner of Edgeware Road and Sussex Gardens. His wife Margaret, known as Rita, was often with him. She was a strikingly good-looking woman and thought the world of Jack, who was having some aggravation at the time. In fact he had just come through a trial at the Old Bailey which had attracted a great deal of publicity.

The story behind the trial was common knowledge in the underworld. Billy Hill had returned from one of his foreign trips to find that Jack had been putting himself about and claiming that he was the governor of the West End. This didn't please Billy at all. On August 11th 1955, in Soho's Frith Street, Jack earned himself a vicious striping at the hands of Albert Dimes (real name Alberto Dimeo), one of Billy's trusted lieutenants. Dimes didn't escape injury. Jack had plenty of bottle and could be relied upon to give as good as he got. The two of them appeared at Marlborough Street and were committed for trial at the Old Bailey. There were two trials, both of them farces, which ended with

Spotty and Dimes being chucked and leaving the court with no (further) stains on their characters.

There had been a touch of the Damon Runyon's about the second trial with mentions of Sonny the Yank, Moisha Blue Boy and a reverend gentleman by the name of Basil Claud Hudson Andrews who, as well as being a retired clergyman, was a very accomplished liar.

Just after Christmas Jack Spot approached Joey with an offer to him to become his minder. Joey was very happy at the Miramar and had a feeling that he might be letting himself in for a load of grief, but it was a step up the ladder and into the big league. Joey took the job.

Actually it wasn't too bad, not in the beginning at least. Only the best was good enough for Jack and it rubbed off on Joey. He was well-tailored, went to the best places and began to see at first hand how the other half lived. When Jack went on a meet Joey would be at his elbow, keeping a sharp eye open for signs of trouble.

Joey made several useful contacts through Jack, and did a bit of minding for some of them, which is how he came to be sitting in a Knightsbridge drinker one day with two straight businessmen, Terry Jennings and Patrick Ryan. They were carrying a large amount of cash, which was the reason for Joey's presence. Anyway, there Joey was, sipping a light ale and at peace with the world, when he happened to glance in a mirror and saw the reflection of Paddy Onions, a villain from South London, holding a chopper with which he is about to split Joey's skull open.

Joey doesn't waste time in taking a dive to one side as the chopper come down and bites into the table top, but he is hampered by the arms of the chair and can't get up. Onions and his mates, three tearaways from the same manor, set about him with knives and razors as he does his best to protect himself with an arm across his face. There is blood everywhere. Ryan has passed out and Jennings is having it away on his toes. There is a lot of screaming and shouting from the customers and some yelling on the part of the staff of the club, who don't care for the sight of a good punter being chopped up on the Axminster. Finally the gang scarper and Joey staggers to his feet, literally soaked in the red stuff.

A couple of the girls did what they could to tidy him up, but Joey knew he had to get to a hospital pretty quickly as he was losing a lot of blood. There was no question of waiting for an ambulance and interrogation by the Old Bill. Joey reeled out into Knightsbridge and he was lucky enough to get a taxi to take him to St Mary's hospital in Paddington. He bunged the driver a good few quid to make up for the bloodstains on the seat and dived into casualty, where they did a rapid job of hemstitching. He made up a fanny about being attacked and robbed, gave a moody name and address and got the hell out of it.

The best thing for him to do now was to go home, where he could rest up and keep out of the way for a while. When he walked in the door, looking like something out of a horror film, poor old Mum nearly passed out and his girl Ellen, who happened to be there, gave him a mouthful, most of which he didn't listen to. After all, he wasn't complaining. He didn't see why anyone else should.

The news that he had been done went round the manor like wildfire. Some of his mates suggested a revenge raid over the water, but Joey had his own ideas about that so he told them to leave it out. The wounds healed fairly quickly. He took the stitches out himself and he was as good as new apart from a few scars. As most of the cutting had been done with razors the scars were hardly noticeable.

He did a few more jobs through Spotty's introductions, but they were dead easy. One of them was to look after a woman club owner who was having aggravation from a couple of so-called villains. Joey put in an appearance for a few nights, which was enough to put the wind up this pair of toe-rags. As soon as they set eyes on him they knew they were out of their class and they faded out of the picture.

Some time later the woman was found dead in her office at the club. She had taken an overdose of sleeping tablets. It was curious that two of her friends involved in the nightclub scene also met tragic ends. The owner of Esmeralda's Barn died of coal gas poisoning and her friend committed suicide. Maybe the going was too tough for them.

There was one woman whose nerve didn't give under the strain. She was Billy Hill's wife Aggie who ran a club called the Modernaires and had more than a finger in other establishments.

One of the more interesting jobs that Spotty put Joey on to was minding Billy Daniels, the Old Black Magic man himself, when he appeared at the London Palladium. Joey expected to meet a right big head, but he turned out to be one of the best, a real down-to-earth bloke who treated Joey more like a friend than a minder. Joey must have made a good impression, for Billy remembered him twenty years later. Visiting the Kray twins in Parkhurst, he sent a signed photograph in for Joey with the message 'Keep your chin up'.

It was in May 1956 that the shit hit the fan so far as Joey Bello was concerned. It started at the Roundhouse pub in Norland Market where he had gone on a meet with Jack, who told Joey that he was taking Rita out for a meal that evening to a restaurant near Marble Arch. The arrangement was that Joey should meet them there after dinner and go to the flat with them.

To fill in the time, Joey took Ellen to the Conduit, which was a few minutes walk from the restaurant where Jack and

Rita were dining. Joey hadn't seen much of Ellen for some time what with one thing and another, so it was a bit of an occasion. Ellen was his steady and, like Joey, one of a large family living on the manor. Her old man was a local character who had been very tasty in his time. He was once involved in a fight where two people died from their injuries, and Ellen's Dad was done for manslaughter.

Ellen and Joey had a lot to talk about and the time passed quickly. He had a good few drinks and, when he looked at his watch, it was half past one in the morning, long past the time when he was due to meet Jack and Rita. Still, there was no use crying over spilt milk, so he spent the rest of the night with Ellen.

In a way he was lucky. If he had been with Jack when he made his way home, Joey would have been dead or, at best, seriously injured, for this was the night when Jack Spot was the victim of one of the most savage and brutal attacks in the history of gang warfare. As Jack and Rita, arm in arm, approached the block of flats where they lived, a crowd of men ran from the shadows and closed in on them. According to Rita, who told Joey the whole story, there were at least six, and she swore that one of them was Billy Hill. Joey couldn't believe that. Billy was no coward, but he wouldn't put himself up front if there was any chance of being identified.

However that may be, the mob certainly made a mess of Jack. They were tooled up with knives, razors, coshes and iron bars, and in the space of a few minutes they had marked him for life. His face was slashed to ribbons, he was stabbed in the body and beaten about the head and shoulders. Rita, who was as game as they come, had tried to defend her husband but was felled by a blow from a club. The attackers fled, leaving Jack stretched out on the pavement in a pool of his own blood.

Joey went round the hospital first thing the following

morning with Rita. Jack was lying there under police guard, his face completely covered in bandages. He was in considerable pain, but he knew he had to do some fast thinking because Rita had put up some names to the Old Bill. Out of hearing of the copper Joey managed to have a few whispered words with Jack.

'I want you to go and see Hill, Joey,' he said. 'Tell him that Rita wants to nick the mob who did me. Tell him I'll talk her out of it if he agrees to stop the aggravation. Will you do that?'

Joey had no choice. He was known as Jack's minder and it wouldn't be long before people would come looking for him. He got in touch with Hill and made a meet with him at his office in Warren Street, just off the Tottenham Court Road. Joey knew he was going into the lion's den, so he took the precaution of tucking a .45 into the waistband of his pants.

As he picked his way through the crowds of car dealers packing the pavements of Warren Street he wasn't too happy. He was even less happy when he went into Hill's office. Billy was waiting for him with Dimes at his side and about a dozen members of the firm standing around. Nobody searched Joey which was a mistake on their part, or perhaps Billy didn't want the shooting to start before he heard the news from Spot.

Joey passed on the message that Jack had given him and was surprised at the way Hill took it. Billy was normally very calm and kept his temper even under extreme provocation. Now he was shouting and almost foaming at the mouth.

'I don't make deals with grasses,' he yelled. 'Listen, son, you're lucky not to be in the next fucking bed to Spot. If it wasn't for Frankie putting a good word in you fucking would have been. You leave this one out. Spot's a wrong 'un. You side with him and you'll get the same treatment.'

Joey didn't like the way things were working out. It was all going wrong, and there was too much chat about hospital beds for his liking. He unfastened his jacket in case he needed to make a quick grab for the shooter and Dimes noticed the movement. He guessed that Joey was carrying and knew that if it came on top he and Billy would be the first to stop a bullet. He cut into the conversation.

'Look, Joey,' he said. 'All we're interested in is seeing that nobody gets nicked down to this. Can you get a couple of our boys in to see Spot and fix things up?'

It all sounded very reasonable. Jack would be in no danger with the Old Bill watching over him, so nothing but good could come out of the scheme. Hill had nothing more to say and Dimes nominated two blokes to go in the hospital with Joey. One of them was Jimmy Woods, who he knew well. He had never met the other fellow. Joey made a meet for the next day at the Fifty One club, which was close to the hospital.

Joey went to see Jack straight away. He was in a dodgy situation because he had to box clever and pretend that he hadn't seen Billy. Jack agreed to see the two fellows to discuss taking the heat off the mob, but was very worried that Hill didn't seem to want to know. His main concern was Rita's safety. Joey promised him he would watch out for her.

Joey turned up at the Fifty One as arranged and Billy was there with Jimmy Woods and the other fellow. Joey left for the hospital with the two men and Billy said he would wait for them at the Fifty One. When they saw Jack the discussion didn't take long. He was pleased to see Jimmy, who had once worked for him, and he listened carefully to what was said. It wasn't easy with the Old Bill earwigging at the end of the bed, but it was agreed that there would be no point in nicking Mad Frankie and the rest of the mob. Jack promised that he would persuade Rita not to go ahead with her plan.

Joey came away from the hospital well satisfied. As they turned to leave the ward, Jack called Jimmy Woods back.

'Seen anything of Billy Hill lately,' he enquired.

'No, Jack. Haven't seen him for months,' said Jimmy.

That was what put the cat among the pigeons. As the three men came out of the hospital gates there was Billy in his car, surrounded by pressmen. The cunning bastard had set the whole thing up. The evening papers were full of it, how Billy had met three men outside the hospital, with full descriptions of Joey and the others and a lot of speculation as to why Billy was on the scene at that particular moment. When Joey saw Jack on the morning after the meet, the latter was livid.

'You've fucking dropped me right in it, Joey,' he said. 'You let that bastard Hill take a right liberty.'

Joe tried to explain that he was the one in the middle and he had only done his best to sort things, but it didn't wash. Joey realised then that he wasn't in the same league as Spot and Hill when it came to pulling strokes. The result was that Rita went ahead with her plan for revenge and five men copped for large doses of porridge at the Old Bailey. In June Mad Frankie Fraser and Bobby Warren were weighed off for seven years apiece and in October Billy Boy Blythe got five. Two other blokes, Dennis and Rossi, got fours. Joey wasn't involved in any of this. Rita was being minded by a very efficient mob known as the Metropolitan Police and had no need of his services.

As far as Joey's own position was concerned he had to do some hard thinking. If Billy had the needle to him there was bound to be a come-back. Although he had a bit of a reputation, Joey was only a kid of nineteen on his own and stood no chance if he was fronted by the Hill firm. As it happened there were some interested parties who had it in for Hill, and when they came to Joey with the offer of two grand if he would have a pop at him, Joey took it on. In the early hours one morning Joey waited in a car outside the Modernaires. He knew that Hill and Dimes were inside. It was just a matter of waiting until they came out.

They eventually appeared about three o'clock, Hill and Dimes and two of the mob. Joey's driver started up and, as the car sped past the group, Joey loosed off five shots with the .45. He had never fired from a moving car before and that, combined with the recoil of the heavy-calibre pistol, affected his aim. Hill, Dimes and company were lucky. So was Joey, because if he had done any of them it was a racing certainty that he would have been up at the Old Bailey on a murder charge.

He reckoned that Hill knew who the culprit was. So did the Old Bill, but there was no reaction from either. Maybe Billy felt that it was beneath his dignity to declare war on a kid, and the Old Bill couldn't have had the necessary evidence to secure a conviction. It all came right in the end. Dimes contacted Joey and offered him a good drink if he would have nothing more to do with Spotty, Joey took the offer and there the whole thing finished.

For poor old Jack it was the end of the road. He was involved in a wounding case in which it was alleged that he striped Tommy Falco outside the Astor club, but this was such an obvious fit-up that it was chucked at the Old Bailey. He later opened a club in Bayswater, but that went up in flames shortly after the first night.

There were a few sick jokes circulating in the underworld at the time. Two samples. 'Billy Hill's the governor. Jack Spot's very cut up about it' and 'Did you know Spotty was born two days before the Titanic went down. Two fucking disasters within forty-eight hours'.

Looking back now at the kid he was in those far-off days, Joey couldn't help laughing. History was being made in 1955. Bank Rate went up from three-and-a-half to four-and-a-half per cent (no kidding), Winston Churchill resigned as Prime Minister, there was a General Election, the independent television service started up and all sorts of people were getting worried about the atom bomb. In the middle of all this was young Joey Bello, unmindful of the earth-shaking events going on around him, swaggering about the West End with a .45 stuck down his trousers and not giving a fuck for anybody or anything. He knew that was him alright. He just finds it hard to believe.

He supposed that, when middle age puts a spare tyre round the guts, we all have thoughts about the good old days.

5. Seven Years

After the Spot episode Joey was at a loose end. He didn't fancy going back to minding which, as he saw it, put him up front for spankings but at the end of the queue when the rewards were being dished out. What he was looking for was a nice tickle, a quick job that would put a lot of cash in his pocket in a short space of time. It came along in the shape of a snatch that was put up to him by a couple of mates, Roy Simmonds and Ray Jackman.

The plan was to lift the payroll of a large dairy outfit in St John's Wood. It wasn't exactly a snatch, which is capturing money in transit, nor was it breaking and entering. It fell somewhere in between. The information came from two inside men, employees of the company, who would get a share of the loot when the job was done.

On the face of it there seemed nothing to worry about. They cased the premises one Friday morning and saw two clerks who, they had been told, were responsible for paying out the wages. They would be no trouble. Put the two of them together and they wouldn't make a man. They already had a floor plan of the offices and the yard and the wages procedure had been explained to them. All they now had to do was go in and lift the reward.

They go out on the job on the Friday morning. Roy had nicked a taxi which he says is not all that quick but will turn on a tanner. Joey remarked that they're supposed to outrun police cars, not go round in circles hoping they'll get dizzy and go home. They arrive at the depot and leave Roy in the taxi. Joey walks to the loading bay with Ray and leaves him there on watch. He puts on one of those funny masks, a big red nose fastened to dummy specs that hook over the ears and goes up the spiral stairs to the door that leads to the wages office. The gun is under his jacket.

He takes a deep breath and goes through the door. The two clerks are there, plus a mob at the window waiting to be paid. One of the clerks goes to grab him so he whips out the gun and hits him over the head with it. He claims the two trays of wage packets and backs out of the door.

The gun is in his hand under the trays. With both hands full it's impossible for him to open doors. The quickest way out is through the sterilising deparment. The news has reached there before him, which isn't surprising, there's a lot of hooting and screaming going on. The women workers, seeing Joey go tearing through with the false nose hanging off and clutching their wages, begin pelting him with empty bottles. He gets through without a scratch, which is a miracle, and rushes out into the street at full pelt.

Ray, on watch outside, hears the scream go up and thinks Joey is captured. He is in the taxi, looking through the rear window. As Joey dashes out of the yard Roy reverses, comes to a halt beside him, he jumps in and they're away.

It was a doddle and over so quick that there wasn't even a chase. The loot amounted to a very healthy sum and, after the two blokes at the yard had their whack, they split the rest three ways. They were all well satisfied.

It was a month later that it came on top. One of the fellows who had given them the info on the job had told his bird all about it, and she grassed them to the Old Bill after they had a row. All five were nicked and duly appeared in the dock at the Old Bailey charged with a variety of offences. In Joey's case it was 'robbery while armed with an offensive weapon'. The prosecution continually suggested that he was in possession of a gun, but it couldn't be proved because nobody had seen the weapon for long enough to swear that it was, in fact, a shooter. Although he had used it to hit the wages clerk over the head, it was then hidden from sight under the trays he was carrying. Just the same, the clerk's injuries proved that some sort of weapon had been used.

They were all found guilty. Raymond Jackman was sentenced to five years, Roy Simmonds got three and the two inside men received two years and four years respectively. Joey copped for seven, even though he was the youngest member of the group. This was because he was the one who inflicted the injuries.

Since he was under twenty-one he was officially what was known as a young prisoner, so he ended up in the YP wing at Wormwood Scrubs, of which he had had previous experience. He was there for a fortnight, but the authorities decided that he was a disruptive influence and transferred him to Pentonville. That suited him fine. He didn't care for the company of kids who were, in the main, petty thieves and juvenile delinquents.

What didn't appeal to him was the prospect of doing seven years' bird. Soon after his arrival in Pentonville he sorted out people he knew and could rely on. Billy was one of them, an old-time villain who had been a boxing champion. He agreed to help Joey escape.

Billy was one of the inmates 'on association', that is he was allowed to eat in company with other prisoners and stay unlocked of an evening to play darts, billiards or table tennis. Those who didn't have this privilege were served the last refreshment of the day around seven o'clock, just before the association men were locked up for the night. The 'refreshment' consisted of a thick, brown, milkless and sugar-free sludge known as cocoa and the serving of this treat coincided with the last physical headcount of the day.

Joey had worked out a plan for a breakout and

discussed it with a selected bunch of mates who were serving long sentences. Billy would unlock Joey after cocoa-time using a key which would be provided. Joey would then sneak up to the top landing and hide in the water storage tank in the recess. Later, when everything was quiet, he would unlock his mates, they would descend mob-handed on the screws on duty, tie them up and depart.

Came the day when the key was ready. Albert Hobbs, unofficial locksmith to the nick, passed it to Joey who handed it on to Billy. Immediately after the cocoa performance Joey set about making a dummy to put in his bed so that he would not be missed when the landing screw made his rounds, peering through the peephole in the door to check that the inmate had dossed down. He hid the dummy under the bed and waited for Billy to turn up.

It seemed like hours later that Joey heard the key turn in the lock, although it could not have been more than fifteen minutes. The door opened and there stood Billy, looking for all the world as though it was quite normal for him to have his own twirl. He pressed the key into Joey's hand and with a 'good luck, kid' he hurried away to join his mates on association. Joey quickly put the dummy to bed, picked up his shoes and left the cell, locking the door behind him. In stockinged feet he crept along the landing, keeping close to the wall until he got to the stairs. Now he had to reach the top landing without being seen. Moving carefully and silently he made it.

The huge storage tank in the recess was filled almost to the brim with the coldest water in north-west London. As he lowered himself in he let out a gasp. Sitting it out for four hours wasn't going to be a picnic. The first hour was bearable and then the cold started eating into him until even his bones were frozen. There was also another matter he hadn't taken into account, but a pint of piss in a hundred gallons of water isn't what might be described as excessive pollution.

He had no way of telling the time but it must have been close on midnight when he felt it was safe to leave the tank. He squelched on to the landing and, lying on his stomach, slid to the edge and looked down on the main hall of the block. He wanted to know where the night staff was, so that he could plan his route for the unlocking. He saw one of the screws straight away. Indeed he couldn't have missed him, because he was coming up the stairs to do a routine check of the landing on which Joey was lying. No way could Joey have claimed him before being spotted so there was only one thing for it. He wriggled back to the recess and climbed back into the tank.

Risking a quick look over the rim of the tank he saw the screw standing and staring at the floor where there was an enormous, Bello-shaped patch of water with a wet trail leading to the tank. The screw turned and ran for the alarm bell and the heavy mob arrived so speedily that Joey barely had time to dump the incriminating key in the bottom of the tank before he was dragged out and off to the chokey.

As a result of this caper he was brought up before the governor charged with attempting to escape. He lost some remission, but the biggest blow was that he was put into patches. This is a way by which escapers can easily be identified. On to the normal prison uniform are sewn bright yellow diamond-shaped pieces of material both front and back of jacket and trousers. Also a red light burns throughout the night in the cell. As a precaution against further attempts to escape, the con must leave his clothing outside the cell when he is locked up for the night. Joey discovered that sleeping naked under threadbare blankets in a cold peter isn't exactly funny.

Not long after the escape episode Joey was in trouble again. He was talking about the diabolical wages they received with Joey Cronk, Alfie and a few others from Notting Hill, and they were wondering what sort of protest they could make. It was Alfie who came up with the idea of doing the canteen and distributing the loot among the cons.

'It would be dead easy for you, Joey,' said Alfie. 'You're on patches. You line up by the canteen every morning before you go to work, don't you?'

Joey agreed he did just that.

'OK then. You're there for about a half-hour, nobody watching you. All you need is a key.'

'That's easy,' said Joey. 'There's a twirl at the bottom of the water tank on the top landing.'

'I'll get it,' said Alfie.

He was as good as his word, and the key which Joey had dumped was smuggled to him the next morning. When the men on patches assembled as usual, Joey was the first in line. As soon as the coast was clear he unlocked the canteen door and nipped inside. It was like being in Aladdin's cave. He grabbed a large empty carton and filled it with snout, sweets, biscuits, jam, tins of fruit and anything else which was handy. It was like winning an 'all you can carry away' contest. A quick look round and he was down the landing to Alfie's peter, where he tipped the lot on the bed.

'Quick, get rid of this,' said Joey. 'Back with some more in a minute.'

Alfie's eyes lit up like Christmas decorations. Joey shot back to the canteen with the empty box and refilled it, while Alfie spread the word. He repeated the performance five times, and Aladdin's cave began to look like Mother Hubbard's cupboard. On the sixth trip, disaster struck. He came out of the canteen and ran straight into the arms of the Governor. He looked at the bulging box Joey was carrying, then over his shoulder to the bare shelves of the canteen. Joey had never in his life seen a man look so astonished.

The heavy mob marched him straight into the Governor's office where he was informed that he would get no more wages until the missing stock had been paid for. All that had been recovered, in spite of a full-scale search of every peter in the block, was the box he had been caught with. Joey worked out that, at 2/6 (12½p) a week, he would be in debt for the next fourteen years.

A fortnight later he was nicked again, but this time it was more serious. At the end of the work period talking was strictly prohibited, a rule enforced with a lot of shouting and bawling on the part of the screws. On this occasion Joey was in the mailbag shop with keymaker Albert Hobbs, Alfie Fraser and a few others.

When the screw bellowed 'stop talking', he was caught with his mouth open, so to speak. His card had been marked over the canteen incident and the screw, one of the so-called 'hard' men, wasn't going to stand for any nonsense. He walked towards Joey.

'Didn't you hear what I fucking said?' he yelled. 'Shut your fucking trap, or I'll shut it for you.'

'Bollocks,' said Joey.

A roar of laughter went up from the cons. The screw's face went purple as he took out his notebook.

'Right, monkey. You're for it this time,' he snarled.

Joey had had enough of the verbal. He stuck one on the screw's chin, who went down spark out, and the alarm bells began to ring. As the heavy mob stormed in, swinging their sticks, a few of the lads decided to have a go. In no time at all a minor riot was on.

They were eventually subdued and dragged off to the chokey block, but not before a lot of damage had been inflicted on both sides. The cons came off worst. The riot sticks used by the heavy mob were fearsome weapons. Once hit with one of them nobody fancies a second dose.

When they appeared before the Governor it was all down to Joey as he was the one who struck the first blow. The others were awarded various minor punishments such as loss of privileges or remission, but sentence on ringleader Joey was a matter for the visiting magistrates. They awarded him twelve strokes of the birch.

Joey didn't know a lot about this birch business. It had been described to him once by a bloke who had experienced a taste of the pussy, but he didn't really listen. Now he was to discover at first hand what it was all about. For a start, after the punishment had been awarded, it had to be sanctioned by the Home Secretary. While waiting for this sanction, Joey was kept in solitary and out of contact with other prisoners.

The next stage in the proceedings, after the con has spent three nail-biting weeks in solitary, is the day when the punishment is carried out. This is known to all the inmates, because they are kept locked up until the ceremony is over, as used to happen in the case of an execution.

When the day came the prison was in an uproar. Cons were shouting from behind the doors of their peters, the boob percussion section (tin mugs on tin plates) started up and there was a general hullabaloo which reached a crescendo when Joey was marched down to one of the workshops where the official assault was to take place. He didn't know what to expect but in the physical sense he was not afraid. He had taken some stick in his time. A bit more wouldn't make all that difference.

Wearing only a suit of overalls, beneath which he was completely naked, his bare feet in a pair of slippers, he was led into the shop which had been specially cleared for the occasion. The first object he saw was the 'horse', a massive wooden framework about six feet high with stout members at the top and bottom equipped with leather straps. Standing around this contraption, their expressions resembling those of the dirty mac brigade at a strip show, were the Governor, a couple of geezers in white coats who turned out to be doctors, the Principal Officer, a few screws and a small collection of civilians.

The performance started. The escorting screws stripped off Joey's overalls, leaving him stark naked, and shackled him to the horse. He had never been ashamed of his body but now, surrounded by this crowd of drooling degenerates, he felt degraded and dirty. The screws' hands were everywhere. A broad and heavy leather belt was clamped around his waist and a hood placed over his head so that he couldn't see behind him and identify the screw who did the birching, a very wise precaution this, for Joey would have claimed the fucking whoreson sooner or later.

The principals in this barbaric ritual now took their places. The Governor stood in front of Joey with one of the doctors at his side. He couldn't see the other medico. He was probably taking care of the arsehole end.

The Governor spoke.

'Joseph Bello, you have been sentenced to twelve strokes of the bitch. This is the first.'

SWISH.

Jesus fucking Christ. Joey felt his body arch in agony. The pain defied description.

'Joseph Bello, you have been sentenced to twelve strokes of the birch. This is the second.'

SWISH.

Joey heard himself yell, get on with it you fucking bastards, the sweat ran down his face, the doctor moved forward.

'Joseph Bello, you have been sentenced to twelve strokes of the birch. This is the third.

SWISH.

Bloody fucking Norah, O my lacerated arse, fuck you all, fuck you, fuck you . . .

'Joseph Bello . . .'

SWISH.

Twelve strokes, twelve bloody fucking awful strokes, Joey's arse and legs were on fire, the contortions of his body had shifted the horse six feet from its original position. They set him free and put lint and plaster over his arse and legs.

The Governor faced Joey.

'The punishment's over now Bello. You took it like a man.'

He put out his hand. Joey's mouth was full of bile and spittle. He let the Governor have the lot, right in the middle of the face. None too gently the screws put him back into his overalls and slippers and hustled him out of the shop. Some of the spectators were grinning. He learned later that they were observers from the Home Office, present to see that justice had been done.

Looking back with the benefit of hindsight Joey felt disgusted. He had suffered at the hands of professionals, people who know how to hurt. He carries scars all over his body as a result of brushes with underworld enemies. These he can forget; but he will never erase from his mind the organised brutality which, under the cloak of legality, was perpetratd by a bunch of upper-class thugs on the body of a manacled and helpless twenty-year-old who committed the heinous crime of punching a pig of a prison officer on the chin. Pain one can forget, but memories last forever.

Having been party to inflicting the injuries, the doctor and his orderlies now seemed extremely concerned to heal them. The wounds, a multitude of red and purple weals from waist to thighs, continued to weep blood and fluid for two months. Joey had to sleep face down, and any incautious movement caused the partly-healed scars to open again. He was allowed to bathe frequently. The pink tinge in the water didn't come from the use of bath salts.

Is the birch a deterrent? Does it make a bad boy into a good one? On the evening of the day on which Joey got the treatment there was a concert in the chapel. It was usual for the blokes in patches to sit on the front row, but for some reason the screws had decided that they should sit at the back.

Men on special watch have few privileges and they tend to hang on to them.

'We'll sit in the front,' they said.

'Oh no you won't,' said the screws.

The men got up and walked out, the rest of the nick followed suit and the concert was cancelled. So much for the birch as a frightener. It didn't deter Joey from taking part in a walk-out within hours of a birching.

There was one by-product of the filfthy business. Joey's mother heard that he had been birched and at once came on a visit. Before he was allowed to see her he was told that he mustn't give any details of his punishment or the visit would be terminated on the spot. To make sure he didn't say a word out of place a screw stood at his elbow. Mum, who was already distressed, was even more upset when he told her that he couldn't talk about what had happened to him. She left the nick in tears. That this affected Joey more than a dozen birchings is to tell no more than the truth.

There came a time, not long after his wounds had healed, when the Governor of Pentonville made up his mind that he wanted no more of the troublesome Bello. One afternoon Joey was collected from the mailbag shop, taken back to his peter and told to get his gear together. The following morning he was on his way to Dartmoor.

Joey did get a bit of satisfaction during his stay at the Ville. Paddy Onions, who had tried to chop him up in a club in Knightsbridge a year previous, was now an inmate. One morning Joey claimed him right outside the Governor's office. He was armed with a heavy salt-shaker in a sock, and Onions went down with the first blow as the solid earthenware of the shaker shattered. Joey then jumped on the luckless Onions and completed the job by ripping his face to ribbons with the pointed shards. He had waited a long time for his revenge, but it was worth it.

6. The Hardest Survive

There were fifteen of them on the Dartmoor party, and a shabbier looking lot of miscreants would be hard to imagine. They wore their own clothes, which had been lying screwed up for months – in some cases years – in some forgotten corner of Pentonville. They lined up to be cuffed. As an added precaution a chain was passed through the fifteen sets of Home Office jewellery terminating in a live screw at each end.

They were loaded into a coach en route for Paddington Station where they would entrain in a reserved carriage for Princetown. As they were shepherded to the platform across the busy concourse they ran the gauntlet of hundreds of curious eyes. Joey couldn't resist the temptation. A well-dressed City gent was in the forefront of the onlookers.

'Wotcher, Tom,' Joey yelled at the top of his voice. 'When did you get out?'

The rest of the cons joined in and there were shouts of 'Be lucky, Tommy' and 'Keep your nose clean'. The City gent, his face puce, made himself scarce and disappeared in the general direction of Mansion House.

'Shut up there and keep moving,' roared the screw at the rear of the column.

They fell about laughing and were still giggling as they boarded the train. There was a kind of holiday atmosphere about the proceedings, a relaxation of the tensions of prison life. Even the screws exchanged the odd joke with their charges. In a way it was a break for them too.

The journey to Princetown took something like four

hours, and for Joey at least it was a troublesome one. Ever since he had undergone the birching he had been having trouble with his bladder and needed to visit the lavatory frequently. As they were all chained together, whenever he had to go for a leak there was a right old palaver. First he had to be released from the main chain, then a shorter chain was attached to the cuffs, one end of which was held by the screw. He stood outside the part-closed door while Joey performed as you might say single-handed.

At Princetown they were loaded into the coach that would take them to the prison. The laughing and joking now came to a stop as the chilly mists of the Moor closed around them. The jail, when they came to it, was grey and forbidding, a huddle of granite buildings stuck in the middle of nowhere like a scab on the face of nature. Over the massive entrance doors, deeply engraved in the stone, was the legend 'Abandon hope all ye who enter here'.

Joey would never forget his introduction to the grim pile in which he was to spend several years of his young life. They filed into Reception where they shed their clothes, the last link with the outside world, and were issued with the ill-fitting garments that comprised the prison uniform. As Joey put on these damp, smelly articles he lost his last contact with reality and became part of the nightmare which was Dartmoor.

Joey's first impresions were etched deeply on his memory. The prison building itself was shaped like a horseshoe with the open end facing the main gate. From the round part of the horseshoe branched the wings, four of them, A, B, C, D, but only three wings were in use. C wing had been reduced to rubble by rioting prisoners in 1930. The punishment block and the church also formed part of the main building. The hospital and the workshops were separate. There was a football pitch, a straggle of outbuildings and a gatehouse. A fifteen-foot-high wall enclosed the whole area. For a prison wall it was surprisingly low, but where did an escaper go when he had got over it? Miles of treacherous moorland lay between him and freedom.

Joey spent the first three days in the chokey block while somebody somewhere decided where he would go and what sort of work he would do. It shouldn't have been a difficult decision to make because D wing was reserved for cons who had served four years of their sentences and the choice of work was limited. There was the mailbag shop, where rows of men sat day after day thrusting a large needle through heavy canvas, eight stitches to the inch and a punctured thumb every now and then. Then there was the smithy, a noisy and badly-ventilated inferno from which the worker emerged stone deaf at the end of each shift.

Nobody wanted the quarry party. Here gangs of men broke up rocks with sledgehammers, hard manual graft which produced in a week what a mechanical crusher would have turned out in a half-hour. The works party was a fairly cushy number, their efforts being devoted towards keeping the prison in an upright position. The cream of jobs was the farm party where the enterprising con could swipe the odd egg or a few spuds or carrots or anything else that was not nailed down.

While awaiting allocation the new entrants were seen by the various prison officials. The Governor was the first on the list. He had earned the title of 'Iron Man' shortly after his appointment to Dartmoor. According to newspaper reports a hundred discontented cons in the mailbag shop were preparing to riot when the bold Iron Man marched in among them and told them to sit down. They did. What the paper didn't say was that the Iron Man was backed up by fifty screws carrying riot sticks. If the gallant Governor had been on his tod he would have been torn to pieces.

He didn't seem to be all that courageous when Joey first clapped eyes on him. The room was large – it was actually three cells knocked into one – and the Iron Man sat at a table behind an iron grill with the Principal Officer by his side and another three or four screws in the background. No way could have an aggrieved felon have got at him. He barked a few questions over the distance of eighteen feet which separated them, didn't seem to worry whether Joey replied or not and the interview was over.

Next on the list was the doctor, and this was a real farce. Drop your trousers. Cough. Right. Next. That was the medical examination. The story goes that one of the cons was marched in to see the doctor.

'Yes,' barked the medico.

'I'm very worried, doctor. I think I'm masturbating too much.'

'Is anything coming out?'

'Yes, doctor.'

'Right. Carry on. When nothing comes out report sick. Next.'

That was one of the funny stories. There were others more tragic of men dying of hypothermia in freezing cells. On the Moor only the toughest survived.

Joey was fortunate in having several friends already on the Moor who were able to pull a few strings. Billy, who had played a part in his unsuccessful attempt to escape from Pentonville, was working in the blacksmith's shop along with another old mate, Yocker Robinson. The working conditions weren't ideal but at least it was warm and the screw in charge was an esay-going bloke. Billy put Joey's name up and he was allocated.

Joey was lucky in avoiding the alternatives, which were the mailbag shop and the quarry party. The 'no talking' rule on mailbags had recently been dropped, but was substituted with another which permitted a man to talk to his right-hand neighbour. The stupidity of this was evident except to the official mind. What the hell was the use of talking to a bloke who wasn't allowed to reply? The dimwits in charge sorted it out and came up with a brilliant solution. You could talk to the man on either side but not to those in front or behind! Bloody marvellous!

The quarry party was to be avoided at all costs. Out there, in the depths of winter and with temperatures below freezing, human beings were subjected to the most appalling conditions as they swung sledgehammers on the huge rock-piles which had been blasted from the moorland granite. Occasionally some frenzied con would swing his hammer against the nut of one of the warmly dressed screws who had unwisely moved too close. But why didn't the prison authorities use mechanical crushers? The answer is simple. Slave labour at half-a-crown (12½p) a week is cheaper.

Joey was still on the escapers' list so he was put into a peter on the ground floor of A wing. The stone walls dripped water even in the summer and no amount of mopping-up could clear the permanent puddle on the floor. Settling down for the night was an elaborate business for Joey. First he would put his clothes outside the door then, balancing the bed-board beween chair and table, he would put the coir-filled palliasse and pillow on the board. Finally, wrapped in three blankets, he would dry his feet, curl up and try to sleep.

Joey's bladder was still playing him up and, though he tried to resist it, the urge to relieve himself several times during the night added to his troubles. The simple business of having a piss was a major operation. The metal pisspot with its ill-fitting lid was within arm's reach and, still swathed in his blankets, he would swing his legs over the side of the bed-board, hold the pot in a convenient position and let go. Considering that all this was done in pitch darkness, it was a miracle he didn't piss all over himself. As it was, there were times when his aim was bad or the pisspot overflowed. The resulting discomfort can be imagined.

The screw who unlocked him in the morning did nothing to improve the situation. He would wrinkled up his nose and put a disgusted expression on his boat-race.

'Wet the bed again, Bello,' he would sneer.

Any reply would mean being put on Governor's report, so Joey kept his mouth shut. The fucking pillock who'd made the remark had come from a warm and comfortable bed after an early rumpo with his old woman. He could well afford to chuckle. It was part of his sensitive and considerate nature.

One of the minor pleasures in a con's miserable life was having a read between locking up and lights out. To enjoy this relaxation it was necessary not only to have a book but also some light to read it by. Books were a problem. They were dished out once a week, three to a cell, irrespective of author or content. Hence a semi-literate bruiser would find himself wading through Tolstoy's *War and Peace* while in a neighbouring cell an educated con-man would be provided with something like *Gunfight at Broken Lance Creek*.

As to the lighting, Dartmoor had swept into the twentieth century with some startling innovations. When the Prison Commissioners realised that electricity had come to stay, the works party was instructed to knock holes in the walls of adjoining cells. A low-wattage bulb was inserted in the aperture, the two sides closed up with opaque glass and hey presto, two peters were lighted at the price of one. Then space-age technology struck a blow for the benighted con. Each peter was equipped with is own light bulb right in the middle of the ceiling to be cherished and cared for, polished and talked to, by the occupant.

There was only one snag. Your Dartmoor con, by definition a brute beast with no social conscience, would find himself with a roll-up and no means of lighting it, having run out matches. Necessity being the mother of invention, the con would twist a piece of toilet paper round a short length of silver foil, jam the foil against the contacts in the bulb holder and create a flame at the same time as he blew the fuses. Half a dozen cells would be plunged into darkness but the con would enjoy his smoke.

The day's routine would start when the cons were unlocked at 7 am. After the 'slopping out', a sick-making performance described elsewhere in this book, they did their best to shave and wash in cold water. The razor-blades issued for shaving were collected in double-quick time in case a suicidal con tried to cut his throat.

They were all perpetually hungry, but the first meal of the day was enough to take the edge off anybody's appetite. There was always porridge, a lumpy mess made from Canadian Pig Meal which tasted of nothing and stuck like glue to the back of the teeth. With this was a cob of bread, a minute pat of margarine and a teaspoonful of jam. This jam, according to reports, was manufactured in the women's prison at Holloway in the same container used to wash the sanitary towels of the inmates.

As an ocasional treat there was bacon or goulash. The bacon was carved in incredibly thin slices, cooked in watered fat and was little more than a mouthful. The ration for the whole of the nick could have been carved from a live porker and he wouldn't have felt the loss. As for the goulash, any resemblance to the Hungarian dish of that name was purely coincidental. Made from left-over potatoes, scraps of meat and stale bread, it was formed into a slab, baked and then divided into portions. It looked and smelled like dessicated cowshit. To wash down the meal there was a pint of coloured water masquerading as tea. It was completely tasteless with a grey scum floating on the surface but it was wet, warm and welcome.

Work began at eight. Although Joey was in the warm smithy, he put on all the clothing available to him. A con could be moved from one location to another at a moment's notice, so it was as well to be prepared. He wore a pair of long johns, a vest, two shirts, a polo-necked jumper, trousers, overalls, two pairs of socks and a woollen hat pulled down over his ears. All that could be seen of the original Bello was a red nose like a beacon poking out from a mass of rags.

There were a few hard nuts who believed in tempting Providence. One of them was a chap called Pearce, who was about twenty-five and came from Bristol. Even on the coldest days he walked about in an unbuttoned shirt and no vest and continually ribbed the rest of the cons. 'What's the matter with you lot,' he would say. 'What are you all wrapped up for? It isn't cold.' One day he was carried off to hospital with some sort of chest infection and died shortly afterwards. He found out too late that Moor weather is not to be trifled with.

Joey's work in the smithy wasn't all that hard. Along with Billy, Yocker Robinson and Albert Hobbs, the keymaker from the Ville, he hammered lumps of metal into various shapes, tended the furnace and generally made himself useful. Albert was always busy making keys and grapnels for blokes who planned to escape. The instructor screw was an amiable bloke who didn't much care what they did so long as they refrained from bothering him. When he was off duty and they copped for one of the discipline screws they had their own way of dealing with the problem. A wet sack stuffed up the furnace flue, a few quick pumps on the bellows and the smithy would be filled with dense smoke. The screw would then become the target of lumps of iron sailing through the air towards him. He got tired of this performance before very long and retired from the scene.

The escape business was almost a way of life for some of the cons. The smithy crew were kept at it turning our escape tackle but most of it was never used. Joey reckoned that the escapers spent so much time discussing the ways and means that their plots were discovered by the screws before they could be put into action. However the task of smuggling gear through frequent searches kept the cons on their toes and provided some excitement in their drab lives.

Of course there were some escape attempts which got beyond the talking stage. Going over the wall presented no real problem, it was what waited on the other side that made escape almost impossible. Guards mounted on ponies patrolled the moors in the vicinity of the prison and the area was full of natural traps. There were deep holes filled with stinkmud into which a man could fall and disappear in a few minutes without trace, and the constant mist destroyed one's sense of direction.

Two fellows who almost made it were Dennis Staff and a chap called Day. Staff had had it away before and got as far as Port of Spain in Trinidad before being picked up. They went over the wall one misty morning, gambling on the mist clearing later on. It didn't, and they became hopelessly lost. Day was leading the way well ahead of Staff when he suddenly disappeared over the edge of a reservoir, which was his lot. The body was recovered from where it had been trapped by a submerged pipe, which explains why Staff couldn't find him.

Joey had a word with Staff after he had been nicked in London and returned to the Moor. Staff told how he had searched for some time trying to find Day. It was sheer bad luck that Day had been trapped under the pipe, for otherwise he would have got away with nothing more than a ducking.

Another pair who made a getaway in 1957 were Babyface Norman, serving 12 years for armed robbery, and Harper Woodward, doing 14 for armed assault. They got well away from the prison but they were outmatched by fifteen hundred prison officers and coppers, who went over the moors with a fine-tooth comb.

A man whose name always cropped up when escape was under discussion was Ray 'Rubberbones' Webb, who could crawl through the smallest of holes, with the exception of keyholes, and boasted that there was not a nick in the country that could hold him for long. He also made an escape from the Moor, but was duly recaptured after a short spell of freedom.

There was one unplanned escape that almost came off. A bloke called Jennings was near the boiler house with one of his mates as an oil tanker was making a delivery. A quick shufti inside the cab and Jennings saw that the driver had left the keys in the ignition. The two men jumped in and roared away, smashing through the rear gates and out on to the road. Pursued by the police, they treated the huge tanker like a cross between a Formula 1 racing car and a Sherman tank, writing off a couple of police vehicles in their juggernaut progress. The tanker finally committed suicide on a treacherous bend and the desperadoes were captured.

In the smithy escape gear was churned out more from habit than for any other reason. Where it all went to was a mystery. There must have been hundreds of items such as keys, grappling irons, jemmies and suchlike circulating in the confines of the prison, enough for dozens of escape parties. Some of them were discovered in searches and impounded. They never came back to the smithy.

One of the jobs taken on by the blacksmith was shoeing the farm horses, which always provided some amusement.

He would be bending over the animal's hoof scraping away with a file when one of the cons would fire a piece of metal from a catapult at the horse's arse. The huge beast would react to this treatment by having a go at the nearest human object, which was the blacksmith, and proceed to do its best to stomp him into the ground. The blacksmith developed a remarkable agility for a man of his age.

Work in the shops stopped at eleven thirty when the cons went in for lunch. This was an unpalatable mess served up in two-tier billy cans, the bottom half holding the main dish while the top part was supposed to contain the sweet. What usually happened was that the con ended up with a mixture of stew, potatoes and custard, but since it was all equally foul it didn't really matter.

There were numerous complaints about the food but they came to anothing. The Governor had himself tasted the grub, decided it was fit for human consumption, initialled the menu book and that was that. In order to test the Governor's palate, one of the cons pissed in a cup, tipped it into a container of soup then called the Iron Man.

'There's something wrong with this soup, sir,' said the con. 'It tastes something terrible.'

The Iron Man dipped a ladle into the soup and took a mouthful.

'Nothing wrong with that,' he declared.

'It tastes like piss to me,' said the con.

The Iron Man poured the rest of the contents of the ladle down his gullet.

'It certainly doesn't taste like piss to me.'

'Well it should,' said the con. 'I've just pissed in it.' The Governor rushed from the wing and the con was put on report. He was only slightly older than Joey and was serving twenty years for armed robbery. He had made up his mind to do his bird the hard way and was constantly up in arms against authority. Twenty years later Joey came across him in Wandsworth. He was still serving the same sentence, which had been added to on account of several misdemeanours, including cutting a screw.

Joey was the youngest prisoner on the Moor and this had its drawbacks. Today, what with 'gay lib' and 'consenting adults', most youngsters know all about poofs and can spot one a mile off. When the odd lot began to home in on the rosy-cheeked Bello, silly fucker that he was he thought they were being nice and helpful, but Joey tumbled what the game was when one of them made a determined attempt to bugger him.

These men were not limp-wristed sylphs, they were hard men who had their 'girl-friends' among the fairies, but they were not averse to a bit of fresh.

Joey put a stop to that little lark in double-quick time. He made himself a chiv and stuck it into one of his more passionate admirers. He got the message and so did the rest of the bum-fuckers. Joey had no further trouble in that direction.

Prison rules lay down that prisoners must be exercised every day, just like dogs, so for one hour after lunch, winter and summer alike, they trudged round and round the yard between A wing and the hospital. When the snow lay on the ground, deep and crisp and even, they sloshed their way through it.

Work ended for the day to the sound of a strident hooter. This hooter played an important part in the lives of the prison staff, since it also went off half an hour before the end of each shift. It was a well-known fact that the screws had it off with each other's wives as a certain Sunday newspaper made plain in an article referring to Dartmoor as 'the sexbed of England'. The hooter was a convenient warning that hubby would soon be home. It was also a signal for the cons to hurl obscene remarks at the screws, whch didn't make for friendly relations. One day the use of the hooter for this purpose was stopped, and the sexy ladies of Princetown had to fall back on the old alarm clock.

The evenings on the Moor were anything but rounds of pleasure. For the first eighteen months of his sentence the con was locked up in his cell after tea and remained there until the following morning. If he had been a good boy, he then went on stage and on two nights a week he was allowed to associate with his fellow prisoners for one hour during which he could play dominoes, darts or draughts. Card games were not permitted. After a further year he went on to stage two, which gave him an extra night on the tiles. The third and final stage was reached after four years, when the prisoner was transferred to D wing and was able to indulge himself for an hour every night in a wild orgy of dominoes, draughts, darts and, the cherry in life's cocktail, a game of billiards or snooker. He could also have a radio sent in from outside.

In Joey's case the first stage was omitted and he went on association shortly after his introduction to the Moor. He managed to acquire a primitive radio, known as a 'W', on which he was able to listen to the Home Service of the BBC. These illegal sets consisted of a diode with a couple of terminals, one of which was earthed and the other attached to the bell push in the cell. Joey's set was made by Donald Hume, who was an electrician on the works party and was doing twelve years for accessory to murder. He was one of the few blokes to get away with murder and his case made criminal history. He was acquitted of the capital crime but later, after his release from prison, he confessed to a Sunday newspaper that he had in fact killed car-dealer Stanley Setty and distributed his chopped-up body over Essex marshes.

Hume skipped off to Switzerland, where he committed

more crimes. He was sent back to England and ended up in Broadmoor, where it is a safe bet that he will spend the rest of his life.

Cocoa time came at the end of the day when the cons were banged up for the last time. At about seven-thirty the cocoa party made the round of the cells carrying jugs of brown liquid with a film of grease floating on the top. Joey got into the habit of saving the meagre ration of sugar which had been doled out at teatime and adding it to the so-called cocoa, which made it drinkable. The nightcap, so he was told, was heavily laced with bromide to repress the sexual urge. Even the small pleasure of masturbation was made as difficult as possible.

Frequent reference has been made to food in these pages, which is not surprising considering that the cons were always hungry. They got up to all kinds of dodges to get a bit extra, bribing the kitchen workers with snout for a few pieces of duff and thieving anything edible that was around. But, although the authorities point with pride at the menus, claiming that they are varied and adequate, everybody on the staff turned a blind eye to the staggering amount of grub that went out of the front gate and turned up in the screws' quarters. These were looked upon as the perks of the job. Nobody cared that the hungry prisoner was left with the scrag ends of meat, watery tea, insufficient sugar and an unsatisfied appetite.

There was no work at the weekends. It was then that most of the visits took place when relatives and friends travelled from all over the country, spending hours on trains and buses, for the doubtful pleasure of spending an hour looking through a sheet of wired glass and talking to the prisoner via a close-meshed grill as a screw patrolled behind him. It must have been shattering for a wife, longing to put her arms round her man, and even worse for the kids wondering why they couldn't touch their dads.

The weekly football match was played on Saturday, an event in which Joey sometimes took part. If he didn't play, he watched the game, a fiercely contested battle during which many of the cons took the opportunity to pay off old scores. Nobody envied the referee, poor sod, whose whistle worked overtime as he did his best to maintain some sort of order. All was not blessed peace and quiet on the touchlines either as the cons came to blows when violence erupted on the playing field.

Part of the weekend was reserved for God. Attendance at the Sunday service was compulsory, but it is doubtful that anyone derived spiritual uplift from the dreary sermons droned from the pulpit. The choir was largely composed of fairies who seized the chance to wear anything approaching a frock. Dolled up in cassock and surplice, wearing the teeniest trace of make-up, they lent a bizarre touch to this parody of religious observance. Add to this a bunch of the choicest villains in the country singing 'Nearer my God to thee' and you have a sight that beggars the imagination.

Joey came of age on the Moor in more ways than one. On his twenty-first birthday, alone in his cell, he scribbled the following lines. He didn't claim that they were great poetry, but they expressed what he felt at the time.

> The gift I shall most like
> I shall most certainly not get.
> Others may get the key of the door
> But not if they come of age
> As I shall, in Dartmoor.
> In Dartmoor they are more careful
> With their keys than that.

The Moor gobbled up five years of Joey's youthful life, and

they were very important years. As a raw kid of twenty he was thrown in at the deep end among a ripe collection of some of the most violent and brutal criminals of that era. At the time he didn't realise what might have happened to him but looking back, with Wandsworth, Chelmsford and Parkhurst behind him, he was amazed that he came through with only a few scars as witness of those early Dartmoor days.

Some events stand out in his memory. The picture of Bobby, ex-boxer and associate of Billy Hill, serving seven for a bloody attack in 1956, is as fresh in Joey's mind as though it were yesterday. Bobby suddenly got religious and marched round the touchline at the Saturday football game calling on God for help and guidance. It couldn't be anything but a joke.

'Turn it in, Bobby,' said one of the spectators. 'You might kid the chaplain but you can't kid God. He can see through you.'

The angel of light, love and mercy turned on the doubting Thomas and knocked him spark out with a right-hander that spread the poor fellow's nose all over his face. This smiting of the Philistine went unnoticed by all but a few of those standing nearby. Perhaps it was even too quick for God to see. Bobby's conversion was abandoned after that incident and it wasn't long before he returned to his former ways. The ex-avenging angel is still knocking people out to this day but not at God's behest.

While on the matter of religion, the church building deserves a mention. Apart from the Sunday services, it also did duty as cinema, concert hall and general entertainment centre. On these festive occasions the six observation posts, three on each side of the hall, were packed with screws as the cons watched ancient films such as 'The Perils of Pauline', the original version of 'Bengal Lancers' and similar masterpieces in numb-arsed boredom.

There were also live concerts at which a few well-known faces put in an appearance, but the other side of the coin was represented by well-intentioned do-gooders who thought that a captive audience would tamely watch any old rubbish. The Womens' Institute soprano giving an off-key rendering of Ave Maria was interrupted by yells of 'Get off you old strumpet' or 'Show us yer knickers'. The performer at a Moor concert had to be good or the act died the death.

There were times when the church also served as an abattoir. This happened when a certain con was marked down for a bit of treatment by some of his fellows, on account of his having offended against their ideas of what was right and proper. The intended victim would take his seat while the attacker chose a place immediately behind him. The victim would have a couple of the attacker's mates ranged either side. As soon as the lights went out the attacker would grab his victim by the hair, pull his head back and go to work on him with a chiv. Following that performance, which was over in a couple of seconds, the victim would be pushed violently forward over the seats in front of him and the chiv thrown as far away as possible.

When the lights went on and the commotion had died down, the injured man would be found some distance away from the scene of the attack. After the screws had sorted things out it was quite likely that several innocents would be nicked for the crime of having blood-stained clothing. It was also more than likely that the real perpetrators would get off scot-free. The authorities were not interested in the finer points of establishing guilt. A man had been cut, you had blood on your clothes, therefor you had been concerned in the incident, so down the chokey you go, remanded for the Visiting Magistrates.

The reasons for these cuttings and stabbings were many and various. The victim might be considered a grass, an informer either to the police or the prison authorities. Again, he might have been sentenced for sex offences against young children or crimes of violence against his own kids. But the main reasons for these attacks, which resulted in serious maiming and sometimes death, were rows over a few pennyworth of tobacco.

The situation normally boiled down to this. A prisoner was paid half-a-crown a week, which was just enough to buy three-eighths of an ounce of tobacco, a packet of cigarette papers and a box of matches. By making his roll-ups very thin and skilfully splitting each match into four with a needle, he would have enough smokes to last him for about four days. The plight of the heavy smoker who had his wages docked for some offence against prison discipline can be imagined. It was then that the miserable con turned to the tobacco baron.

The baron played an important part in the prison economy. Snout was the currency of the cons. Betting on horse races, purchasing favours, bribing the kitchen party for extra food, all these transactions were carried out on the snout exchange. The baron was a con who, via outside contacts and bent screws, was able to build up a store of this valuable commodity and he was a king in the nick, literally having the power of life and death over the other inmates.

This was how it worked in practice. The con would go to baron A and get the loan of an ounce of snout, to be repaid plus fifty per cent interest on the next pay day. Unable to meet the deadline, he would go to baron B and borrow enough snout to cover his original debt. Finally he would end up owing far more than he would ever be able to repay from his pittance of a wage. He then had two courses open to him. He could apply to the Governor under Rule 43 for segregation from other prisoners or he could brazen it out.

The con who chose the latter course of action was on a hiding to nothing. Obviously the baron could not allow such a liberty as non-payment of the debt, which would undermine his authority in the nick. Thus the defaulter would meet with a serious accident which landed him in hospital or, in some cases, the mortuary. A life for a few bobsworth of snout! Seems incredible, doesn't it? Yet in the nick small grievances are magnified out of all proportion.

South London Jimmy had a bet on with another con, the stake being a portion of dinnertime duff. This duff was almost uneatable but very filling. The debt was not settled, either deliberately or through forgtfulness, and Jimmy stuck a pair of scissors into the other bloke, who died as a result. The killer had another ten years added to his sentence and the victim was put underground for ever. All this for what amounted to no more than a handful of flour.

Joey was a non-smoker, but he still managed to get himself involved in a tobacco barons' war between a team of Londoners and a Scottish mob, as a result of which he ended up in hospital with serious cut to his face and back. Wondering about the attitude of the authorities towards the trafficking in tobacoo, Joey came to the conclusion that they turned a blind eye to it. They knew who the barons were and it would have been a simple matter to turn them over regularly and confiscate their stocks, which would have put them out of business. So why wasn't this done? Well, as long as the cons fought each other they wouldn't be fighting against the system that was the cause of the bother in the first place.

There are two memories of the Moor which Joey would carry as long as he lived. One is that he spent his twenty-first birthday banged up in a cold, wet peter. The other is that, when the news was brought to him that his father had died, he was refused permission to attend the funeral by some snotnose bastard sitting behind a desk at the Home Office.

7. Brotherhood

At last the great day came, the day when Joey left behind him the dirt, depression and degradation of Dartmoor. He returned to London in style in a chauffeur-driven Rolls Bentley sent by courtesy of his mates in the Dale.

It's a tradition among the brotherhood of villains that any one of them who has been away for a long stretch gets a 'welcome home' party. Joey's was a real slap-up affair. Publicans and bookies from the Dale had clubbed together with his brothers and some mates from the manor and taken over a large house in Notting Hill for the night. When Joey got there the party was in full swing. Booze was unlimited and there was a fair ration of birds.

It wasn't long before Joey was feeling on top of the world what with the drink and the food and all that, so he cast his eye around for a bit of the other, of which there was plenty available. Joey captured a right little raver and wasted no time in whipping her outside the room and into the passage. He had intended to make for one of the bedrooms but his feelings got the better of him. She wasn't wearing any knickers, which meant that she was open for business, so he lifted her dress and got stuck in and it was lovely after all those years of dreaming about it.

Joey was about to shoot his load when the door of the room was flung open and what seemed like an army rushed past them. The bird gave a scream, hooked herself off the rod and scarpered. Joey thought it was a police raid and rushed down to the street, where a real battle was going on. About a dozen blokes from the party were knocking bags of shit out of a couple of geezers, giving them a proper seeing-to before throwing them into a pile of dustbins. Eventually they all went back indoors, where Joey discovered what had caused the ruck.

It seems that one of the birds was looking out of the window and saw these two blokes messing about with one of the cars, a white Jag which belonged to one of the tastest villains in the Dale.

'Hey, who owns the white Jag,' she yells above the tumult.

The owner, thinking he has scored, chirps up right away.

'It's mine, darling. Fancy a ride?'

'Not really,' replies the bird, 'but there are two blokes down there who do. They're trying to nick it.'

That's what caused the stampede. Joey couldn't help but feel sorry for the two poor sods who'd copped for a spanking. They must have been overjoyed when they saw this long line of expensive motors just waiting to be nicked. Even if it came on top the worse they could expect was a half-hearted chase by a few flabby company directors. How they must have felt when they were dropped on by a dozen of the most diabolical villains in London can be imagined.

As was usual the boys had a whip round for Joey, so he wasn't short of marching money. Some of the top lads chipped in with a few hundred, which was decent of them. Joey took a few days holiday during which he saw some old chums and generally picked up the threads of his life once more.

One day Joey was approached by a little firm from the West End who owned a hotel in Pembridge Gardens. This gaff had been run by a chap called Serge Paplinski, a sort of adopted son of Peter Rachman. He had allowed it to get into a run down state, but the firm who took it over had tarted it up and filled half the rooms with brasses.

Tarts and trouble go together as the hotel's new owners quickly found out. Their proposition was that Joey should mind the place, in return for which he would have his own flat and a handsome earner, and it would be up to him to use his own methods to keep the peace. It was an offer he couldn't refuse. He moved into the flat, which was nicely furnished and very comfortable, and settled down to enjoy himself.

The work wasn't hard and he had plenty of time on his hands, so he was able to keep an eye on his other interests. However he spent a lot of time at the hotel, where he was on good terms with some of the younger brasses who had just started on the game and weren't all that shop-soiled. If one of them fancied a bit on the side Joey duly obliged. It was what he called his 'fucking perks'.

The head girl in this establishment for naughty ladies called herself Annie Laurie. She was a right hard case and knew all the tricks of the trade. She came from Australia and was a great favourite with the lads from down under, who nicknamed her 'The Witch'. Joey wasn't on very good terms with her on account of the fact that she was aware of his encounters with some of her girls. A strict moralist, she didn't approve of them doing it for nothing.

One evening Joey was standing in the foyer when one of the girls came in with a punter, a well-dressed geezer carrying a brief case. Annie stepped forward.

'Good evening, sir,' she said. 'I'll have your case taken care of.'

She turned to Joey and snapped her fingers.

'Porter. Take the gentleman's case up.'

Joey didn't know whether to laugh or belt her one. Anyway he copped for the case and led the way upstairs, then nipped back sharpish to have a ruck with the saucy cow. Needless to say, she had done a disappearing act.

The basement part of the building was a club, all legal and above-board, run by Jeanette Roberts and her husband Roland. His real name was Kofi, and he was press attache to the Ghana High Commission. He was a very well-educated man and spoke several languages, and it was due to him that the Garden Club, as it was known, numbered among its members three ambassadors and an assorted bunch of foreign diplomats.

Joey spent some time in the club and was on good terms with Roland, who came to rely on him to a great extent in keeping the premises free of trouble. There wasn't a lot of that for the punters were on the whole very well-behaved, but if the clouds began to gather Roland would give Joey a signal by stroking the back of one hand with the other. Joey would sort out the offender, ease him out of the door and attend to him in the yard. On these occasions he was always on to a good drink.

Roland ran into trouble in 1965, when he collected some unfavourable publicity and was recalled to Ghana. Two years later he was nicked along with a wealthy young Lebanese called Kazoun, and sentenced to four years at the Old Bailey for possession of cannabis.

Joey was going very nicely at Pembridge Gardens and money was rolling in from other ventures in which he had a share. He made some good friends on the way to prosperity but he also made some enemies. This led to a tragic happening which left him with unhappy memories.

Veronica was a stunning bird with a great personality whom he met in one of the clubs. She wasn't a slag, just one of the good-time girls who enjoyed life and went around with a permanent smile on her face. They hit it off together and she moved in with Joey at the flat. He took her around with him most of the time and they were seen together in the various clubs and restaurants by a lot of people, some of them not all that friendly to Joey. He should have seen the red light, but he didn't.

He was at his club in Kensington one night, having gone there on his tod to sort out a little problem that had cropped up when he was called to the phone.

'Bello,' said a male voice at the other end of the line.

'Who's that,' said Joey.

'Better get home a bit sharpish, mate, we've just done your bird five-handed.' There was a loud mocking laugh and the line went dead.

Joey was out of the door and in his motor in seconds. He drove like a lunatic along Kensington High Street, jumping traffic lights, ignoring halt signs and overtaking everything in front of him. Over the top of Campden Hill by the water tower he went, hand on the horn and headlights blazing, hoping all the time that it was a bit of kidology, some comedian winding him up, but feeling in his heart of hearts that this one was for real. He pulled up in front of the hotel, leaving the lights on and the engine running, and dashed into the flat.

He had seen some terrible sights in his time but this one beat them all. Veronica was spreadeagled on the bed, stark naked, her wrists and ankle secured by cords which passed under the mattress. A handful of paper tissues had been crammed into her mouth, blood dripped from her lips, her face was a bruised and swollen mess and her body was covered with angry red weals. A sharp smell of semen and sweat lingered in the room. She was making small moaning noises through the gag, moving her head from side to side, the look of a wounded animal in her eyes. Joey was sickened.

He untied her hands and feet and took the gag out of her mouth. As he did so four of her teeth fell out on the pillow. Her ready smile had been one of her most attractive features, but it would never be the same again. Her hands moved to cover her sex where a raw patch oozing blood from several tiny wounds showed where one of the rapists had torn out a handful of her pubic hair. Joey tried to comfort her but it wasn't on and she wouldn't tell him a thing about what had happened. She sat around the flat for a couple of days in a dressing gown, drinking heavily and not saying a word. One morning, while Joey was out on a bit of business, she packed her bags and left. He never saw her again.

Joey did his best to find the animals who had done this thing. Apart from what had happened to Veronica, this was a liberty aimed directly at him and he couldn't let it go unpunished. He had word that a firm from the Bush was missing from its usual haunts and the rumour was that they had gone up North. He spent a few days hunting round the Leeds and Manchester areas but drew a blank. Perhaps it was just as well that he didn't find them for he had every intention of taking a spectacular revenge. He would have had no compunction in castrating the bastards and watching them bleed to death very slowly with their severed goolies stuffed down their throats.

Poor Veronica came off worst in the affair, but that's the way life goes. When the knives are out the innocent suffer along with the guilty. She should have known that if you play with fire you're bound to get burned sooner or later.

It was some time before Joey recovered from his fury over the event. His resentment and desire for revenge abated and, with hindsight, he realised that Veronica wasn't the stuff of which gangsters' molls are made. A villain's dolly bird needed to be tough and resourceful and should, above all, possess an instinct for survival equal to that of an alley cat. At times she might be called upon to fight like a man, particularly when some rival moved in on what she regarded as her territory.

Joey remembered one incident which more than proved the point. It was in a club in Shepherd's Bush and a few faces had assembled to celebrate the fact that one of them had brought off a fairly large tickle. Each villain was accompanied by his bird, for on these occasions the wives were left indoors. The drinks flowed fast and furious, the music was loud and all were having a wonderful time when suddenly it came on top. The partner of a West London villain, a good-looking blonde by the name of Caroline, took exception to one of the club hostesses who was showing out in no uncertain fashion to her escort. The exchange of insults between the two girls was short and to the point.

'Fuck off out of it, you slag,' said Caroline.

'Bollocks,' replied the hostess, and the battle was on.

Caroline slid off the bar stool, grabbed her opponent by the hair and stuck a right-hander into her ribs with all the accuracy of a professioal pugilist. The hostess, who was obviously no mug when it came to taking care of herself, gave a little gasp, stepped back and raked both long-nailed hands down Caroline's cheeks. The blood flowed and the crowd cheered.

'Stand back,' roared the villain who was the cause of the row. 'Let 'em fight it out.'

The two girls did just that. After swapping punches they came to grips, tearing at each other's hair and clothes until, half-naked, they rolled on the floor, treating the spectators to a close-up of tits and pussy that would have delighted the audience at a strip show, only it was all for free.

The end came suddenly. Caroline took hold of the other girl's right arm, rolled her over so that she was face downwards on the floor and very neatly snapped the arm across her leg. There was a loud crack, the hostess screamed and the fight was over.

The proprietor of the club, who had been hovering in the background, came to the fore.

'Alright, ladies and gentlemen,' he said. 'Cabaret time's over.'

Looking back at that display of female brutality Joey saw quite clearly the distinction between the public and private lives of those who, like himself, regarded villainy as a way of life. In the domestic environment the villain kept his wife and family contented by supplying the wherewithal. On social occasions the wife was present along with other wives in a supporting role, indulging in gossip while the husband chatted with the other husbands. Everything was proper, bad language was strictly out of order and any invasion of privacy on the part of members of the public outside the privileged circle was dealt with in summary fashion.

In his private life the villain was another man completely. He drank, gambled, cursed, screwed and immersed himself in any form of depravity that took his fancy. When he copped for a bit of bird, the wife took on the job of family provider, faithfully visiting her spouse as and when the regulations permitted. It was all part of a pattern which regularly repeated itself.

When any questions were asked about the husband's whereabouts there was a stock answer. He's away, the wife would say, which did not mean that he was disporting himself in the sun on some foreign shore but was slopping out and performing other menial tasks as an unwilling guest of Her Majesty.

8. The Villains

In the Spring of 1964 Joey had a lot on his mind. Though he took no part in that caper of all time, the Great Train Robbery of August 1963, the activity on the part of the Old Bill affected all those who had something to hide. More than two and a half million sovs had gone missing, and that had to be recovered. Added to that there had been interference with Her Majesty's Mail, an offence only slightly less serious than interfering with HM herself. The Old Bill put themselves about and the waves they made were felt throughout the British Isles.

In the upshot Scotland Yard's Detective Chief Superintendent Butler led the team that captured practically all of the mob and they were now being weighed off at Aylesbury Assizes with Mr Justice Edmund Davies in charge of dishing out the porridge. The leading members of the gang copped for thirty years each, a result which sent shivers down the spine of every villain in the country.

There had been plenty of newspaper comment on this job and books have been written airing all kinds of theories about the master-mind who set it up. There is a man who had the contacts and the organising ability to do it but he must be nameless. He wasn't among those who got away because he was never there. Joey was not the only man who knew his name and has yet to meet the man who would have the guts to publish it. One day, after a famous funeral, the truth will be told.

Every villain has a 'one that got away' story. Knowing how

luck plays an important part in any blag, many of them must be true. In Joey's case this one was the real McCoy.

A couple of pals brought him some genuine information about a diamond merchant's in Hatton Gardens which is, by the way, one of the best policed areas in London. Burglar alarm technology in the early sixties was not what it is today, but some trust was placed in security guards. Being human they often fell by the way, and this particular geezer on duty in the building was prepared to leave the premises unguarded for an hour for a cash consideration.

Joey had to have a good peterman or safe-blower for the job because the diamonds were kept in a massive old Miller safe. One of Joey's mates brought in the Professor – he was really known by that name – and the four of them set out one night to do the job. They met in a pub just off Hatton Garden and had a couple of drinks while they waited for the nod from the security man.

The guard turns up on the dot, comes into the pub and tips Joey the wink that he can go to work. They have one hour. They go over to the office building, enter by the main door and go up to the third floor. There is enough light coming in from the street so they don't need torches. John is on the stairs where he can see into the street from a window. Joey and the Profesor go into the office where the Miller is all on its own in a corner. The Professor gives it the once-over, says it will be no trouble and sets about packing explosive round the lock. Joey wanders about in the office, which is also a small workroom, collecting anything lying around on the benches. Finally the Professor has finished. He sets the detonator and runs the wires out into the passage while Joey takes up the carpet and drapes it over the safe and opens the windows so that the blast does not blow them out. They get the all-clear from John on the stairs, the Professor touches the wires to the terminals of the battery, there is a dull thud and the office fills with smoke. They go into action. While Joey closes the windows to prevent the tell-tale smoke from drifting out into Hatton Garden the Professor tugs at the door of the safe which has opened a little way and then jammed. Another charge is needed so they repeat the process. The door remains stuck in the same position. Joey tries to squeeze his arm inside to get at the contents but the gap is too small. There is no more Jelly and the hour is almost up.

They give the safe a few hearty kicks but without result and finally have to leave before the guard gets back. Their total haul from the workbenches goes to the dabbler for a couple of grand. They have risked a ten stretch for five hundred apiece.

Their feelings can be imagined when they read in the mid-day paper that the office cleaner came in, pulled at the door of the safe – and it opened. There was only a quarter of a million quid worth of diamonds in it! To say they were choked is putting it mildly.

Not all Joey's operations were a piece of cake. There is a darker side to the underworld of which the public knows nothing. There violence is a commonplace as teams of villains carve each other up over some incident or other which might seem unimportant to the outsider. Few of these affrays come before the courts unless a grass informs the Old Bill.

The professional criminal regards the grass as the lowest form of animal life and every man's hand is against him or her. Whatever the rights or wrongs of a dispute it should be settled without turning to the law, either by a straightener or a battle between the two sides.

Jack Spot's wife Rita was looked upon as a grass since she had been directly responsible for Frankie Fraser and Bobby Warren being put away, so when she walked into the Magic Carpet club in Shepherd's Bush with a villain called Jimmy

Emmett there was some resentment felt that she had been let in. Joey was one of those who said that the team who owned the club had been out of order, and they got the needle. Out of this single incident came a row that ended with the complete destruction of the Magic Carpet and another club owned by the same team.

What happened was that the Shepherd's Bush mob sorted out a couple of Joey's mate and knocked them about pretty badly to give him the message that they didn't like his attitude in the Rita Comer business. If Joey hadn't done something about this by way of retaliation his name would have been mud on the manor, and he couldn't afford that. He got a team together and one evening they dropped in on both clubs and wrecked them. They never re-opened.

The thing about violence is that once it starts it spreads rapidly. You have a ruck with somebody and they can't get back at you so they have a go at someone close, like a mate or a member of your family. Joey's brother Tommy was out one night with his wife having a drink in a local pub. It was a small place with an outside toilet. Tommy went for a slash but no sooner was he outside the door than four blokes jumped out of a parked car and set about him with knives, coshes and razors. They cut him up badly, slicing off part of an ear and stabbing him in the body, then they got back in the car and had it away. So far as they were concerned Tommy could have been a goner.

Joey's brother didn't die but he was marked for life. He had, however, recognised one of the mob and rough justice was done a few nights later. In the dead of night two blokes got into this geezer's house and, while one of them held him down on the bed the other went to work with a chiv, giving him all that Tommy had received and a bonus. Without going into detail it would be a miracle if he ever fathered kids.

Perhaps the most frightening aspect of violence is the use

of shooters. As a trained boxer Joey could take care of himself in a punch-up because he knew how and where to hit. The other fellow also knew this, so if he was fronting Joey single-handed he would provide himself with a gun. Since you can't explain Queensberry rule to a bullet and a pair of fists is no match for a .45, Joey was sometimes forced to carry a shooter himself. There's also another side to the question. The finest fighter in the world is no match for a mob armed with knives and coshes.

A shooter is an excellent weapon of offence or defence but carrying has its dangers. For starters, if you happen to be carrying and you get nicked it's a cert that five years will be added to your sentence whatever else happens. Joey was lucky when he was nabbed in Shepherd's Bush because of his youth. If he'd been older they would have thrown the book at him. Ronnie Kray was also one of the lucky ones when he made one with Bobby Ramsey and Billie Jones in '56. He was carrying but he got away with three years.

There is also the hazard of accidental discharge. Noller Knowles, a mate of Joey's, carried a shooter which had a faulty safety catch. He was fishing for his keys outside his front door when he touched the trigger. The bullet went straight through his chest, killing him instantly.

Going back to boxing, the Bello's were a real fighting family. Even Mum could perform with the best of them as she proved on one occasion. Joey's brother was at a party with Yocker when some woman got the needle and smashed a bottled over Nobby's head. Naturally he could not retaliate in kind but he popped off home and, while Mum attended to his wounds, he told he what had happened. Nothing would satisfy Mum but that this female should get her deserts, so when the doctoring was finished she piled into Yocker's car along with Nobby and they went back to the party.

When they arrived Mum sorted out the woman and

squared up to her, giving the surprised female a right whacking, left jabs and right crosses, the whole business, finishing the job by knocking her out with a right cross of which Cassius Clay would not have been ashamed. There the matter would have ended but this cow nicked mum who was bound over to keep the peace at West London. This put an end to Mum's boxing career which, according to Yocker and Nobby who had ringside seats, was a pity. She showed championship potential.

In the sort of life that Joey led it doesn't do to be taken by surprise. There's always the possibility of being almost axed in half, cut to ribbons or shot at so, in any uncertain situation, it's best to take immediate action and leave the apologies until later. For example, Joey was walking along King Street in Hammersmith one day when he noticed a bloke coming towards him and giving him the once over. As they passed each other the bloke shot out a hand, grabbing Joey by the arm and mumbling something or other. Joey's instant reaction was to swing round, bring his knee up sharply into the chap's balls and put a right-hander into his chops. Leaving him groaning on the pavement, Joey had it away.

He thought he had foiled just another villain-inspired attack, but this was not the case. The 'villain' was a plain-clothes Old Bill and he was done for assault and resisting arrest. There is a little bit of justice left in the world because when Joey explained the copper's method of arrest the beak gave him the benefit of the doubt and put him on probation.

It would be impossible to write about the underworld and its violence without mentioning the Kray twins, whose exploits both in and out of prison have made headlines over the past quarter of a century. Books have been written about them and they have figured largely in the memoirs of retired coppers. Nowhere in the vast mass of words is what could be described as the simple truth about them. It can be expressed in three words. They were villains.

What is a villain? By definition he is a violent, malevolent or unscrupulous evil-doer who is low-born and base. What the dictionary does not say is that he lives in a separate world apart from normal society, a world that has its own rules and very rigid codes. It is something the outsider can never hope to understand completely. On the inside, where Joey was, the understanding of these matters is the difference between survival and extinction.

Like Joey and many others, Ronnie and Reggie Kray were natural-born villains and villainy was their business. When they went out to capture their sometimes very considerable rewards they made their own rules which had nothing to do with Acts of Parliament. They could be expressed in a few words. The loot was shared out fairly and if you were nicked you didn't grass. Fail to obey the rules and you were either seriously injured or dead.

So where did the Krays and the Richardsons and the Tibbs and the rest fit into society? The answer is they didn't fit in at all. They killed and maimed each other for a variety of reasons and the only members of the public who were involved were the idiots who tried to have a go and came off second best. There are certain facts of life of which everyone should be aware and one of them is that the maintaining of law and order is best left to the Old Bill. By and large, when the amateur interferes in a row between professionals he will invariably get the shitty end of the stick. Put it this way. Who but a raving lunatic would jump into a ring where Cassius Clay and Joe Frazier were belting hell out of each other and try to interfere with the battle?

There's also another important point to be borne in mind. The Old Bill and the villain, both professionals in their respective fields, have the measure of each other and if a situation that looks like ending in bloody murder can be resolved by a touch of bribery and corruption then all's well that ends well. There's no trial, which saves the taxpayer's money, the overcrowded prisons don't become more overcrowded, the Old Bill cop a few bob and the villain skips off to Spain with the loot. The only lot to lose out are the insurance companies and they can well afford it. The whole set-up may be illegal and immoral but it's practical.

As in any other section of society, vendettas and feuds happen in the underworld but they last longer and are more violent than a quarrel between neighbours in suburbia. Some of the firms seemed to adopt a principle of 'if you're not with us you're against us'. In the mid-Sixties, when gang battles in the London area were giving the Met all kinds of headaches, Joey must have put a foot wrong somwhere.

The first indication of trouble came one evening when he was at a birthday celebration in the Jack of Clubs, a Mayfair nightspot. He was with friends who owned a pub in Seven Sisters Road. Minding the club at the time was a fellow called George Cornell who was later to get a bullet through the head in the Blind Beggar pub in Whitechapel. The man who fired the fatal shot was Ronnie Kray, but that's another story.

Joey had known George in prison and they got on quite well together. He came over to Joey's table and chatted for a while, wished Joey's friend a happy birthday and left. Joey had no suspicion that there was anything wrong, so he was surprised when one of the waiters came over and warned him in a whisper that Cornell was on the phone arranging for a firm to sort him out. Joey lost no time in gathering his party together and having it away. From the end of the street he watched as two car-loads of heavies pulled up outside the club. It was either the All-in Wrestlers' annual night out or Cornell's reception committee. Joey didn't wait to find out.

About a fortnight later a bloke called Bello, but no relation to Joey, was grabbed by a team and stabbed before being driven away in a van. Thinking he was dead the team had wrapped him up in a carpet, but in fact he was very much alive, and when he came to he started chucking himself about and screaming and yelling. This was too much for the driver and his mate. They obviously didn't fancy explaining to the Old Bill why their carpet was having a fit. They left the van with its load intact and scarpered.

It may have been that this villain was mistaken for Joey or vice versa, or maybe it was another villain altogether who was down for a bit of treatment. It wouldn't be the first case of a mix-up in gangland feuds which were becoming a feature of a criminal landscape in the Sixties. Ginger Marks got himself shot outside the Carpenters Arms in Cheshire Street late one night, but it was all a mistake. Somebody else should have been on the receiving end.

It was a curious thing that the body was taken away and not left where it had fallen. The only other case in Joey's recollection concerned Frank Mitchell, whose body also disappeared after a shooting. Maybe there was a connection between the two incidents. There was also Jack McVitie, again a vanishing body, but he was stabbed to death according to an eye-witness. Of these three killings only one was solved. Reggie Kray was convicted of McVitie's murder at the Old Bailey in 1968, although the defence claimed that Ronnie Hard wielded the knife that sent McVitie on his last journey.

These killings and many others were the outcome of underworld vendettas which are being carried on right up to the present time. Those concerned claim that it is nobody's business but theirs and even the Old Bill seem to accept the situation with some reservations. Joey had the feeling that somewhere high up in the private councils of the Met a cynical group took the view that the more the villains bumped each other off the less work the law would have to do.

It appeared logical to Joey that the law should turn a blind eye to some of the goings-on until the time arrived when they had to do something. Then there would be a grand round-up, a spectacular trial at the Old Bailey with cars, vans and motor-cycles dashing around, screaming sirens and all the rest of the paraphernalia. All this may have terrified the public. It didn't frighten the villains one little bit. They let the dust die down and then carried on with the vendettas.

In 1970 David Knight, a younger brother of Ronnie Knight, was stabbed to death in a London night club. Tony Zomparelli, adopted son of Albert Dimes, was found guilty of killing and served four years for manslaughter.

In 1974 Zomparelli was shot dead in a Soho amusement arcade. Ronnie Knight, Nicky Gerard and George Bradshaw were brought to trial for the killing. Knight and Gerard were acquitted.

In 1978 Michael Gluckstead was shot and stabbed in the Norseman club in Dockland. Nicky Gerard received seven years for grievous bodily harm.

In 1979 Johnny Mangan was shot at and left for dead in the East End. He survived. The man charged with attempted murder (and acquitted) was Brian 'Little Legs' Clifford who was later shot through the head while asleep in his bed.

Mickey Hennessey, Peter's elder brother, was blasted by a shotgun through the side window of his car. His attackers escaped.

In 1980 Alfie Gerard, father of Nicky Gerard, was found dead in mysterious circumstances in a Brighton boarding house.

In 1981, during a fight in a club at the Elephant and Castle, Chris Byrne had his throat cut with a broken bottle and died from his injuries. The attacker, a man called Peter Kelly, was convicted of manslaughter and jailed for four years.

The body of Colin 'Dukey' Osborne was found on Hackney Marshes. He was on the run from the police and evidence indicated that his corpse had been dumped from a moving car.

Club owner George Bell, a close friend of Peter Kelly who had ben jailed for the manslaughter of Chris Byrne, was shot twice in the stomach outside the City club near the Angel at Islington.

Towards the end of 1982 Nicky Gerard was shot to death outside his home. The two men who committed the murder made their getaway.

Patrick O'Nione, known as Paddy Onions, lies dead outside a South London wine bar, shot by an unknown assassin.

A fitting comment on this grim recital of murder and serious injury was provided by Barbara Windsor, actress and ex-wife of Ronnie Knight.

'This has been going on for years,' she said. 'When is it going to stop?'

9. Violent and Dangerous

Came the Spring and Joey was in trouble again. He had a good run and pulled off several jobs but the law caught up wit him and he was in Brixton on remand on several charges of robbery which he reckoned would earn him five years. There was nothing to be done so he settled back to enjoy the period of remand.

Being on remand isn't all that bad. A prisoner is allowed to wear his own clothes and have grub sent in from outside. Also, since he is innocent until proved guilty he can't be put to work. This, as can be imagined, doesn't go down too well with the screws. So far as they are concerned a con is a con and shouldn't be permitted to strut about the boob smoking his head off and indulging in big eats. To even things up the screws go out of their way to make things difficult for visitors bringing in the goodies.

When they tried this performance on with his Mum, Joey got the dead needle. She had come all the way from the Dale to pay him a visit only to be turned away by the screws at the gate. Joey heard about this through the prison grapevine and went on Governor's application right away, determined to create a hell of a stink. Joey had quite a lot of experience of prison Governors. Some of them are fair-minded men who are prepared to listen to what a con has to say but others are just arseholes, full of their own self-importance, having doors opened for them and being saluted wherever they go in the nick. The Brixton Governor was one of the arseholes. When Joey was escorted in to see him, a screw at his elbow, he didn't bother to look up from the papers on the desk in front of him.

'Yes, Bello,' he says.

Joey tells him what happened to his mother and all he does is snigger and the Chief Officer standing beside him has a quiet grin. Joey looks at this pair of bastards enjoying a joke at his Mum's expense and he's almost beside himself with rage. What the hell can he do? He must do something.

'I don't see what you expect me to do about it, Bello,' said the pompous shit.

This is the last straw. Joey has been dying for a piss while waiting outside the office and what follows is almost automatic. Quick as a flash he unzips his fly, takes his prick out and before the screw beside him can do anything to prevent it, he has sprayed the Governor with a cascade of steaming hot piss. All hell is let loose. The screw jumps him and starts screaming for help, more screws rush in and Joey is carted away, still pissing, to a padded cell in the hospital wing.

The news went round the nick like wildfire. Prison history had been made. There had been many previous instances of piss-pots being emptied over screws and senior officers but this was the first time in living memory that a Governor had been deluged with the freshly-made article. Even some of the screws had a good laugh. The Governor wasn't all that popular with most of his staff either.

Joey was kept in the hospital wing until the date of his trial but received no punishment for his breach of the 'thou shalt never piss over the Governor' rule. There was now no doubt in his mind that the authorities suspected that he had gone round the bend and were treating him like a fully-fledged lunatic. At the Old Bailey he duly marched up the steps, copped for three years and was whipped off to Wandsworth where he was locked up in the hospital. Joey's inspired guess was confirmed when he was transferred to

Tooting Bec hospital and placed under observation in a mental ward.

It's an ill wind that blows nobody any good, as the proverb says. As Joey walked round the ward muttering to himself like the rest of the loonies, he soon decided that having it away would be easy. Choosing the right moment he smashed a window and was three quarters of the way to freedom by the time the staff realised that one of their prize nutters was leaving them without permission. Hands closed round his ankles but the ratio of Bello outside to Bello inside was about three to one and the heaviest part won.

Joey was wearing his own clothes so he didn't stand out as an escaping jailbird, but he had to get off the streets as soon as possible. The Old Bill was liable to be out in force. An old mate lived in the Tooting area. Joey picked his way through the back streets, arrived at his house and knocked on the door. It was opened by his pal in person.

'Blimey, Joey,' he said. 'I thought you were away.'

'That's right. Away from Wandsowrth,' said Joey. 'For fuck's sake let me in.'

With a new rig-out and a few quid in his pocket Joey was on his way the following morning.

He had his freedom but he was on the run, which meant that he could not be seen about in his usual haunts. He tucked himself away south of the river, emerging from time to time for a spot of screwing the proceeds of which built up his cash reserves, but he was just marking time. As usual trouble was waiting for him round the next corner.

It was Ronnie Biggs going over the wall at Wandsworth that gave him the idea of making one on behalf of an old friend. Freddie was doing twelve and it looked as though he would do the lot in Wandsworth, the most horrible prison in the British Isles. Joey could sympathise with him wanting to be out of it.

The escape party was five-handed. Adgie was at the wheel of the red Jag as they pulled up about thirty yards from the main gate of the jail just after one o'clock in the morning. There were two other blokes and a bird in support. Joey was the one to go in with one of the other fellows helping with the gear, a knotted rope fitted with a grapnel, a rope ladder and a pair of bolt cutters.

The first hurdle was easy, the low wall of a house which led them directly to the main wall of the jail behind which was the hospital wing. Joey swung the rope, the grapnel clanged against the wall and fell back. He had another try with the same result. At the third attempt the grapnel lodged itself firmly on top of the wall and they were ready to go over. They waited for a few minutes in case the noise had aroused anyone either in the house or on the other side of the wall, but all was silent. They swarmed up the rope and sat astride the wall, looking out over the roof of the storeroom to the row of cell windows which formed part of the hospital wing.

Speed was now essential. They dropped down on to the roof and fixed the rope ladder to the guttering from where it hung down into the yard. Freddie was expecting them and a glimmer of white showed where he had thrust his towel through the bars. Climbing down the rope ladder they were soon beneath the window. Freddie had already let down the drop-type frame behind the iron bars. Now all that remained to be done was to cut through those bars. Joey had tested the bolt cutters which sheared through inch square steel as though it was butter. What he hadn't taken into account was the fact that he would have to use them with his arms stretched up over his head. He couldn't get a leverage in that position so they had to do a quick scout round to find something to stand on. Fortunately there was a pile of bricks close at hand from which they made a rickety platform. Bolt cutters at the ready, Joey jumped up and there was Freddie's pale excited face only a few inches from his.

The first bar was cut in no time at all and Joey was just starting on the second when the scream went up. Somebody inside the prison had pressed the alarm button. Freddie looked over his shoulder at the cell door behind him, which was slowly opening.

'Quick, have it away! It's on top!' he gasped and his face disappeared from Joey's view as he dropped back from the window.

Joey dropped the cutters and ran. His mate was close behind as they shinned up the rope ladder and shot across the storeroom roof. Lights were going on all over the place, the guard dogs were barking their heads off and there was enough row to waken the dead. They went down the ladder in double quick time and piled in the Jag. Adgie was on the move before they had closed the doors. There was no need for words, it had obviously gone wrong and it was now up to Adgie to get them clear.

The man was pure magic with a car. In no time at all they were across the Common and into the back streets behind Tooting High Road. At the Broadway a couple of police cars had formed a road block. Adgie dropped down a gear, mounted the pavement and shot through, scattering Old Bill in all directions as he floored the accelerator. They were pursued for a while, Adgie doing things with the Jag which would have brought a set of tens from the 'Come Dancing' panel and a cheer from the Jaguar design team. In the end they got clean away.

There was no mention in the papers of the attempt to liberate Freddie which, coming so soon after Biggsy's escape, was bound to raise questions about the Micky Mouse security at Wandsworth. There must have been a few red faces at the Home Office, which was some reward for their efforts.

Freddie was finally freed in tragic circumstances. He collapsed and died in Hull prison. Had Joey's attempt to free him had been successful he might have been alive and well today. Who knows.

After Joey's brief career as escape organiser he lay low. The need to earn some cash led him to team up with an Irish lad who was known as Tony Jenkins though his real name was Doyle. He was one of the two uninvited guests who joined the Biggs-Flower escape from Wandsworth in July. From what he told Joey the getaway was a well-organised doddle for which Paul Seabourne and Ronnie Leslie, the organisers, got top marks.

'We were out at exercise,' Doyle told Joey. 'Biggsy and Eric Flower was near the wall when these two ladders came over and the two of them were halfway up before the screws realised what was happening. Some of the cons tackled the screws. It must have been all arranged. Anyway I though I would have some of this so I went over with another chap.'

'What did Biggsy have to say?' asked Joey.

'He was OK,' said Doyle. 'Nice as pie. He dropped me and the other fellow at the station at Wandsworth Common. Wished us both good luck.'

Joey thought it was very generous of Biggsy. To see a pair of blokes crash in on a scheme which must have cost him thousands could have led to recriminations all round, but he must have taken the view that his own escape had come off so it was a bonus for anyone who got in on it.

Tony had a nice little earner lined up for them, a two-handed job which required that one of them would have to be diguised as a copper. What they would have to do was capture a uniform. They cased a flat where an Old Bill lived and waited for him to go out. As soon as he left the premises with his little shopping bag they went in through the front door as bold as brass. They locate the uniform, make it into a tidy parcel and prepare to leave.

What they don't know is that they have been spotted entering the house and some nosy public-spirited character has rung the law. Joey opens the front door to be fronted by a copper with an Alsatian on a lead backed up by what appears to be the entire duty roster from the local nick. He slings the uniform at the dog and a right-hander at its handler and the fists begin to fly. While the dog is worrying the uniform thinking there is a body inside it the rest of the force descends on the two felons and the battle commences. The outcome is inevitable. Joey and Doyle are bundled into the paddy-waggon and carted off to the local nick where the duty sergeant is overjoyed to have a couple of notorious escapers brought back to the fold.

So it was back to the old routine, an appearance at the Magistrates' Court charged with burglary and assault, a remand in custody to await trial at the Old Bailey and a long spell in Brixton while the prosecution assembled the case against them. Finally the day came when the might of British justice was ready to deal with the malefactors Doyle and Bello.

Joey had a word with his counsel in the cells underneath the Old Bailey before the trial started. Counsel wasn't very comforting.

'It looks like ten this time, Joey,' he said.

'Bloody lovely,' Joey replied, which was a sarcastic way of indicating that he didn't think it was lovely at all.

'Mind you,' counsel went on, 'we could try a plea under Section sixty and sixty-five of the Mental Health Act.'

Joey pricked his ears up at this one.

'What's it about?' Joey asked.

'Well, it works something like this,' said Joey's personal Rumpole. 'It says here in the depositions that you pissed all over the Governor at Brixton, which indicates that there might be something wrong in the top storey. Then you've got a history of persistent violence dating back to Borstal. Now if we make a plea under the Act this would squash the three years you were serving when you escaped plus you would be sent to hospital for observation and reports.'

Joey gave this idea some thought and it looked good.

'So how does it work out in practice?' Joey asked.

'You won't get a sentence,' said the brief. 'If the plea come off you'll probably go back to hospital at Tooting Bec. They'll keep you there under observation, give you some treatment. As soon as they decide you're OK you'll be released. You should be out in six months or so.'

'Bloody lovely,' Joey said. This time he wasn't being sarcastic. 'Let's have a go.'

Joey was indeed well pleased. Instead of sowing mailbags and slopping out old barmy Bello would be lying in bed eating grapes brought in by daily visitors and living the life of Riley. He almost skipped up the steps to the dock when his case was called. The charges were read out, Tony and Joey pleaded not guilt as a matter of form, the judge nodded off and the trial got underway.

To cut a long story short Tony came out of it with just over six years after the consecutives and the concurrents had been sorted out. Then Joey's turn came and the old judge really let himself go. According to him Joey was a violent and dangerous character who rampaged around like Attila the Hun, leaving a trail of serious injury and destruction in his wake, and was suitable to be dealt with under the Act as a potential homicidal maniac. He made an order for detention and treatment under the relevant sections of the Act and that was that. Good old Joey he thought as he danced down the steps. Tooting Bec here I come.

Alone in a cell in what had been the bowels of the old Newgate prison he took stock of himself. Here he was, not yet thirty years of age, branded as a nutter by his own choice but knowing in his heart of hearts that he was completely sane. As he saw it he had taken the only way out of an impossible situation, impossible in the sense that he had been forced to choose between a long sentence of imprisonment and a temporary period during which he would be treated as a loony. Fine and dandy, he thought, I'll play the game according to the rules and make sure that I come out on top in the end. Or so he thought.

There was a rattling of keys and the cell door opened. A beefy copper he had not seen before stood outside.

'Right, Joey,' he said. 'Let's get going. Use the toilet now. We've got a long way to go.'

A long way to go? Tooting Bec hospital was less than an hour from the Old Bailey. Joey did a quick piss and followed his escort out to the waiting van. Joey had no option but to follow him because he was attached by a set of Home Office jewellery. When he saw that half-a-dozen Old Bill were sitting in the van he began to have misgivings and he felt even worse as the vehicle headed North.

'Where are we off to then,' said Joey to the copper to whom he was cuffed.

'Didn't you know?' replied the copper. 'We're off to Hampton.'

10. Criminally Insane

Hampton. Somebody had taken it seriously. What the hell had his brief done to him? He had heard stories about Hampton, each one more horrifying than the last. What made it even more terrifying was that the rozzers in the van were humouring him, treating him as though he was a real nutter and a dangerous one at that. Not that there was much conversation. He had the feeling that the sooner they got rid of him the better pleased they'd be.

The welcoming committee at Hampton was a bunch of screws – Joey learned the hard way that they weren't screws but nurses ha-bloody-ha – and he'd never seen a more wickedelooking mob. They had evil grins on their faces and were obviously looking forward to introducing their new victim to the delights of the institution. It was Joey's guess that they had been tipped off that he was a hard case because as soon as they got him inside they went into a punching routine as they hustled him down a corridor.

'Think you're a hard man, Bello,' said one of them. 'We'll teach you. We tame lions in here.'

Joey kept his mouth shut and didn't retaliate as he was wheeled into a cell, known as a side room for some reason. There they stripped him stark bollock naked, took his clothes and left him locked up for about an hour. Then two of them came in and proceeded to shave off every scrap of body hair, pubic hair and the lot. One of them took hold of his prick as he wielded the razor.

'You won't need this for a few years,' he said. 'Might as well fucking whip it off, eh?'

His mate laughed. 'He could piss out of his fucking arsehole, couldn't he?'

They cracked a few more coarse jokes at Joey's expense. Every other word was four-letter Anglo Saxon. Then, still naked, Joey was led into a bathroom.

'Right. Get your dirty fucking body in there,' said the screw.

The water was boiling. Joey looked for the cold tap but there wasn't one.

'I can't get in there, guv'nor,' he said. 'I'll be scalded.'

'Say sir when you speak to me. Now fucking get in there or I'll fucking put you in.'

No way was Joey going to step into that bath. The 'nurse' stood for a moment then went to the door and let out a yell into the corridor. In a twinkling the bathroom was full of them, large beefy blokes who had clearly been waiting for a signal. They were five-handed and each man carried a knotted towel.

'Right, cunt-face. Get in that fucking bath.'

'Bollocks!'

'OK. You fucking asked for it.'

They set to work on Joey after they had soaked the towels in water. By the time they had finished he was on the floor, feeling as though he had been put through a concrete mixer. A knotted towel soaked in water doesn't sound like an offensive weapon but it can do some damage when there's a fourteen stone geezer at the delivery end.

That was Joey's introduction to Hampton, but it was only a taster of what was to come. He had never been frightened of anything or anybody in his life but he began to know the meaning of fear. In an ordinary prison a con is able to take steps to protect himself not only against other cons but also against the odd screw who takes a dislike to him. In Hampton where the screws – Joey couldn't bring himself to refer to them a nurses – all seemed to be related, they ran the place. Not a day passed without some act of cruelty taking place. There was no discipline as such. The inmates were controlled by fear and the screws were responsible for the reign of terror.

Joey's card was marked for him one day by a screw who didn't care for the look on his face when he passed him in a corridor. He gave Joey a pull right away.

'Come here you fucking toe-rag,' he said.

Joey kept his distance. He had already been introduced to the screws' sport of 'spine-dropping', kicking an inmate's legs from under him so that he landed with a crash on his arse.

'Right you fucking monkey,' said the screw. 'I'll be watching you. We can keep you here forever. Don't fucking forget it.'

Joey had no intention of forgetting it, just as he had no intention of staying in that hell-hole forever. He was in ward D2, a section reserved for violent and dangerous men, and he was treated as such. He was not allowed to shave himself, this was done for him on a hit and miss principle that left him looking like a mangey poodle. The same went for the haircuts. It was all part of an overall scheme to rob a man of the last vestige of his self-respect.

There were some sorry sights on the ward. There was Bernard, a bent and feeble figure confined to a wheelchair who, Joey was told, had been a fitness fanatic. Now he was a broken man with a pathetic waggling head and a pair of huge cauliflower ears. The stories about him were legion, how he had taken on whole gangs of screws and beat the shit out of many of them before he hit the deck. Whenever Joey looked at him he saw what he might become after a few years. The screws gave him a wide berth. He had not lost his bottle and would still have a go, even though his attempt usually ended up with him lying on the floor. It was then that the screws put the boot in.

Another pitiful case was a blind bloke called Jimmy. The screws tormented him something rotten, sneaking up behind him and clapping their hands over his ears so that he almost jumped out of his skin. Everything would go quiet as Jimmy tried to identify who it was. Is that you, he would call and then wait for an answer. He knew the voices of all the men on the ward, but the screws would gesture to them to keep silent and the poor blind sod would wonder who was having a go at him.

A particular butt of the screws' perverted sense of humour was a big fellow they called Bonzo who would sit for hours dragging on an unlighted cigarette and muttering obscenities. Two or three screws would come into the day room and make out that Bonzo was a dog. The performance would go like this.

'Come here, Bonzo.'

'Wuff, wuff, wuff.'

'Louder you fucking tripehound, louder.'

'WUFF, WUFF, WUFF.'

'Who's fucking shit on the floor then?'

'WUFF, WUFF, WUFF.'

Bonzo would then be on the receiving end of a good kicking and ordered to lie down in a corner. It was sickening to watch this degrading and humiliating spectacle but nobody dared protest.

In an ordinary nick, if you had a complaint you went on Governor's application and stated your grievance either to the Governor himself or his assistant. In Hampton the system was different. In the corner of the ward was a box with a slot in the top. If an inmate had a complaint he was supposed to write it down and put it in this box but he must first of all show it to the so-called staff nurse. Since most of the inmates were illiterate they were automatically ruled out. If the complaint was against a member of the staff it was torn up. To get in secret a written complaint into the box was impossible. It added up to a sense of isolation from the real world that in itself was frightening.

Early evening was treatment time in ward D2 but no pills or medicine were dished out. The treatment was the screws' method of punishment for offences committed during the day and was administered in an office at the end of a corridor leading from the ward. The proceedings were unofficial but then so were most of the goings-on at Hampton.

It would start with the name of the offender being called out by one of the screws in the dayroom where the inmates sat around playing draughts or dominoes or staring at a blank television screen. The miscreant would then walk along the corridor to the office where four or five screws would be waiting. The treatment would then commence with a volley of abuse followed by punchball practice in which the body of the inmate was used as the bag. Then would follow a booting. If it went too far and a man was seriously injured the screws would sort out one of the right idiots, accuse him of fighting with the injured geezer, lock them both up and make out a report on the fictitious incident.

Joey witnessed one occurrence which filled him with horror. One of the big fellows, a real loony but harmless, spoke out of turn to a couple of screws. They grabbed him and shoved his arm repeatedly through a window until it was slashed to ribbons and there was blood all over the place. The poor bloke was screaming in agony. One of the screws held him down while the other gave him an injection in the arse which put him spark out. They then made out a report that the man had tried to escape through the window. Joey remembered very vividly the expressions on the faces of the two screws as they were performing. They were enjoying it.

Not all the inmates were timid characters being subjected to brutalising by sadistic screws. Some were hard, tough and very dangerous. They were the ones who kept out of trouble in the main. Those who copped for most of the whackings were the big simple blokes. Joey tried to figure out what made the screws tick, why they seemed to enjoy brutalising fellow human beings, but he couldn't come up with a satisfactory answer. A partial explanation was, he supposed, that they had too much power and tended to abuse it, added to which their jobs would be pretty boring if they didn't have a bit of excitement to look forward to.

There were a few decent men on the staff who tried to do a good job but they were very much in the minority and helpless in the face of the Nurses' Mafia. The hard core of brutes, long-serving screws with family ties and roots in the locality, were in command and God help anybody who went against them. If the ex-Governor of the Scrubs is to be believed when he referred to his prison as a penal dustbin, then Hampton was a bomb-site, a derelict wasteland littered with bits and pieces of useless humanity, a property nobody wants to develop.

At some time in the distant past some official had the bright idea that the dreary lot of the inmates would be made more tolerable by allowing the sexes to mingle at a weekly dance. At the time Joey was there the inmates numbered about a thousand, six hundred men and four hudnred women. They looked forward to the dances as the high spot of the week.

Joey went to a few of them. The scene beggared description. Something in the order of four hundred male and female loonies jigged about to the music of a record player, their main object being to work their way to the centre of the crowd where, surrounded by jostling bodies, they would try to have it off. As soon as they were spotted the screws would dash in and separate them and they would be dragged from the room. What happened to the woman was anybody's guess but the man was given the treatment which was more painful and less satisfying than the quick fuck he had in mind. The whole business was ludicrous anyway. To pack three or four hundred sex-starved men and women into a room and permit them to have close bodily contact was asking for trouble. They had been certified as mentally unstable and many of them were sex offenders. Whoever thought of the idea in the first place must have had a macabre sense of humour.

After a few months during which Joey watched points and kept out of serious bother, he began to get himself organised. He knew from the off that Hampton presented problems different to those encountered in an ordinary nick. To start with he was surrounded by lunatics which could be a bit of a nuisance. There were two blokes who were very retarded, childrens' minds in grown-up bodies, who latched on to him and tried to hold his hand when they were out at exercise. Another geezer looked on Joey as a father confessor and sorted him out to talk about his troubles. He was in for sexual offences against little girls and was an absolute nutter. He would corner Joey and describe in detail how he used a razor to enlarge their vaginas then go off muttering to himself about the shortage of little girls in Hampton. It was sickening because the bloke really believed he had done nothing wrong.

There were a few fellows in the same boat as Joey, completely sane but stuck away in Hampton for one reason or another. They tended to stick together, which was one way of preserving each others' sanity. Joey also had as many visits as the rules permitted, which had the effect of keeping the screws off his back to some extent. They weren't too keen on persecuting an inmate who had regular outside contacts. The man without friends or relatives was an easier mark.

Towards the end of the first year Joey started having trouble with his back. The knotted-towel-cum-spine dropping treatments had resulted in a bone being displaced. The pain was almost unbearable and there were times when he couldn't walk. At first the screws laughed off his complaints but in the end the doctor had to be called in. He was a young chap and very bright. After he had given Joey a thorough examination in his surgery, they got to chatting.

'What are you doing here, Bello?' said the doctor. 'You're not mental.'

Joey told him the whole story and he laughed.

'You've only yourself to blame,' he said. 'You should know better than to try and buck the system. However, I'm calling in an osteopath to see to your back. It looks as though you will need to wear a corset for a while. By the way how did you come by the injury?'

'I was lifting a bed,' said Joey. 'Then I got this sudden pain . . .'

He didn't have to say any more. In the upshot he was fitted out with a steel-braced corset and transferred from ward D2 to the main hospital where he was put on light duties. He was also recommended for release, went before a review tribunal and was passed for discharge.

That wasn't the end of it. Joey was out of D2 and away from the real loonies and all he had to do as a cleaner was to walk around with a duster in his hand, but every day he was shitting himself in case something went wrong. He woke up one morning and there was a black, furry thing on the pillow next to his head. He jumped out of bed, grabbed a shoe and was about to beat the thing to death when he realised that it was a clump of his own hair which had simply fallen out of his scalp. Worry does strange things to a man.

It was to be a year before the Home Secretary put his signature to a piece of paper which stated that Joey Bello wasn't mad any longer, three hundred and sixty-five days each one of which seemed like a week. He came out of Hampton a wiser man, for it was there he learned the real meaning of words like fear and brutality and, above all, the depths of man's inhumanity to man.

11. Demanding with Menaces

Joey's coming out of Hampton was like being released from a nightmare into a world peopled by real human beings, although a reminder of that hell-hole was by his side all the way to Notting Dale. The regulations laid down that he must be accompanied to his home by a screw, but he was so relieved at getting out that he wouldn't have minded being taken home by old Lucifer himself.

When they arrived at King's Cross Joey fell out with his travelling companion who wanted to go on by tube. Joey wasn't having any of that. He was now on his own manor, back in the smoke, and it was a taxi for him. He debated giving his guard the slip but decided it wasn't worth it. The result was they turned up at the Dale in a cab and Joey felt like a member of society again as he paid the cabbie and invited the screw indoors for a cuppa.

Mum was, as always, glad to see him but the screw put his foot in it once more, rabbiting about how much money Joey had on him and suchlike as though he was a naughty kid who couldn't be trusted. Joey soon put a stop to that.

'Look, mate,' he said. 'Leave that out. Sit down, have a nice cuppa and then I'll buy you a drink before you go back.'

The screw got the message. Just then Joey's two brothers, Billy and Nobby, walked in the door. He marked their cards about the screw, who was invited to come and have a drink with them. They intended to get him well pissed and send him back to Hampton in a right old state but it didn't work. He had a light ale at the local and went on his way. Joey wasn't sorry to see the back of him. With his departure he was finished with Hampton .

For a few weeks things were a bit strange. Joey stayed on the manor because he felt secure among the people he knew, but even some of them gave him funny looks now and then as though they expected him to suddenly foam at the mouth or swing from a chandelier or something like that. Yet what disturbed Joey most was Mum's reaction to him. She had always been a jewel, visiting him when he was away, looking after him when he came home cut to pieces and never questioning the way he lived. Now she had a long talk with him and made it plain that she was getting too old to put up with this sort of lark, so if he got into trouble again the door was closed.

During the two years Joey had been away there had been some big changes. The Old Bill had been very active. They had nicked the Richardsons who, in June of 1967, were put away for a very long time. Charlie Richardson copped for twenty-five years. Then in May of 1968 the Kray firm was also nicked, three months before Joey was let out of Hampton, and were banged up in Brixton awaiting trial. Naturally everybody who had had any sort of connection with the Krays was a bit jumpy, including Joey who ran the risk of being pulled in for questioning.

About that time there was an outbreak of demanding with menaces in the pubs in the Notting Hill area. Quite a few of them were smashed up and several people got cut, so the publicans got together and brought in the Old Bill to clean things up.

Joey is in the Derby one night with a few mates when somebody comes up on him from behind and sticks a shooter into his back. The band is belting away and there is a lot of noise. The bloke whispers right in his ear. 'You're nicked, Joey,' he says. Joey starts to walk out of the pub with this geezer treading on his heels. The band stops playing and Joey sees men being hustled out of another door. Out on the street Joey is shoved into a car, an ordinary saloon with no markings. As he sits there a pitched battle starts on the pavement. A police van comes swingings round the corner and a dozen Old Bill jump out.

It was a real round-up. Joey heard later that half the villains in Notting Dale got their collars felt. So far as he was concerned he was done, along with three others, for robbery and damage to a pub and remanded in Brixton. The Kray mob was also there but they were kept in a special cage well away from the other prisoners. Joey had a feeling that there was something funny going on and when he heard through the prison grapevine that Nipper Read, who had personally nicked Ronnie and Reggie Kray, was spending a lot of time interviewing villains in a private room at Brixton, he knew that his feelings were right. The last thing he needed was to be involved in the Kray trial. As things turned out he couldn't avoid it.

Chief Superintendent Leonard Read, to give the Nipper his official title, was in charge of the operation of building up a cast-iron case against the Kray twins. As soon as the pair were safely banged up in Brixton he put himself about to gather a mass of evidence against them, most of which came from villains who were already inside either serving sentences or awaiting trial. It was all very simple. They grassed the twins, the law granted them certain favours and everybody was happy. All except Ronnie and Reggie, that is.

That was where Joey came into the picture. When he and his three co-defenders went on trial at the Old Bailey on the menaces charge, Joey cocked up a story with one of them to the effect that he would say that he had met Joey in prison. It was an old dodge, but such a mention would necessitate a new trial at which there might be a chance of getting chucked or coming out with a lighter sentence. Now what does this louse do but change his plea to guilty halfway through the trial and throw himself on the mercy of the court while dropping Joey right in the shit. The rat had obviously done a deal with Nipper Read to give evidence against the Krays. Although he had more charges against him than the other three put together he got off with two and a half years. The two others got eighteen months and nine months respectively. Joey copped for four years. He was sent to the model prison at Blundeston to serve his sentence.

The Kray trial opened at the Old Bailey on the 7th January 1969 and was to continue for two months. The twins were up on charges of murder. Ronnie was accused of shooting George Cornell in the Blind Beggar pub, Reggie of stabbing Jack 'The Hat' McVitie to death in a house in Evering Road, Stoke Newington. Joey was brought from Blundeston to give evidence for the defence but for all the good he did he might just as well have saved himself the journey.

Blundeston was like a convalescent home and, as compared to other prisons in which he had served sentences, it was a dream. The majority of the inmates were habitual criminals but most of the staff, from the Governor downwards, treated them like human beings. There was none of the usual shouting and bawling, 'Get in line', 'Lead on', 'Stop talking' and that sort of thing. The buildings were modern and purpose-built. There was always free access to toilets at any time so the degrading 'slopping-out' routine wasn't necessary. Incidents of violence were very rare indeed. It was the smoothest-running prison Joey had ever been in. It was also the only prison where he was never on report and didn't lose a single day remission. His four-year sentence thus became two years and eight months.

The inmates of Blundeston enjoyed many privileges. Chris Wilkins, one of Joey's old mates, wanted to get married while serving his sentence and applied to the Governor for permission. It was granted and Chris was let out, under guard of course, for the ceremony. Some of the inmates decided that the occasion should be celebrated so they threw a party for him. With the help of a friendly screw they got together the necessaries, including a supply of booze, and had a high old time. Joey was to see a lot of Chris in the ensuing years. They often had a good laugh about what must have been the most unusual wedding breakfast of all time.

Joey had his reward for being a good boy. The last six months of his sentence was spent in the hostel attached to the prison and he was allowed to go out to work from Monday to Friday. He was fixed up with a job at a local factory, a sort of knacker's yard where dead animals unfit for human consumption were processed for all kinds of purposes. It wasn't the kind of job he would have picked for himself but it made a change. He worked on the ramp where the carcasses were loaded on to a conveyor belt from the delivery lorries and though it wasn't the most pleasant of tasks to handle meat in various states of putrefaction, there were compensations. The carcasses contained masses of fine, healthy maggots and he did a roaring trade with the local fishing enthusiasts. He didn't want for pocket money.

He had a few visits from Vi and Charlie Kray, the twins' parents. In spite of their own troubles they still found time to make the journey from London to see him. He knew, of course, that the twins had got life with a recommendation that they should serve thirty years, and brother Charlie had got ten for allegedly having helped dispose of Jack McVitie's body along with Freddie Foreman. Joey really felt sorry for Vi, but she didn't wallow in self-pity. She went all out to try and help her sons in any way she could. There were a lot of people who missed her when she died in 1982. She was a very remarkable woman.

The day came when Joey was released but he didn't go home. Mum had stuck to her word and put the bar up, for which he really couldn't blame her. He went to work on the Kentish Town manor where he teamed up with a Greek in the mini-cab business, and also opened a fruit stall in Leyton Road just outside a pub called the Gloucester Arms.

It was reported in the press, merely another robbery in the catalogue of London crime. The time was ten thirty on the evening of Monday 7th February 1972. In the Duke of Edinburgh, a pub on the corner of Queensway and Moscow Road, Mrs Nora Clarke was drinking with her friend, a young man by the name of Dennis Rice.

Mrs Clarke was a regular customer at the pub where she was known as a good punter. She threw her money about at the same time as she flashed a load of high-class tom, which was an invitation for any villain looking for an easy mark. The three met sitting in the Austin Cambridge saloon parked in Moscow Road had accepted the invitation. The lady was due for a shock.

Shortly after eleven o'clock Mr Price and the lady emerged from the Moscow Road entrance – or should it be exit – to the pub. Mrs Clarke's two small dogs cocked their legs against the nearest lamp post while the lady leaned affectionately against her escort. A few yards away two men sprang from the back of the Austin and stood waiting as the couple approached them.

There was suddenly the sharp odour of lemon juice in

the air as the men discharged the contents of the plastic containers they carried into the faces of their victims. As the lady screamed and her escort staggered blindly on the pavement one of the men put a full nelson on her and fell backwards into the rear seat of the car. The other man leapt in beside the driver. The car was off into Queensway scattering pedestrians to right and left. In Inverness Terrace, barely a mile from Moscow Road, the car came to a halt. By that time the unfortunate lady had been stripped of her rings, bracelets, brooches and watch, everything save the keys of her flat had been taken from her handbag and she was left dazed and helpless as her attackers climbed into another car and sped away.

The lady was not hurt. The Old Bill took her to the nearest hospital where she was treated for shock, given a cup of tea and sent home. Some months later Joey was to be charged with taking part in the robbery.

To return to the Kentish Town scene, Joey put in a lot of work at the mini-cab business which became a money-spinner. Greek Andy, his partner, ran the garage in the downstairs part of the premises. Joey had an office on the first floor over the garage from which, with the help of a controller, he ran the fleet which grew bigger every day. Only an idiot could fail to make money at this game. The drivers owned their vehicles and all Joey had to do was take them on, fit them out with radios and collect a weekly payment from them. The drivers paid all expenses including hire and reward insurance and petrol and were responsible for repairs and maintenance. Greek Andy carried out the repairs in the garage, so there were two bites at the same cherry.

Advertising was no sweat. He plastered the whole area with cards and the business rolled in. He didn't bother much with account customers. Cash was what he was after and it was cash he got, so he always had a wallet stuffed with readies and bollocks to the Commissioners of Inland Revenue. The game was so good that many villains with a bit of cash to spare jumped on this profitable bandwagon and, as the competition hotted up, took to using shooters to enforce their territorial rights. This was in the future. At that time his only worry was Greek Andy, who was turning out to be a very dodgy character indeed.

Joey turned up at the office one morning and found a stranger sitting at his desk and going through the books which, although rough and ready, still gave a good idea of the state of the business.

'Who the hell are you?' asked Joey.

The man looked up. 'I'm Andy's brother-in-law,' he said. 'I just wanted to see how you were getting on.'

'That's none of your fucking business,' said Joey. 'Come on. Out.'

The man go up meekly enough and Joey carted him off downstairs to sort things out with Andy. The two of them began jabbering away in Greek. Joey soon put a stop to that.

'I don't know what you pair of shitecunts are up to,' he said, 'but don't mess about with me.'

A worried looked appeared on Andy's face. he knew what Joey was capable of doing to anybody who tried to work a flanker on him.

'Nothing to worry, Joey, nothing. My brother-in-law own lease. He renew it for us.'

Remembering the old saying, shake hands with a Greek then count your fingers, Joey was not convinced, but he was fairly sure that Andy wouldn't do anything silly. He couldn't have been more mistaken. The lousy little bastard set him up which he discovered when he arrived one morning to find the place swarming with Old Bill. The premises had been broken into and cleaned out and it was obvious that it was Andy's work. With his form Joey had no chance, he was the prime suspect and he was nicked. A grinning Andy watched him being taken away.

12. The Big Escape

Once more back in Brixton on remand Joey is seething. That little Greek bastard has worked a right flanker on him and here he is, nicked down to nothing.

Since the last time Joey was in residence there Brixton has become even worse. The conditions are terrible, the screws are leaning on everybody and Joey's card is marked because of the episode when he pissed all over the Governor. He met up with a few old pals, among them Chris Wilkins who had been with him in Blundeston.

All the remand men are really pissed off and one fine sunny day they do something about it. At the end of the morning exercise period they sit down in the yard and refuse to go back inside. There isn't much the screws can do about the situation. The men don't indulge in any violence, they just sit there on their arses and refuse to budge.

The deputy Governor comes down and does a bit of shouting and hollering but for all the difference it makes it is a waste of his breath and the cons' time. Lunch time comes and goes and they are still sitting there, but it's not very comfortable since it's a very hot day and there's no shade in the open yard. They are all dying for a cuppa and something to eat. Joey is sitting with Chris and a couple of other blokes, Ray 'Scarface' Pegler and Richie Payne, who is called 'Honeypuff' because he is such a clumsy sod. As Joey looks round the hundred or so fellows who all have the same idea about protesting he realises that a bit of geeing-up is all that's required to start a mass break out.

Joey's little group begins chanting, stuff like 'why are we waiting' and so on and some of the others take it up, but it comes to nothing. Most of the geezers tumble what they're up to and don't want to be involved in anything serious so they get up and go back inside. By the evening it's all over but Joey is still thinking about the possibility of stirring up a mass escape.

In any remand prison escape fantasies flourish. Irish gas meter bandits put it about that they can organise their mates in the IRA to blow a hole in the wall. Then there's the bloke with the friend who's a helicopter pilot who gives out with a load of verbal about Fearless Fred hovering over the exercise yard as swarms of cons climb rope ladders to freedom. Others claim to have a team on the outside who will storm the wall, come over the top brandishing knives, choppers and shooters and open the gates. After listening to some of these merchants Joey thinks he's back in Hampton.

Joey gives some thought to the busines and it doesn't seem to him to be all that difficult, so he collects a little team and asks them what they think. There's Chris Wilkins, Ray Pegler and Richie Payne who are all for it, and they rope in big Harry Turner and Leroy Davies. Davies was later to turn informer and put a lot of men away. Then a good man by the name of Obie O'Brien gets interested and says he will make one. Joe is building up a little mob who can be trusted to perform when the moment arrives.

There is a small fly in the ointment. A geezer called George de Buriatte has got a whisper and he comes to Joey asking to be let in. Somehow he doesn't trust the fellow so he laughs it off and tells him he's dreaming. Joey still feels uneasy and he tips his partners off to keep clear of this merchant.

The first step in the plan is for a couple of them to be

unlocked in the evening so Ray and Joey get on to a works party which is doing a bit of painting on the wing. They wangle this through an old mate, Jimmy Moore, who is well in with the screws as he does some of their bookwork for them. The two are unlocked at six every evening, issued with paint and brushes and then left more or less on their tod to get on with the job. After a few days they have the routine pretty well taped and fix on a Sunday night as being the best bet. They have discovered that there is only a skeleton staff on duty.

They pass the word during exercise on Sunday afternoon just before they are locked up. Ray and Joey are in adjacent cells on the ground floor of A wing, the others are on the fours. Joey has a mug of tea beside him but he can't drink. During the next two hours the tensions mounts. Will the screws unlock him and Ray on time? Has the plot been sussed? The excitement has a reaction and Joey wants to piss. He's wearing a suit under his overalls so he's sweating like a pig. He fingers the fifty pence piece in his pocket and wonders if he will get to spend it on the outside. Then suddenly it's six o'clock and he hears the welcome sound of a key being turned in the lock of his peter.

The screw pokes his head in. 'Painting tonight, Bello?' he says. Joey tells him he won't be a minute and steps out just as Ray is being unlocked. Stuffed inside his overalls is a real double-lively hard porn magazine which is going to be bait for the older of the two screws, who is a right dirty old fucker. Joey winks at Ray and they start getting their gear together. Then, right on the dot at five minutes past six a bell rings on the fours. Chris Wilkins' finger is on the button. It's all part of the plan.

It works out as they thought it would. The old screw looks at the indicator.

'Oh shit,' he says. 'Up on the fucking fours, Nip up and see to it, Fred. Your legs are younger than mine.'

It's all going for them. As soon as Fred starts his climb to the fours Joey pulls the mag out from inside his overalls.

'Here, guv,' Joey says. 'Got a new mag here. A right beauty.'

He holds it up so that the screw can see the cover, which is very lurid indeed. Joey banks on him walking over to take it so that he can be bundled into the peter, laid out and tied up. It doesn't come off.

'Let's have it, Bello,' says the screw, holding out his hand.

Joey has no option but to go over to him and hand him the magazine. The screw takes it without a word and moves over to the recess where the light is better. As he turns the pages his eyes are almost popping out of his head. Joey looks over at Ray who nods his head.

Joey goes into action and reaches the screw in a few quick strides. He claims him, clamps his hand over the screw's mouth, kicks his feet from under him and they hit the deck together. The screw's hat has fallen off in the struggle and the silly old sod tries to bite Joey's hand as Ray rushes up with some pieces of rope. Joey grabs the screw by the hair to pull his head back and finds himself holding a handful of wig. Then, all at once, Joey's other hand is full of false teeth. Christ, he thought, the poor bugger's coming apart in my hands.

Nothing else falls off him so they tie him up and stick a gag in his mouth. They carry him into the recess, Joey cops for his keys and they are ready for the next stage which is to claim the other screw who by now should have reached the fours. Then it starts to go wrong.

When a con rings the bell in his cell a metal indicator drops outside the door. The screw on his way to the fours notices that there is an indicator down on the threes and has gone to see to it. Consequently as the two cons reach the threes landing there is the screw a few yards away giving them both a hard look. Next minute he's off down the landing like a greyhound. If he reaches the alarm bell that's the end of the escape. He doesn't. Ray and Joey collar him with yards to spare.

He isn't a lot of trouble. In fact as they drag him into the landing recess and proceed to gag him and tie him up, he shits himself. They don't waste any time wiping his arse. They have other things to do. Ray bags his keys and the two set out on an unlocking spree. The first to be let out are Wilkins, Payne, Davies, Turner and O'Brien and they are out of their peters like shots from a pump-gun.

The plan is to unlock as many prisoners as they can. Joey gets busy on one side of the landing, Ray takes the other side. Joey comes to Ken Lawrence's cell and unlocks him.

'Want to have it away, Ken?'

'Cor, not fucking much, Joey.'

'Right. See you down below.'

The next one is Lionel Galloway. He's a big blond fellow, a fraudsman facing charges on a million pound credit card swindle for which later he was to get eight years. He's very bright and doesn't need to be told what to do. He's off down the stairs like a flash to join the others. Joey carries on with the job. Every peter he comes to he says 'If you want to have it away, get downstairs', and the looks on some of the faces have to be seen to be believed. There are no refusals until he comes to de Buriatte.

This is the bloke who only that afternoon had been telling Joey that he would make one in an escape.

'Coming George. We're off,' says Joey.

The man backs into a corner of the cell and starts screaming.

'Bang me up, bang me up. Put the bolt on.'

Hello, thinks Joey, here's one who's lost his arsehole. He bangs him up and carries on. He can still hear the shouting which worries him because sound carries a long way in the huge open spaces of a prison wing. However time is getting on. Ray and Joey call a halt to the unlocking and go down to the ground floor.

It's a strange sight. All the geezers who have been so unexpectedly freed are hanging around as if waiting for a coach to take them away. Some of them are wearing overcoats and sheepskins and carrying all their personal belongings, radios, books, bundles of case papers and letters. One bloke has got an enormous cardboard box full of canteen gear, tins of fruit, chocolate, biscuits and tea bags. Maybe he thinks there is a famine on outside.

Ray nudges and points toward the main door leading to the other wings. Lionel Galloway has been told to stand there and claim any screws who happen to come through. He's dressed to kill, smart suit, silk tie and highly polished shoes and he's wearing a stocking mask over his face. They nearly piss themselves laughing.

The next step is to capture the security room, which is the nerve centre of the prison. The communication sets carried by the screws pass through the control panel there and a direct line to the Old Bill is part of the installation. That's as much as they knew about the place apart from its location. Joey tells the mob to be quiet and he and Ray creep to a gate which leads on to a passage and then on to the security room. Very gently Joey turns the key in the lock on the gate and they both tiptoe down the passage. They reach the room and barge in.

A Principal Officer is sitting before the control panel. As he jumps up and makes a dive for the alarm Joey gives him a left hook which puts him out, but they don't notice a screw sitting behind the door. He has it away sharpish down the passage and he's moving so fast that his impetus carries him right through the crowd of potential escapers.

According to Chris, who told Joey about it later, Leroy Davies takes off after the screw with Kenny Lawrence and

Obie O'Brien right behind him. Leroy jumps on the screw's back but the fellow keeps going. The screws from B wing have heard the racket and open the gate as the four men reach it and they all go through in a tangle of arms and legs. A screw bangs up the gate and locks it and Joey has not only lost three members of the gang but the scream has gone up.

Meanwhile Ray and Joey are busy wrecking the security room. The various plugs and wires mean nothing to them so they rip out the lot. There's banging and flashing and clouds of smoke in the midst of which the PO who had copped for a left hook from Joey slides through the door and gets away. Only a moment later Chris rushes in followed by Richie Payne and Harry Turner.

'It's on top, Joey,' yells Chris.

'Where's the others,' said Joey.

'Scarpering back to their peters.'

In all the confusion on the wing Joey reckons tht his little band won't be missed for some time. He signs for the others to follow him and unlocks the gate leading from the wing to the kitchen. They move quickly and quietly to the kitchen door.

'Straight in and claim the screw,' Joey tells his mates. He silently turns the key, leaving the door close, then it's one, two, three and in. Joey claims the screw and shoves him against the wall, telling him to put his hands on his head and keep still. There are three cons in the kitchen and they stand flabbergasted with their mouths open.

Padlocked to the wall is a light extension ladder. They don't have a key but Richie has something just as effective. He wraps his huge hands round the padlock and wrenches it off. As he is performing Joey sees out of the corner of his eye that the screw is edging along the wall towards the alarm. He lets out a yell.

'Chris. Shove that fucker in the fridge.'

The screw goes white. 'No, no, don't do that. I'll freeze to death in there,' he cries.

'Well jump up and down,' says Joey.

Chris bundles the screw into the fridge and slams the door. Joey turns to the three cons who still don't seem to realise what is happening.

'We're going over the wall,' he says. 'Any of you want to come?'

The three of them shake their heads.

'Right,' says Joey. 'Give us five minutes then let cookie out of the fridge.'

He grabs one end of the ladder and Richie takes the other end. Ray, remarking that it might come in useful, cops for a fire extinguisher. They come out of the kitchen by a door that leads directly into the grounds and the wall is right in front of them. It's like stepping out on to the stage at the Palladium. All the lights are on. Ray, who is in the lead, tests the fire extinguisher with a quick burst in the air. He should have tested the wind first. The foam blows back, covering them with streaks of white.

It's like something out of a Mack Sennett comedy as they run down the side of the administration block, Richie and Joey carrying the ladder, Ray in front waving the extinguisher and Harry and Chris trotting along in the rear. Suddenly three screws with Alsatians come round the corner. As soon as they see the escapers they let the dogs go. Richie and Joey drop the ladder and prepare for battle, but Ray waits until the hounds are almost on them and lets go with the fire extinguisher right in their muzzles. The effect is dramatic. The dogs slide to a stop then turn and run, their tails between their legs. As they skedaddle round the corner, yelping their heads off, the screws follow them.

The escapers make for the wall where they are out of sight of the reception block. The lighting is brilliant and they are in full view of the closed circuit television cameras, but it's a safe bet that they weren't working after the performance in the security room. They run the ladder up against the wall and let it out to its full extent. Joey goes up it like a rocket. It's a seventeen foot ladder and the wall is twenty-five feet high. Joey can just reach the top with the tips of his fingers. Chris is right behind him and takes in the situation.

'Right, Joey, stand on my shoulders,' he yells.

Joey feels himself being propelled upwards. He reaches the top of the wall, sits astride and reaches down to give Chris a hand. Between them they get the other three up to join them. Now all they have to do is drop down on the other side, which is easier said than done. About a third of the way down is a jutting ledge which has to be cleared.

Joey goes first, pushing himself out so as to clear the ledge. As he lands the shock travels right up to the top of his head. Ray follows him and, as his knees bend to absorb the shock, his arse hit the deck, his glasses fly off and his knees smash him under the chin. Joey retrieves the glasses as Richie and Harry, both heavy men, land safely. Funnily enough Chris, an ex-paratrooper, does his ankle in and he has to be helped along as they head for the main road.

All they need now is transport and they decide to stop the first car that comes along. Joey is hoping for something in the XJ6 line but it turns out to be a Mini. He steps into the road and holds up his hand. The car stops, Ray and Joey go round to the driver's side, Harry and Richie stand in front of the vehicle and Chris limps to the passenger door. The driver is an elderly man and there is a woman beside him. Joey opens the door.

'Police,' he says. 'Would you mind stepping out of the car, sir.'

The man sits there and looks at them. Ray reaches past Joey and cops for the ignition key.

'Look mate,' he says, 'we're escaped prisoners. We need your car. Just come out and nobody'll get hurt.'

They are out of the car in a flash, which goes to show that it sometimes pays to tell the truth. They all pile in, Ray takes the wheel and they are away, leaving the old couple on the pavement in a state of total bewilderment.

A successful escape falls into three parts. First you get out then you get away and then you stay out. The first part had gone well. As they rolled along through the back streets towards Clapham Common the second part of the enterprise seemed to be in order. Near the tube station Joey spotted a church with a large open space in front.

'OK Ray, drive in here,' he said.

Ray parked close to the wall of the church. There was no-one about. They crawled out of the Mini and, as Joey wriggled out of his overalls he felt a hard lump in the pocket. He had completely forgotten that, as he left the security room, he had nicked the master key of the prison from its glass case on the wall. He hung on to it, threw the overalls in the back of the car and followed the others as they strolled across the road to the station.

All they had between them was a fifty pence piece. Joey bought five tenpenny tickets and, as they walked to the escalator, they heard the wail of sirens as police cars sped to Brixton. Joey looked at the station clock. It was six-fifty, just forty-five minutes since the caper had started. They made their way to the northbound platform, got in the first train that came along and sat on different seats in the same carriage.

It wasn't long before the reaction set in. Sitting opposite was a bird in a very short skirt and, as Joey looked at her, he also caught Chris's eye. He smiled and Joey smiled back. Then he began to laugh and Joey laughed too. The other three in different parts of the carriage took it up, and there they were laughing their heads off and not quite knowing why. Laughter is infectious. Very soon some of the passengers joined in. What they were laughing at, of course, was a vivid remembrance of some recent scenes. A couple of screws trussed up like turkeys, one of them with his pants full of shit. Lionel Galloway in his stocking mask and Saville Row suit. Three Alsatian dogs falling over each other to get away from them. And above all they were laughing because they were free.

They left the train at Charing Cross and Joey made a transfer charge call as a result of which there would be a couple of cars at the Embankment entrance to the station within fifteen minutes. All of a sudden he noticed that Chris was missing, then he heard his voice. There was one of these fire-and-brimstone merchants spouting and Chris was verballing him from the crowd. Joey weeded him out just as the cars arrived.

The mate who provided the cars was an old friend who owed Joey. He expected that they would be taken to a safe flop for the time being so he was surprised to find that their destination was a luxurious penthouse in the heart of the West End. It was a smashing pad, deep carpets, modern furniture, colour tele, the lot. There were two birds living there, Julie and Angie, both hostesses at Churchill's club.

'What's the score, Charlie?' Joey asked as they made themselves comfortable in the lounge.

'Only place I could think of Joey,' he replied. 'Don't worry. The girls are as good as gold. It'll cost you, but I think you'll find it's worth it.'

He was minding a couple of grand for Joey so he was able to see that the girls were well sweetened, and they didn't seem to object to having a few husky blokes about the place. The only snag was that the rent was paid by a sugar-daddy but he wasn't expected to turn up in the near future so that was alright. Being five-handed they had to double up in the spare bedrooms but that was better than being three-up in Brixton.

During the next couple of days news came out of the prison about what had happened after they went over the wall. For a while nobody knew that anybody had escaped at all, such was the confusion. The cons who had gone back to their cells believed that Joey and the others were banged up in the chokey. It wasn't until the ten o'clock news reported that five prisoners had made a getaway that they realised that their efforts had not been in vain. They shouted and cheered, yelling the news from the windows and banging on the doors of the cells. The only bloke who didn't do any cheering was George de Buriatte, the fucking grass who did all he could to wreck Joey's plan. This merchant later admitted in an article in *Weekend* magazine that he had been responsible for putting more than a hundred and fifty men away.

A message came out to Joey via Leroy Davies' brother Glen that there was a right old fuss going on over the master key Joey had nicked and Leroy, Kenny Lawrence and Obie O'Brien were having a lot of aggravation. The bloody thing was no use to Joey but he gathered that it would go down on the credit side if the key found its way back to its rightful place on the wall of the security room. He made arrangements for its return by 'special' messenger.

That same day Big Harry left them. He'd done his bit during the escape and they were really sorry to lose him. He went off to see his wife, who persuaded him to give himself up so, like the little nigger boys, now they were four, Ray, Chris, Richie and Joey. Poor old Chris was in a bad way. His foot, which he had injured when he jumped from the wall, was swollen to twice its normal size and had turned all the colours of the rainbow.

They got hold of a nurse who could be trusted to keep her mouth shut. She came round to the flat and, when she had examined Chris's foot she made no bones about it. He had smashed the ankle and needed hospital treatment. That being out of the question, she bandaged the foot and packed ice-bags round it to reduce the swelling and ease the pain.

'He ought to have a crutch,' she said.

Joey volunteered the information that he already had one and anyway it was his foot they were worried about, not his balls.

'That's the sort of remark I would expect from you,' she said. 'I mean a crutch to help him walk.'

'So where do we get a crutch?' asked Richie.

'Knowing you lot you'd probably snatch it from a cripple in the street,' she said.

That afternoon Richie and Joey set out to capture a crutch. Richie was at the wheel of Angie's little Ford. They had already decided that it would be too risky to march into John Bell and Croydon's and buy one, which might have led to some awkward questions, so they made their way to Westminster Hospital. Richie parked the car and they strolled in. As things went, they could have nicked the bloody hospital because they were never challenged. Joey picked up a white coat which was hanging about doing nothing and slipped it on. Now he looked like a thug in a white coat.

They roamed around the corridors and finally they spotted it, a lovely aluminium crutch sitting on a trolley waiting to be nicked. Joey picked it up and, with Richie at his side doing a crutch salesman act, they walked out of the door past the porter and got into the car. Joey slung the crutch into the back seat.

'OK, Rich,' he said. 'There's no rush now, let's have a little drive round.'

13. Solitary

Richie was just as keen as Joey to see the sights. As they swung into Victoria Street Richie glanced in the mirror.

'Heads up Joey. It's the filth,' he said.

'Where?'

'Right up our arse.'

Joey looked through the rear window. The distinctive white Rover with its red markings was right behind them.

'Keep going Rich,' Joey said. He leaned back and shifted the crutch, making sure the occupants of the following car got a good eyeful. It was as though he was saying 'You wouldn't nick a cripple, would you?' It didn't have any effect. The law followed them round Parliament Square and up towards Westminster Bridge. They crossed the lights by the Houses of Parliament and Joey spotted an opening on the left.

'Turn in here and keep going,' he said.

Richie dutifully did as he was told, and the Old Bill also turned as if the two cars were tied together with a piece of string. Suddenly Joey realised where they were. The opening they had turned into was Cannon Row and they were in Scotland Yard, the headquarters of the Metropolitan Police.

'Hold it, Richie,' Joey said. 'Just do a quiet U-turn and go back.'

The police car stopped as Richie made the turn and drove slowly past to join the bridge-bound traffic. It made no move to follow. Richie turned left on to the Embankment.

'Jesus Christ,' said Joey. 'I thought they'd sussed us.'

Richie came up with a classic reply.

'Maybe they don't read the papers,' he said.

It is Monday the 9th June 1972 and the time is a little after eleven o'clock in the morning. A silver-blue Ford Corsair 2000E saloon is speeding along Cranbrook Road in Ilford. E is for Executive, but there is nothing of the executive about the four men in the car. They are not wearing striped suits but their faces are covered by striped scarves worn balaclava fashion and with eyeholes cut in them.

Chris is at the wheel. The other three occupants are 'Honeypuff' Richie, 'Scarface' Ray and Joey. They are on their way to make a withdrawal of a substantial sum of money from the National Westminster Bank, Ilford branch. None of them have cheque books but Ray and Joey are carrying sawn-off shotguns and Richie is armed with a pickaxe.

Chris makes a tyre-screaming turn into Beehive Lane, then turns left and slams the car up on to the pavement outside the bank. He stays at the wheel and the other three leap out and burst through the doors. Joey shouts 'Don't anybody move. This is a raid', and makes for the security door with Honeypuff right behind him. Scarface stays by the door and orders the customers to lie face down on the floor. Some of them don't seem too willing but Scarface waggles the gun at them and they are persuaded.

The security door is locked. Joey shouts 'Open this door or you'll get shot'. It's opened in double-quick time and Joey and Honeypuff get behind the counter. Somebody has pressed the silent alarm which is connected directly with the local nick. This action also closes and locks the cash drawers. Joey points the gun at the cashiers and orders them to lie on the floor. Honeypuff goes to work with the pickaxe, forces open the drawers and loads the cash from them into a capacious bag. There's a sudden commotion at the main door. A women is walking in, looking over her shouder at the car parked up on the pavement. She turns, see Scarface and lets out a scream, but she's soon down on the floor with the rest of the customers.

Honeypuff has captured the loot. He goes through the security door as Joey backs out, the sawn-off at the ready. They meet up with Scarface at the main door. There is a shout from one of the geezers behind the counter.

'You've missed most of it,' he yells.

He's wrong. Joey is well pleased with what they've got. They sprint to the car and pile in, Chris lets the clutch out and makes a quick U-turn. Down Cranbrook Road they go like an arrow from a bow. They ditch the Corsair in Dersingham Road in Manor Park and switch to another car, then drive slowly back to the Mayfair flat. Once inside Honeypuff tips the bag out on to the floor. The carpet is covered in readies.

'Not bad, eh?' he laughs.

'Did you cop for that feller,' says Scarface. 'You haven't got it all, he says. That's the slippery bastard who set off the alarm.'

They go out shopping that afternoon. There's a gaff in Shepherd Street called Quincy's and Ray, Chris and Joey have a look round at the gear. They get the odd look from one of the salesmen, and the next thing they know somebody has slipped round behind them and locked the door. They give each other the nod. If there's any move to the phone they all go out straight through the plate glass window.

They've picked up a few articles, so they go to the counter and pay for them, something like sixty-odd quid. The bloke who had locked the door slyly unlocks it and they leave the premises. It would have been a bit of an anti-climax to be nicked for shoplifting after doing the bank.

*

Later on that evening they sat round the television having a drink. Ray had gone out to meet a mate, and they were just discussing going clubbing soon when the ten o'clock news came on. Joey doesn't remember which talking head it was but he well remembers what it said.

'One of the men who escaped from Brixton Prison a few weeks ago was recaptured earlier this evening after a brief car chase through the West End of London. The man, Scarface Ray Pegler, was recognised by a police officer on routine car patrol.'

The news was a bit of a facer. Ray was driving an MG with a distinctive number plate. It had been parked outside the flat on several occasions and may have been spotted by the Old Bill. Also, though it wasn't likely, Ray might have been carrying a letter which would give a clue to their whereabouts. One thing they knew for certain was that Ray wouldn't grass them up. They decided to get out of the flat right away and meet next day at Valerie's flat in Halley Road, the other side of Ilford. They packed their gear and cleared out.

It was about quarter past three in the afternoon when Joey arrived at Val's place. It was a nice roomy flat on the upper floor of a Victorian house. Chris and Richie had already arrived and were brewing up in the kitchen. They had hardly sat down when the phone rang and Valerie answered it. She picked up the receiver, held it to her ear for a few moments then replaced it.

'What was that, Val?' Joey said.

'Oh, some nutter,' she replied. 'Didn't say anything. Just rang off.'

Joey jumped from the chair and picked up the phone. As he thought, the line was dead. Whoever had rung hadn't replaced the receiver at the other end. It was a typical Old Bill trick to prevent a call being made out when they were ready to move in. Joey went to the window and looked out and, sure enough, the street below was swarming with law, five or six cars and a couple of vans and Old Bill with shooters all over the place.

Joey turned to the others. 'Quick, it's on fucking top,' he yelled. As Chris and Richie made a dive for the bedroom Joey dashed into the kitchen. He had a few grand in readies which he stuffed into an empty chocolate box and dropped into the rubbish bin. An amplified voice boomed from outside the house.

'We are armed police officers. We have a warrant to search this house. Stay where you are.'

As Valerie went to the head of the stairs Joey made for the loft, threw back the cover and climbed up. From his hiding place he heard the Old Bill rush into the flat and drag Chris and Richie out of the bedroom. He knew it was only a question of time before his turn came and he was dead right.

'You in the loft. You've got a minute to come out before we fire through the ceiling.'

Joey had no chance. He pulled the cover to one side and lowered himself ready to drop. As he did so one of the armed coppers smashed the butt of a rifle against his ankle and he fell to the floor. He was in agony.

'Tut, tut. You shouldn't have done that officer,' said the Detective Inspector in charge of the raid. He was laughing all over his face.

'I thought he was going to run away sir,' said the rozzer, smiling happily.

All Joey could think of was getting into the open air where there would at least be a crowd of bystanders to witness any further brutality. He closed his eyes and pretended to faint. He was dragged out to a waiting car by a couple of heavyweights and ended up in West Ham nick.

The DI, whose name was East, and another officer travelled with him.

Joey held to the rule that it's best to say nothing after a nicking but he had to get one thing straight.

'You'll find there's some money in a chocolate box in the kitchen – in the rubbish bin,' he said to East. 'It's down to me.'

'Oh, really,' said East. 'Part of your share of the loot?'

'Don't know what you're talking about, guv'nor. It's my life savings.'

'So what's it doing in the rubbish bin?'

'Always hide my money there. Lots of thieves about.'

East laughed. It didn't really matter what Joey said. It would come out East's way in the verbal, but Joey was anxious that possession of the money wouldn't be down to Chris or Richie. As it happened the bin was not searched until about two hours later by a pair of Detective Sergeants from the Regional Crime Squad. The three thousand odd pounds had shrunk to two hundred and eighty-five. Actually the two scoundrels had done Joey a favour. The less money found the greater his chances of getting away with a charge of robbery.

Later that day they were all taken to Ilford nick. Chris, Richie and Joey were charged with armed robbery and receiving. Val, poor cow, was charged with receiving and harbouring escaped prisoners. But Joey's troubles weren't over by any means. Out of the blue came a DI from Paddington to interview him about a Mrs Clarke who had been assaulted and robbed in Bayswater earlier in the year. He copped for that one too. It never rains but it pours.

Chris and Joey were taken to Ilford hospital to receive attention for their injured ankles. Needless to say they were heavily escorted. When the doctor asked Joey how he had received his injury he told him that a copper had whacked him with a rifle-butt.

The doctor turned to one of the coppers.

'Is that true?' he asked.

'No sir,' came the reply. 'He fell off the wall at Brixton while escaping.'

There are no prizes for guessing which explanation was accepted.

At the Magistrates' Court hearing the three men were remanded in custody. Poor cow Val got bail. Joey didn't need a vivid imagination to envisage what kind of a reception was awaiting them at Brixton. They had tied up a couple of screws, locked another one in the fridge and Joey had personally chinned a Principal Officer. It was a safe bet that somebody was going to be hurt and the three were in the frame as prime favourites.

They had an escort worthy of a Prime Minister going to address a meeting of unemployed. They went into the reception area, Chris and Joey leaning on each other's shoulders with only two good legs between them. There were far more screws about than was usual and it looked as though it was going to be off. The escort handed them over, their property was checked and they were told to lead on through the tunnel that led to the second reception and the baths.

This was where it would happen and Joey clenched his fists in anticipation. As he came to the end of the tunnel a screw was standing there and, as he passed him, he saw out ot the corner of his eye as he raised his hand. Joey swung round, ready to ride the blow and reply in kind, but all he got was a friendly pat on the back.

'Well done, Bello,' said the screw.

Joey couldn't believe his ears. When he heard him say the same words to Chris and Richie he was even more flabbergasted. They were a dozen screws waiting at the desk which was normally manned by a single officer. They were laughing and cracking jokes.

'Right you buggers, you won't get away this time.'
'We've got you taped.'
'No more birds and booze now, eh?'

There were many similar comments but not one of the screws raised a hand against them. Joey reckoned that they had a sneaking admiration for them and didn't want to add to their troubles by coming the heavy, which they could quite easily have done. It was one of those cases of let bygones be bygones but we'll make sure you don't do it again. The surprising thing was that they received no punishment at all for the escape attempt. They were brought before the Governor and were later interviewed by the Brixton police and asked a lot of questions to which they gave a load of rubbish in reply. They were put on special watch with two screws on constant guard outside their cells, but other than that they were treated as ordinary remand cases.

Ray told them the details of how he was captured. He was upset in case Joey thought he had grassed them but he was put right on that score. Some of the blokes they had unlocked gave them full marks for trying, so all in all they didn't come out of it badly. There was one little matter that Joey saw to personally. He had a chat with de Buriatte and made sure that the grass understood that his behaviour on the night of the escape was out of order. He got the message.

Joey settled down into the routine very quickly. He had no more thoughts of escaping. All he had to worry about was facing the charges against him and that was quite enough. His first appearance before the judge and jury was on the burglary charge in connection with the garage from which he had run the mini-cab business. He was assured by his brief that the evidence against him was pretty flimsy and he stood a good chance of getting chucked. Consequently when he went up the steps at the Inner London Sessions he was quite cheerful.

One of the nice things about the British judicial system is that the accused, within reason of course, can call as many defence witnesses as he likes. Joey told his brief that certain persons now being held in Brixton were essential witnesses so Chris, Richie, Ray, Leroy and couple of other merchants found themselves having a day out and a decent lunch which Joey arranged to be sent in to them. Of course they weren't called, they just sat around chatting and smoking.

The case didn't take long. Andy the Greek and his lousy brother-in-law were not very convincing in the witness box and the judge quite properly slung the case out. That didn't mean that Joey left the dock without a stain on his character to emerge into the outside world as a free man. He returned to Brixton to await the next development in the Bello saga.

In November Joey was at the Old Bailey before Judge Edward Clarke on a charge of robbing Mrs Clarke (no relation to his Lordship) of money and jewellery. The judge was no stranger to Joey. He was the one who sent him down on the pub affair when he appeared with the Mills brothers and Charlie Canavan so Joey's card was marked. He had the sort of face that is not easily forgotten.

The chief police witness was a Detective Inspector Ridley, a bent copper who was later, in 1982, sentenced to twelve months. He came out with a load of verbal about Joey having been a drinking companion of the lady, which she denied very strongly and also said that Joey confessed to the crime in West Ham nick, which was a load of rubbish. He overstepped the mark when he rabbited on about Val being brought into the nick by DS Hayday of the Regional Crime Squad, thus linking Joey with the Ilford job before he had been tried for it. Anyway it made no odds, the damage had been done and Joey was weighed off with four years.

So it was goodbye Brixton and the privileges of sent-in meals and unlimited canteen facilities. Joey was carted off to Wandsworth, rigged out in yellow patches and put on the A list. What this amounts to is that the prisoner is issued a book with his photo and description in it. This is handed to the screw in charge of him at any given time. He is responsible for the A man until he hands him over to another screw. This serves a double purpose. If the man manages to get away it will be a miracle, secondly the prison authorities will have somebody to jump on in case he does escape.

In some ways being an A man had its advantages. He was always at the head of the queue when it came to seeing the Governor or the doctor or the welfare. On the other hand security in the mailbag shop was very tight and the precautions taken on excercise had to be experienced to be believed. Joey never knew when he was going to go walkies until a screw came into the shop and called his name out. Then there was the irritation of special searches when the A man could be stopped at any time and given a rub-down.

It was one of these special searches that landed Joey in trouble. A chap called Jackie Jury, who later died in Hull prison, was carrying more snout than he was entitled to when the two screws who carried out these searches turned up in the mailbag shop. Jury got the wind up. Joey was right beside him.

'What shall I do, Joey?' he said out of the corner of his mouth.

'Go for a piss and ditch it,' Joey said.

One of the screws, a nasty specimen who wasn't very fond of Joey, noticed the talking.

'You. Face the front and shut up', he said.

Joey took the chance to create a diversion which would give Jackie an opportunity to get rid of the snout.

'Who the fucking hell do you you think you're talking to,' he said. 'You dressed-up prick. I've eaten better things than you before breakfast.'

All Joey wanted to do was to take the screw's attention away from Jackie but it went wrong. The screw dived for the alarm bell and the heavy mob was on the scene in no time. They claimed Joey and frog-marched him out of the shop. He went quietly, it wasn't worth starting a fight, but the screw who'd set up the scream had other ideas. As Joey was hustled down to the chokey he suddenly kicked him in the kidneys. As Joey turned the heavy mob took this as a gesture of defiance. They rushed him into a cell and really set about him. He didn't fight back. He could have claimed two or three of them but that would have given them a holiday with pay on so-called sick leave and he would have had to face the serious charge of assaulting a prison officer so he covered up and yelled blue murder as the sticks and boots went in. After a while the heavy mob gave up. Joey was black and blue all over, but it could have been worse.

The next day Joey was up before the Governor and made a formal complaint which was refused because it wasn't in writing. He made a written complaint which was considered by the Visiting Magistrates who referred it back to the Governor with a recommendation that Joey should be punished for making false and malicious accusations. The substance of the allegations, that he had been savagely beaten, were shoved on one side. Over the coming years Joey was to fight for the right to take action in the civil courts against the bastards who had hammered him. All he got from the authorities was delay, prevarication and outright obstruction.

All screws aren't tarred with the same brush. The majority are quite decent fellows who do a difficult job to the best of their ability. It's the minority of spineless shits who cause the bother. Delve into the causes of the riots at Hull, Chelmsford, Parkhurst and other prisons and somewhere along the line is a small group of bullying psychopaths dressed in prison officers' uniform who, instead of being weeded out, are protected by authority in the name of prison discipline. They treat men like animals, brutalise them and subject them to all sorts of humiliation. Complaints against them are disregarded. No wonder the wretched con reaches a point where he says 'Fuck it' and takes the law into his own hands.

By April of 1973 conditions had become so bad in Wandsworth that the inmates were in a mood verging on open rebellion, particularly with regard to the 'no talking' rule. Individual complaints to the Governor proved useless, so twenty-one cons made a group application for the order to be relaxed. Joey was one of them. The next thing he knew he was up before the Governor and put on Rule 43, solitary segregation for the good order and discipline of the prison. Joey was the only one singled out for this treatment which went on for seven months, the only break being the few days he spent at the Old Bailey when he stood trial for the Ilford job.

There were three of them standing in the dock, Joey, Chris and Richie. Valerie should have been with them but she was in hospital after having taken an overdose of sleeping tablets. Scarface Ray was safely tucked up in jail somewhere and the best of British to him. The outcome of the trial was in no doubt. They were all marked down for hefty doses of porridge, so it was just a matter of going through the motions and some of the proceedings would have made a cat laugh.

DI Ridley, the Paddington terror, had a field day in the witness box with pages of verbal along the lines of 'fair cop, guv' and 'you got me bang to rights', the kind of phoney dialogue used by TV writers which bears no relation to the real speech of genuine villains. He went into a song and dance about bringing Valerie to the West Ham nick, saying he was led to do so by 'humane considerations'. Joey's brief caught him out in palpable lies more than once.

Another comic turn was DS Hayday of the Regional Crime Squad who came up with such gems as 'I'm no snout', a term used by the Bow Street Runners to describe a grass. Chris, said Hayday, came up with 'if you've got any witnesses let's get on with the IDs (identification parades). I was well masked'. Joey and Chris looked at each other and they both had to laugh. Then Richie pulls one out of the bag with evidence that he was in Austin Reed's emporium in Knightsbridge at the same time as the bank was being done in Ilford. Everybody knew where he was, including the filth, but they couldn't prove it.

Joey's brief called the copper who had smashed his ankle with the butt of his rifle.

'How did Bello come by the injury to his ankle?' asked the brief.

'Escaping from Brixton prison, sir,' said the idiot.

Previous evidence had shown that the robber alleged to be Bello had been leaping about like a gazelle in the course of the raid. Even members of the jury had to smile at this barefaced piece of fiction.

Eventually the trial came to an end. Surprisingly Richie got chucked and walked from the court a free man. The jury, by a majority verdict, found Chris and Joey guilty of receiving but not guilty of robbery, which showed what they thought of the way the prosecution had presented the case. It also indicated their opinion of the comic act Ridley and Hayday. But, though the jury decide guilt or innocence, it's the judge who does the sentencing. Despite the gaping holes in the evidence and the comic opera nature of the trial, he gave Joey eight years and awarded seven to Chris. Val, poor cow, came up some months later and got chucked.

Joey was sure that, had it not been for the silly copper

who said that he had done his ankle at Brixton, he would have been found guilty of robbery. He also thought that the jury did not take kindly to being treated like a bunch of half-wits in being asked to believe the verbal garbage by Ridley and Hayday.

Joey read somewhere that Lord Kilbrandon, addressing the International Commission of Jurists in 1976, said 'the verbal is becoming a music hall joke'. He must have read the transcripts of the trial of Joey, Chris and Richie.

It was back once more to Wandsworth and solitary. Joey missed the daily trips to the Old Bailey where he had at least been able to talk to somebody. Now he could only talk to himself. He put up the best performance possible in these one-sided conversations but found it hard to laugh at his own jokes. He'd heard them all before. On a serious note, though solitary is not recommended as a life-style except for Trappist monks, it does exercise the old thinking machinery. There's not much else to do.

One morning, out of the blue, Joey was told to pack up his belongings as he was being moved to another prison. He didn't bother to ask where he was going. Anywhere must be better than Wandsworth. Eventually, after some shuttling around, he ended up in Chelmsford, a place about thirty-odd miles from London with a cathedral, a golf course and a museum. There was also a prison, which wasn't mentioned in the guide books.

Joey was quite wary as he walked into reception. As a potential escaper he was well escorted and his A list status would be known to the prison staff. Joey's surprise can be imagined when the reception screw stuck his hand out.

'Hello, Bello,' he said. 'No hard feelings, eh?'

Joey wondered what the hell he was talking about. He had seen the man somewhere before but he couldn't quite place him. The screw saw that Joey was puzzled.

'The last time I saw you, you were tying me up in Brixton,' he said.

It all came back to him then, and he felt a bit of a shit. Here was this merchant who had it in his power to make things tough and get his own back, and he was holding out his hand. He took the hand and shook it heartily.

'Look,' said Joey. 'I'm sorry about that. You know how it was.'

'Sure. I know. All water under the bridge now, isn't it?'

Joey was choked. Later on when he got to know him better, the screw turned out to be a first-class bloke and he did Joey many a favour during his stay at Chelmsford.

It's a small world and full of coincidences. The following day, under escort, Joey was allowed to watch a match being played on the football field, quite a treat for him after his stretch in Wandsworth where all he ever saw was a wired-in exercise yard. There was a bloke in civvies standing on the touchline. It was 'Mad Mike' who ran the Rugby Club in Notting Dale when Joey was a kid. Joey thought he must be a member of the staff because he evidently wasn't a con.

Joey could see he was trying to figure out who he was.

'Joey Bello from Notting Dale. Nobby's young brother,' he said.

'Oh, yes. I remember,' said Mad Mike. His manner was a bit frosty.

'What are you doing here?' enquired Joey.

Mad Mike gave a slight smile.

'You'll find out on Monday morning,' he said, nodded and walked away. This was Saturday afternoon.

On the Monday morning Joey was on parade outside the Governor's office. This was usual procedure. The Governor or his deputy sees every new inmate as soon after arrival as possible, but only on weekdays. Joey had been delivered on Friday afternoon. As an A man he ws at the head of the line and he marched into the office with a pair of screws in close attendance. Sitting behind the desk, a Principal Officer at his elbow, was 'Mad Mike', now Governor of HM Prison, Chelmsford. Joey rarely blushed but, remembering the familiar way he had greeted the man, his face turned slightly pink.

The Governor acted as though he had never been on the football field on the Saturday, which was understandable, but when he was delivering the usual homily about being a good boy, keeping out of trouble and so on, there was a twinkle in his eye. Joey was duly marched out but Mad Mike obviously had a word with the PO because there wasn't any of the aggro which happens to an A man when he changes prisons. Actually he was surprised at the amount of freedom he was given. Although the rules were carried out to the letter, it was the interpretation of the rules which made Joey's life easier.

To a tough nut who had taken Dartmoor, Wandsworth and Hampton in his stride Chelmsford was a piece of cake, despite the category A label. Joey settled down nicely and got himself involved with an organisation inside the prison which called itself Recidivists Anonymous. They produced a regular magazine with official sanction, but it was only for circulation within the confines of the jail and subject to censorship, so it was a pretty weak-kneed effort. He wrote a few articles and helped with the production which gave him something to do in his spare time.

Joey didn't know why he suddenly upset the apple-cart. On the whole the screws were a decent bunch and it was bad luck that the one who stopped Joey outside his cell was one of the few bastards. He had a sneering look and a lot of venom in his voice.

'Pack your gear, Bello,' he said. 'You're changing cells.'

Joey had put in a lot of work on his peter, scrubbing the table and chair, keeping the floor clean and sticking up a few pictures on the walls, so he wasn't keen on moving and really the only reason for the move was the rule that said an A man's cell should be changed from time to time.

'Come off it, mate,' said Joey. 'I like this peter.'

'Say sir when you speak to me. And don't fucking argue, you cunt,' said the screw.

That did it. Joey stuck one on his chops, which took the sneer off his face, but then two other screws joined in the battle. For a moment Joey thought of chucking in the towel, but then he thought of Wandsworth and how far he didn't get by going through the proper channels, so he steamed in and soon had the three of them in trouble. By the time the heavy mob came up at the double Joey had decked two and was putting the finishing touches to the third. Then the big sticks started swinging and that was his lot.

He went through the rigmarole of chokey, Visiting Magistrates, loss of remission, fourteen days bread and water, loss of privileges, in fact loss of everything except self-respect. The three screws went on extended sick leave on full pay and Joey went on the transfer list, destination Parkhurst. A few months later HM Prison Chelmsford was burned to the ground. Whoever or whatever caused the blaze remains a mystery.

All prisons are bad news but, apart from Dartmoor, the gaggle of ugly buildings just outside Newport on the Isle of Wight ranks very low on the list of Her Majesty's holiday camps. There are three penal establishments in the huge complex. Camp Hill is a red-brick Victorian prison which was at one time a Borstal but is now used to house short-term young prisoners. Albany is a more modern place entirely, equipped with all the latest and most up-to-date contrivances for cutting off the malefactor from the outside world. Parkhurst proper is the ugly sister of the trio, an ancient mausoleum of crumbling brick steadily falling to pieces as a result of the ravages of time and the regular convict riots.

There were a number of cons in the green coach that left Wandsworth where Joey had spent the night in transit. The designers of the vehicles must have been under the impression that cons have specially sprung arses because there was no padding on the seats. The screws were wise to that. They brought their own cushions. At Portsmouth the coach was driven on to the ferry that plied between the mainland and the Isle of Wight and there the cons were, a sort of peepshow firmly manacled to their seats.

Joey had never been much of a seaman and he wasn't looking forward to this trip across the choppy waters of the Solent. To begin with, the ferry was an old tub with flat ends, not the most efficient design for a smooth passage through water. Also the engines weren't up to much, they seemed to be doing their best to shake the vessel to pieces. What with the constant vibration and the crashing of the waves against the flat bows Joey was beginning to get a bit panicky.

'What about taking these cuffs off, guv,' he said to one of the screws. 'If this fucking heap goes down we've had it.'

'You'll be alright, Bello, it won't go down. If it does I'm a good swimmer.'

You'd better be, mate, Joey thought, because if anything does go wrong, I'll cling to you like a fucking leech. However nothing did go wrong and, twenty minutes after leaving the ferry they were being driven through the forbidding gates of Parkhurst. Joey went through the reception routine, including a vigorous search by the reception screws known as the 'burglars'. What they expected to find he didn't know as he had just come from Wandsworth which isn't exactly a freedom centre. He was allocated to A wing.

He was lucky enough to meet two old friends as he went

on the wing. They knew the ropes and helped him to wangle a decent cell and some furniture. Bertie he had met years before in Dartmoor. He was in his late forties and a fitness fanatic, wearing shorts and singlet whatever the weather and dead keen on weight-lifting. Patsy Fleming was one of the old school villains who had escaped from Nottingham in 1955 along with Alfie Hinds. He was doing eight years for a wage snatch at a South London printing firm. What Patsy didn't know was that the Old Bill had been tipped off that it was to be an armed raid. He was most upset when his car was fired on. He didn't believe in shooters. Bertie on the other hand had no such scruples. Part of his ten stretch was awarded for firearms offences. Shooters or not, it made little difference. They all landed up in the same place.

Joey arrived at Parkhurst shortly before the festive season, but Christmas in prison is no cake-walk. It was a pretty sad and miserable time for the family men and not exactly a bundle of fun for the others. The cons all got an extra twenty pence from the Common Fund to spend on riotous living and the food on Christmas Day and Boxing Day was an improvement on the usual fare which was diabolical by any standards. Joey did get to see a couple of fairly up-to-date films, 'The Sting' and 'The Three Musketeers', but that was the extent of the jollification.

After the so-called celebrations it was business as usual and the prison settled down into the old routine, near-inedible grub served on plastic plates, heavy punishments for minor offences and the daily monotony which changes men into human vegetables.

14. Home for Criminals

Parkhurst is the home for criminal 'headliners'. Stand on a corner of the exercise yard and you will be passed by some of the most infamous characters in British criminal history.

There were the Hussain brothers, a pair of Asians who kidnapped the wife of a national newspaper executive and held her to ransom. When the money was not forthcoming the lady disappeared and the brothers were convicted of her murder. Joey had a long chat one day with the elder brother and out of curiosity tried to find out what had happened to the lady's body, which was never found.

'They almost pulled the farm to pieces looking for it,' said Hussain, laughing all over his face. 'We wouldn't be so stupid as to bury her on the farm. She's in the last place you would ever think of looking, but it's one place where you could expect to find her.'

This one was a real funny fellow. Whenever Joey saw him he was running as though he had to get somewhere in a hurry. Even the way he ran was peculiar, a high-stepping trot like one of the performing horses in a circus.

Another famous fellow was a bloke called von Bulow. He was walking along a road in Caterham when a police car pulled up and a copper stepped out, wanting to know what von Bulow had in the bag he was carrying. It turned out to be a Luger pistol which the suspect promptly emptied into the officer's body, killing him instantly. The murderer ws hunted for four weeks by posses of armed police, much to the disgust of the Surrey villains who were forced to stay indoors at nights due to the activities of the Old Bill. The name von Bulow was assumed, deriving from an ancient German prince, all part of a Teutonic obsession. He used to stroll about constantly clenching and flexing his fingers as though practising a quick draw with a six gun.

There was also the Parkhurst platoon of the IRA, Welch and Armstrong, convicted with the Price sisters of the bomb attack at the Old Bailey. There was also one of the team responsible for the Birmingham bombing. In discussion with them they advanced valid reasons for what they had done, but it was hard to forget the innocent victims of their actions.

Johnny Brook had been convicted of the murder of Muriel Patience at the Barn restaurant on Guy Fawkes night 1972. Another man was twice tried and twice acquitted of the same charge. He was George Ince, a former associate of the Kray twins and Dolly Kray's lover. Brook was a loner. He had an artificial right eye which gave him a rather peculiar expression. This glass eye looked right at you while the other roamed about all over the place.

Danny Allpress and Bryan Turner were two outstanding characters. Danny had been put away by supergrass Bertie Smalls and kept a budgerigar in his cell which he had taught to say 'Bert is a fucking grass'. Danny and Bryan had pulled off robberies at the Ilford and Wembley branches of Barclays bank amounting to close on four hundred grand.

The man christened the Cambridge Rapist by the popular press was a queer fish. Joey had expected to see some sort of super athlete when he first laid eyes on him, but he was an insignificant figure about five feet six with long hair below his shoulders. He had a profitable business renting out his court depositions for tobacco when he first arrived. They put the hard porn magazines to shame.

Ex-commando Harry Roberts, who killed three Old Bill in Braybrook Street near Wormwood Scrubs, was one of the hard cases. After the killing, when every copper in

London was looking for him he stayed at liberty for a month, hiding out in Epping Forest. Another cop-killer was Fred Sewell, who shot an inspector in Blackpool and later was mixed up in an attempted break-out from Gartree. He told Joey how one of the screws copped for one of the escapers and repeatedly smashed him over the head with a claw-hammer, which sparked off a riot. Then there was Bill Skindle who also killed a copper by putting nine bullets into him.

Johnny Kellard, serving sixteen years for bank robbery, was captured after a bizarre incident in Kensington High Street, a fashionable shopping area. The gang, waving their shooters, were making a getaway from the bank when out of the blue a copper came on the scene. He was leaving his post at a local embassy and, like all Old Bill on that sort of duty, he was armed. Proving the point money, especially bank money, is more valuable than lives, the copper sprayed the surroundings with bullets, shot Johnny in the thigh and also wounded another member of the gang by the name of Hart. Johnny was nicked but Hart managed to make his way to the multi-storey car park where he had left his car. He bled to death beside it.

There were many others serving long sentences either for armed robbery or murder and all of them at one time or other had been in the Special Security Block known as the SSB. This was a two-storey building about the size of a large detached house, which had electronic locks, closed circuit television cameras, a wired-in exercise yard and batteries of floodlights. It was considered ecape proof but there were three cons who didn't agree with that. They were bank robbers Johnny Kellard and Cyril Burkett and cop-killer Bill Skindle. One afternoon they broke out of the block, cut through the wire-mesh fence enclosing the exercise yard and were away. They split up, Kellard and Burkett making for the houses and the chance of nicking a car, Skindle for the woods near the prison.

The two bank robbers were recaptured within the hour but Skindle, a lifer with nothing to lose, had not been found by nightfall. The following morning armed police with an SAS unit were out combing the area and a helicopter was also brought into the hunt equipped with a detection device which could pick up a human body from its heat radiation. Poor old Skindle. He didn't have a chance.

As usual the Home Office over-reacted. They didn't just close the door after the horse had bolted, they nailed it, screwed it, padlocked it and barred it, shoved the horse back through the only window and then bricked that up. Actually the SSB was immediately evacuated and the prisoners shifted under heavy escort to other jails all over the country. Then, working on the principle that the best way of holding up a pair of trousers is belt, braces and six-inch nails through the hips, the brains went to work. First they replaced the perimeter fence with a steel-lined concrete wall, topping it with an overhanging rubber coping incorporating a pressure-pad alarm. Then they built a tunnel-proof exercise yard, alarmed all the windows, installed enough searchlights to illuminate Piccadilly Circus and finally ringed the area with a dozen television cameras. When this work had been completed the prisoners were brought back to their hermetically-sealed environment.

One of the old mates Joey was glad to see again was John Thorne, who was doing fifteen years for armed robbery. He had a very interesting tale to tell for he was one of many who had been sent down on the evidence of a new breed of law enforcer known as the supergrass.

What is a supergrass? He is, quite simply, a criminal who buys immunity for his own crimes by informing on fellow criminals on a mass scale. Maurice O'Mahoney turned Queen's evidence when John was charged in connection with the armed robbery of a Securicor van in Heston in 1974. They were on this job together. Four other men were also concerned.

The scene of the robbery was Phoenix Way, Heston, the date 1st June 1974. The security van was rammed by a low-loader and four men in another van parked nearby leaped out, captured the loot and escaped in a stolen Jag. The following extracts are from the statements made by O'Mahoney to the Old Bill which were the basis of the evidence he gave at the trial.

'As I was sitting in the back of the van waiting I had a touch of bottle and said to John (Thorne) "What am I doing here, I've got a lovely wife and kids at home" and he said "If you don't get out of this van I'll blow your fucking head off". He then pointed the shotgun at my head.'

Later in the statement:

'The driver then opened the inside door which leads to the back of the van because Thorne threatened to shoot the guard in the legs and as the guard was getting out I got in and saved the guard from getting shot in the legs because I was in the line of fire. If it wasn't for me that man would have been shot dead.'

Further on in the statement this poignant cry from the heart:

'It was too much. Thank God the security man didn't die, I'm going to help the police and tell them a number of other jobs I've been on. I just wish to God I'd never got involved with crime and these sort of animals I've been associating with. I repeat I'm glad it's over, thank God.'

Now who was this fellow O'Mahoney who provided the evidence to put away dozens of other criminals? Between 1969 and 1974 he was in on over a hundred jobs, the loot totalling more than two hundred grand in cash and goods.

Armed robbery, conspiracy, receiving, house, shop and warehouse breaking, practically every crime in the calendar was committed by this man who suddenly became an upright and model citizen after being nicked and leaned on by the law.

What was his punishment? He was given a five year sentence, spent twenty months in a police cell having it off with his bird when he felt like it (so much for the lovely wife and kids) and going out on parole at the end of the twenty months. He didn't even see the inside of a prison.

Joey didn't envy the man for, in his book, it was better to keep one's mouth shut and do the bird with a clear conscience. That was also the opinion of John Thorne who took it all very calmly and merely remarked that the supergrass was just one more hazard in a very risky profession. In conversation Joey expressed the view that the law had every right to collect evidence from any source, including supergrasses. What seemed wrong was this 'cough and all is forgiven' business. When the Old Bill virtually said 'go and nick as much as you like, come and tell us all, throw in plenty of bodies and you can go home' there was the smell of an unholy alliance which didn't reflect much credit on the dignity and impartiality of the law.

Thinking things over Joey came to the conclusion that the criminal always seemed to get the shitty end of the stick. It was little wonder that they went over the top and started riots. After all, he mused, they're on a hiding to nothing. Once the riot has started there's no chance they can get away, all they can do is give in at the end. Looking at it from the prisoner's point of view, which very few people do, they must be in a desperate state to risk further additions to their already long sentences.

A villain commits a crime and goes down for it and he doesn't expect to be sent to a convalescent home. On the other hand, having been deprived of that most precious thing, his liberty, he has the right to demand that he gets comparatively decent treatment providing he behaves himself. For example, a con is expecting a visit from his wife and kids and they don't turn up. He worries himself sick wondering what might have happened then, days later, he gets a letter from his wife saying that she phoned the prison saying why she couldn't come. He makes enquiries. Yes the message was received but 'what the fucking hell do you think we are, a messenger service?' Of course they're not a messenger service but what does it cost for a screw to pass on a message, 'tell so-and-so-so his wife isn't coming, she'll write later'. Actually one of the decent screws would do just that. It's the bastards who love to dish out the mental torture.

At the bottom of it all is the absence of an effective system for considering legitimate grievances. Under the present system the prisoner has no chance, he is a liar and guilty before he opens his mouth. The Governor believes the screw, the Visiting Committee believes the Governor and the Home Office will believe anybody bar the prisoner.

Knowing the true circumstances of prison life Joey found it hard to blame cons who riot or take hostages. It's their only way of being heard. Surrounded by secrecy and cover up they reach a stage of desperation where drastic action is called for, so they take it. It's not just mindless violence. They are up against a repressive system that has been perfected over centuries and secrecy is an essential part of it. Prisons are insulated from the outside world. If the public knew only one-tenth of what goes on in these places they would join in the riots too. Brutal discipline, lack of adequate medical treatment, denial of access to legal advice, restriction and censorship of letters, monthly visits and the petty irritations of prison rules add up to the creation of a situation which is bound to explode in violence sooner or later.

The worst feature of the system comes to the fore towards the end of a sentence. It is then that the con is eligible for release on licence, commonly known as parole, and this is how it works. When a prisoner has done one-third of his time his case comes in front of the Local Review Committee who decide whether it should go to the Parole Board. Once past that hurdle the Board considers the prisoner's dossier. If parole is turned down no reason is given and there is no right of appeal against the decision. It works out in practice that a prisoner serving twelve years is considered for parole after serving four. If he hasn't been a good boy he gets knocked back. His case then comes up again after a period of time during which he is kept in promise land. What can happen, and often does, is that a con serves his full time but during eight years of it he is kept in a state of nail-biting uncertainty. Beat that for refined torture.

Of course there is every reason to say that the con has committed a crime, he has been given twelve years and he should serve it. Fine and dandy, then abolish the parole system and don't burden a man who has enough on his mind with vague promises of release. The Parole Board, whose activities are shrouded in secrecy and who are not accountable for often inexplicable decisions, are above common justice and humanitarian considerations. Like cunning old Fury in 'Alice in Wonderland' they are judge and jury, they try the whole case and condemn you to death. In Joey's case he served six years of an eight year sentence but then he wasn't a good boy so he couldn't expect much by way of time off.

When Joey had the dust-up with the screws at Wandsworth he had been granted permission, for what it was worth, to consult a solicitor about taking civil action for assault against the two screws who'd given him a kicking. This business had been going on for the best part of five years. The Home Office put every obstacle in the way, holding up letters, making it difficult for the solicitor to see Joey on various pretexts and in fact doing everything possible to prevent the case coming to court. For example, one letter to the Home Office requesting certain details was not answered for twenty-two months.

At the same time as this palaver was going on Joey had a claim for some clothing which had gone missing from his property, again at Wandsworth. Admittedly the place was full of thieves but that was hardly Joey's look-out. He hadn't put them there. The Home Office started off by denying all responsibility but finally paid £80 into court, a cunning dodge well known in legal circles which meant that, if he continued with the action with the hope of getting a more substantial sum, all costs would be down to him. He cut his losses and took the cash. The affair had its humorous side because Joey had bought the Crombie overcoat and the other gear out of the proceeds of crime. It was also a giggle that an expensive battery of lawyers had been hired by the Home Office to administer a legal licking to a lowly con.

When the case against the screws finally got to court it was the 3rd November 1977. Joey was sent up from Parkhurst for the hearing and given temporary accommodation in that 'penal dustbin' Wormwood Scrubs. The comic opera opened when Joey appeared before the court to conduct his own case clad in prison clothes and carrying a bulging briefcase. The two screws were represented by solicitors provided by the Prison Officers' Association and Lord Harris of the Home Office had Treasury counsel. Ranged against this small army of legal talent Joey prepared to do battle. In the event it was a nonsense.

The judge listened for a while to the legal prattle then put a stop to the proceedings by declaring the action out of time. The delaying tactics of the Home Office had arbitrarily decided the outcome before Joey had a chance to present his evidence. The judge gave the legal eagles a mild ticking-off, recorded his disapproval of the way the Home Office had behaved and then, because it was legal procedure, awarded costs against Joey! It is a sad reflection on the law that, had Joey been a free man, the matter would have been disposed of in three months at the outside. So much for going through the proper channels. Joey swore there and then that the next time a screw laid a hand on him he'd punch his fucking head in. Arseholes to a system that denies common justice to a man because he's a con.

As Joey was led away under escort the two screws were outside the courtroom. They stuck out their tongues at him and laughingly gave the two-fingered salute. It was fortunate for them that Joey was cuffed up because, if he'd had his hands free, he would have taught both of them a right lesson.

During the few days he was in the London area Joey was shuffled about between the Scrubs and Pentonville. This business of being kept on the move was intended to make it difficult for any of his mates to visit him and thus save the long trip to the Isle of Wight. He heard later that quite a few of them had been turned away, being told by the screws that his whereabouts were not known. A queer bloody prison system, thought Joey, that doesn't know where its prisoners are. Another thing that got up his nose was that, as he went from one nick to another, all the papers in connection with his case were read over and over again by screws who were animated by curiosity and not security. By the time he got back to Parkhurst his documents were in rags and tatters.

At the Scrubs and the Ville Joey met up with old

acquaintances and learned of the reception accorded to ex-Commander Virgo and his confederates who had been sent down for corruptly accepting bribes in the notorious pornography trials. These former pillars of the police force, who were quickly transferred to the open prison at Ford, refused to leave their cells, shit-scared that some of the cons would take it into their heads to even up a few old scores.

Joey's attitude to these men was uncompromising. A villain is a villain and makes no secret of the fact, but he had no time for men who masquerade as enforcers of the law and use their privileged positions to break the law they are pledged to uphold. Later when, as a free man, he assisted in the Countryman enquiry, he made his feelings quite plain.

Having been away from the Scrubs for some years Joey was quite interested to note the changes that had taken place since he was last in residence. When he came up from Parkhurst he landed in a cell with a couple of kids and was surprised to say the least that he, a hardened villain, should be brought into close association with juveniles. One of the kids, a twenty-year-old, was serving a first sentence of four years. He cried himself to sleep every night. The other kid was a harder case but then he'd had a spell in Borstal and was only serving twelve months, a cake-walk as he proudly said. Joey could see that he had the makings of a right villain, accepting bird as one of the natural hazards of his chosen profession.

Joey was not the only hard case mixed in with the kids. There was a bloke called Cheeseman who had done a long stretch in Broadmoor where he murdered another inmate, a fellow by the name of Reed who had robbed and killed a taxi driver and a chap called Powell, a very hard man indeed who had done eight months in chokey on the Moor and was now in the Scrubs awaiting re-allocation. To house such men as these under the same roof as a bunch of impressionable kids was asking for trouble and, as Joey heard later, it wasn't long in coming. It culminated in the resignation of the Governor who sent a letter to *The Times* stating why he had decided to get out of the prison service. He is a lone voice crying in the wilderness but then so was Winston Churchill once upon a time.

After the heady excitements of the Metropolis and the delights of the Scrubs and the Ville, Joey returned to Parkhurst just before Christmas. His parole application was due to come up early in the New Year and the way he saw it the authorities would be happy to be rid of troublesome Bello. Still there was some way to go and who knows what was waiting round the corner.

Joey went back to his old job as a cleaner. One day a call went out for volunteers to clean out the empty cells which were splattered liberally with pigeon shit, dead mice and the odd deposit of human excrement left by a con who had been caught short. Joey was approached but turned the job down, but a couple of blokes did take up the offer. They were budgerigar fanciers so they probably felt at home among the heaps of birdshit.

There were quite a number of budgie fanciers in Parkhurst. They kept the birds for company and many a cell door bore a notice 'Do not enter. Budgie loose.' The little things were well-trained and very tame and flew about the wing without any attempt to have it away which they could have done very easily without being brought before the Governor for trying to break out. There was one bloke who acquired a young bird from a breeder with the intention of making it the tamest, sleekest, fattest, most beautiful and well-spoken bird in the nick. He lashed out on an exotic cage, birdseed, millet, cuttlefish and all the paraphernalia available to the besotted owner of a pampered bird. It died that very night. The following morning the bereaved owner picked up the stiff little body and, holding it in front of his face, gave forth. 'You fucking ungrateful bastard,' he yelled. 'I spent a fortune on you and all you can do is fucking snuff it.'

Apart from keeping budgies there were many ways in which the cons passed their time. Model making, using matchsticks as material, was one of them. One bloke made a church about four feet high with pews and altar and all the interior fittings. It was beautiful. There were any number of boats of all shapes and sizes from ancient Spanish galleons to cabin cruisers, all made from odd bits of wood and correct down to the last rope. There were also a few budding Picassos who spent their money, such as it was, on oil paints. Some of their work was good enough for exhibition in any art gallery.

One of the lifers was an opera singer who often felt the urge to let himself go. He would choose a time when the table tennis room wasn't being used and would walk about, hands behind his back and filling the air with extracts from various operas in a glorious tenor voice. Even the roughnecks stopped watching tele to listen to the performance. Music hath charms to soothe the savage breast.

Joey never ceased to be surprised by some of the unusual and remarkable happenings inside the grim walls. There were some four hundred inmates living in conditions of almost indescribable squalor, denied sexual relationships and working out their frustrations by slaughtering each other or having a go at the screws. Yet when Ron Strutton suddenly collapsed and died one morning while drinking a mug of tea the whole prison rallied round. His daughter was due on a visit that day. She was met at the gate and told that her father was ill and could not be visited, and so was saved the misery of a journey home knowing that she would never see him alive again. The Governor gave permission and a collection was taken up for Ron's widow which raised the considerable sum of three hundred pounds, most of it coming from the meagre wages of the cons. It tended to restore one's faith in humanity.

Prison life was not without its humorous incidents though they were few and far between. On the 18th September 1987 a football match took place featuring a Parkhurst side and a Sport and Showbiz eleven. It was reported in the local paper. In all seriousness the sides appeared as follows:

SPORT AND SHOWBIZ XI	PARKHURST PRISON XI
Tosh Chamberlain	No. 224057
Johnny Evans	265876
Dennis Puttock	756452
Joe Wallis	245098
Barry Francis	768743
George Francis	675698
Roy Francis	875321
Dennis Pinching	987874
Tony Sutton	843125
Joey Singleton	245376
Jimmy Langley	256879

No kidding! The writer lost a chance of an extra bit of comedy. He could have referred to Dennis Pinching's opposite number as Charlie Thieving.

One day a bunch of cons were watching television when a programme came on called 'Day by Day'. It wasn't Sir Robin talking about himself but a news and comment affair. An item was shown about an aircraft race from Southsea to Lydd and, as the competitors were being introduced, the picture switched to an aerial view of Parkhurst. 'Parkhurst prison,' said the commentator, 'home of England's blackest villains where tonight the men have bet their last ounce of tobacco on their Deputy

Governor winning the race'. The 'blackest villains' didn't even know he was competing. Then came a picture of the aforementioned prune in a Micky Mouse plane with a Volkswagen engine. The television room echoed to derisive roars and jeers, Next morning, pinned to the notice board and read by everybody before it was taken down, was the following epic poem:

On Day by Day the other night
The viewers all were told
That we, the blackest villains,
All had hearts of gold.
We loved our dear old deputy
And would all scream and shout
To hear that he had won the race,
We'd backed him with our snout.
But they had got it slightly wrong,
The snout we'd pay with glee
To someone who could fix his plane
To come down in the sea.
Happy? We would raise the roof
And cheer quite fit to burst
To hear the lifeboat got there late
And the sharks had reached him first.

Just the sort of comment that could be expected from England's blackest villains.

On 8th May 1978 Jacques Mesrines, the most notorious criminal in France, made a spectacular escape from La Santé prison in Paris. A few hours before he went over the wall another less well-known malefactor was let out through the gates of HM Prison, Parkhurst, Isle of Wight.

Joey was out but not really free. As a convict on licence he was under the control of the Home Office probation service and for the next eight months his movements would be closely supervised. He would have to lead an industrious life, keep away from bad company and generally behave himself. If he stepped out of line he stood a good chance of being back in the boob in double-quick time. He had a few drinks on the ferry and took a long, luxurious piss in a clean, sweet-smelling lavatory for the first time in years. At Portsmouth he boarded a train and, in a little over an hour, was at Victoria Station.

15. Big Business

It wasn't a bundle of laughs being on parole as Joey soon found out. Although the probation officer was no trouble Joey had to steer clear of his old mates, who came under the heading of 'bad company'. The usual coming-out party did not come off. It would be organised by villains, attended by villains and would be bound to attract the attention of the Old Bill. Also Joey had to get something that looked like a job of work in order to comply with the 'honest and industrious life' bit which was one of the conditions of his licence.

Within a couple of days of coming out he had a meet with Billy who, with his brother Eddie, was in a big way of business over Ilford way. They had come a long way since Joey had first met them when they were up at the Old Bailey on various charges in connection with a gun battle outside their mini-cab outfit in Ilford in '71. Eddie was shot in the leg and Billy was severely cut about the face, but they were both nicked and charged with causing an affray.

Eddie had it away but the Old Bill caught up with him in Leicester, and in the end both sides in the battle came up for trial in March of '73. Joey made a statement for the defence, which was not used, but in the result both Eddie and Billy got chucked. Joey was up at the Bailey about the same time and later on the brothers paid him a visit at Chelmsford. They also came to see him at Parkhurst.

Over the years the brothers had no further trouble with the law. Joey had postcards from them from all over the place, Tenerife and Torremolinos when they were on holiday, Austria, France, Sweden and Denmark when they toured with the pop group 'Status Quo' and one letter in which they let him know that he would be looked after when he came out. One postcard Joey remembers particularly for Billy had understamped it and Joey had to pay 22p from his wages before he was allowed to read it.

'Hi, Joey, having a great time,' it read. 'I'm still working with the Quo, went to a party with the group, plenty of hansom(?) birds. We're in Austria at the moment, might be going to the States. Friend for life, Bill.'

Joey went out on the town with Billy and, when they parted company in the early hours of the morning he pressed a wad of notes into Joey's hand and told him to come over to Ilford as soon as possible and Eddie would fix him up. Two days later Joey turned up at the office in Seventh Avenue, Manor Park, and got quite a surprise. The brothers had organised themselves into a very profitable business selling ice-cream and hot dogs to the tourists from vans and trolleys at some of the best pitches in the West End.

Eddie explained to Joey how the system worked. The blokes on the vans and trolleys bought their ice-cream cones from him at 70p each and were given the ice-cream free. The workers paid their own expenses, maintained the vans and it was then up to them how much they earned. From some of the stories Joey had heard about what was known as the 'ice chop', foreign tourists being charged a couple of quid for a cornet and up to any price for a hot dog, Joey reckoned that the brothers must be on at least thirty grand a week in readies during the season, and that was money.

The brothers were a striking pair. Eddie himself was just over six feet tall, powerfully built and very fit. He didn't smoke and drank very little. At the time he was around thirty-eight but there was nothing middle-aged about his habits. He was up early every morning, went for a swim in the pool at his luxurious house in Mill Road in Aveley, Essex, and was always at the yard by eight-thirty to get the vans and trolleys on the road. What struck Joey most about him was his determination. If he wanted something he went all out to get it and didn't allow anybody or anything to get in his way.

Billy was a different proposition to his brother, being shorter and lighter with a tendency to put on weight, but he was a hell of a battler. He had more bottle than any man Joey had ever met and certainly didn't know the meaning of the word 'fear'. Joey got on very well with him for he was much more approachable than Eddie, who had a way of keeping people at a distance.

After putting Joey wise to the 'ice chop' side of the operation, Eddie gave him an outline of the rest of the business empire. He owned a lot of property in the Ilford and Manor Park areas and was into the pop scene in a big way, selling souvenirs and T-shirts at all the big festivals not only in Britain but on the Continent as well.

'We need good men, Joey,' he said. 'If you want to come in there's a place for you.'

Joey pointed out that he was on licence and had to be a bit careful about getting into trouble, but Eddie laughed that one off.

'We're respectable businessmen,' he said, with a wink at Billy. 'You might have to give somebody a slap now and then, but that can happen anywhere. We handle a lot of cash. You would be a sort of security man. It's all the fashion these days.'

Joey had to laugh at that one. Even Eddie had a smile behind his beard. He changed frequently from being bearded to a close-shaven appearance, a dodge to make positive identification more difficult.

'What about my probation officer?' Joey said. 'I'll have to give her some sort of story.'

'No sweat. I've got a legit property company. You'll come in as a manager.'

That was how Joey came to work for the brothers. There were a lot of doors closed to an ex-con fresh from Parkhurst and the bullshit about a man having paid his debt to society didn't cut much ice with prospective employers. Joey wasn't forced to take on this job, in fact he rather looked forward to doing it because it was right up his street and the money was good. In any case he wasn't mixed up in any criminal business. Eddie and Billy had to protect their interests and they adopted their own measures to do so. When it came to looking after cash in transit or indeed anywhere, there was no difference between Bello and Securicor except that Joey wouldn't wear a crash helmet, swing a baton or travel in an armoured van.

Joey fitted into the organisation quite well. One of the first things he noticed was the loyalty the brothers were able to command among their workers. The only time he had witnessed that kind of loyalty being shown was when Ronnie and Reggie Kray were at the top of the tree in the sixties. Not that there was any real comparison between the twins and the brothers. Eddie and Billy were dead clever and, apart from the mini-cab trouble in '71, they had kept well clear of the law. Joey guessed that the local Old Bill was well straightened because Eddie got away with some diabolical liberties on his own manor.

The brothers had come up the hard way. They came from the Paddington manor in the first place. Joey remembered their old man who worked at the same dairy in St John's Wood that Joey had blagged all those years ago. Their mother was Spanish and one of the most trusted men on the firm was a relative called Jose Larios known to everybody as 'Pepe'. He wasn't all that to much look at, a thin wiry geezer with a Zapata moustache who spent a lot of time pulling the birds, but he was a wily sort and up to all the strokes. Joey heard that what was called the mini-cab war was down to Pepe because he had stepped out of line with a bird from the other mob and started off the chain of events that led to the Old Bailey.

Joey was impressed by Eddie's colourful life-style. He was big in every sense of the word. In the restaurants he frequented he would march in, sit down and expect the staff to give him their complete attention. His car was equipped with a police-type siren which he would switch on whenever he encountered a traffic jam. Then he would tear along on the wrong side of the road, ignoring traffic signals and scattering pedestrians. One time he was going from Manor Park to the West End and a copper on duty at a crossroad waved him on against the red light. One morning Joey arrived at the yard to find everything in a turmoil. Some thieving sod had knocked off the siren and Eddie was doing his nut.

There was one incident that almost led to a nicking. Eddie had his own personal van which he took out occasionally to do the rounds and he was in the vicinity of Madame Tussaud's when there was a stabbing involving an ice cream seller. The first Joey knew about it was when he and Eddie were sitting down to lunch in one of Eddie's favourite restaurants, an Italian joint in a side street near Marble Arch. The van was parked up on the pavement outside and they were just taking their first forkfuls of spaghetti when the Old Bill turned up in force. They copped for a right going-over and the van was searched thoroughly but nothing was found to tie them in with the stabbing. Joey was lucky because, if he'd been nicked, he would have been back inside double-quick. Actually the stabbing wasn't down to them but was the result of a personal grudge between a couple of merchants who had no connection with the brothers.

Joey was in the office one morning having a chat with

Eddie when a call came through from one of the workers who operated from a stall outside Tower Hill station. This was one of the most profitable sites in the set-up. From what Joey could gather as he listened to the conversation, some comedian had fly-pitched his ice-cream van next to the stall and started selling.

'Tell him I said to fuck off,' said Eddie.

'I've told him but he won't go,' said the plaintive voice at the other end of the phone. 'He says he's got as much right here as what I have.'

Eddie slammed the phone down.

'Come on, Joey,' he said. 'We'll sort this little lot out.'

They shot off in the car and were at Tower Hill within minutes. As they walked towards the station entrance Joey saw no sign of the comedian, who had got the message and made himself scarce, but some other merchant had nipped in with a load of rubbishy souvenirs. Joey recognised him as a member of a little firm from North London.

Eddie walked up to this geezer. He didn't waste any words.

'You,' he said. 'Fuck off.'

The idiot started to argue.

'I've got as much right here as anybody,' he said.

'No you haven't,' said Eddie.

'Who says so,' said the idiot.

'I say so,' said Eddie. 'Now pack up and fuck off.'

The idiot must have fancied himself as Jack the Lad. He had certainly recognised Eddie so he should have known better than to turn his back on him which was a very silly thing to do. Joey grabbed his shoulder, whirled him round and hit him on the chin. He went down like a sack of potatoes and stayed on the deck.

Joey said, 'Do you want some more?'

The idiot shook his head. Joey took a couple of steps

forward and kicked the stall up in the air, and then walked back with Eddie to the car.

These minor incidents of violence were infrequent. Generally the mention of Eddie's name was enough to scare off anybody who fancied their chances of setting up in competition. There were the odd cases who were silly enough to argue, and then Pepe was ordered to discourage them. A stink-bomb thrown into the van, a dollop of engine oil in the ice-cream or a knife-thrust in the tyres was usually sufficient. There were no persistent offenders.

Joey saw the logic of the brothers' actions. They had a very large stake at risk and elimination of the competition couldn't be achieved by price-cutting owing to the nature of the business. It was the man on the spot in the fly-pitching game who did the trade and made the money. Since fly-pitching was against the law it was a matter of dog eat dog, and the dog with the loudest bark, and of course teeth to match, got the bone.

When Joey joined them the brothers were already into the pop scene in a sizeable way. The venues at Wembley, Earl's Court and the Hammersmith Odeon and the open air festivals at Reading, Knebworth and Blackbushe attracted tens of thousands of fans. Inside the halls, or the enclosures in the case of outdoor events, the sale of souvenirs, refreshments and so on were in the hands of concessionaires who paid the promoter a fee, but outside it was a free-for-all. Eddie and Billy, who saw no reason to pay for something when they could get it for nothing, were on the outside. Conditions here were different to those in the ice-cream and hot dog trade because there were some right villains attracted by the quick and easy money to be made and that's where the trouble began. The brothers were no pushover and in the struggle for the best pitches somebody had to get hurt. Eddie and Billy made sure that it wasn't them or their workers who suffered.

When the workers set off for a concert they carried the usual gear for sale, pirated programmes, T-shirts, badges and souvenirs. They also carried Irish Tony, Kevin and Martin whose job was to protect them and keep the opposition in its place. When the firm moved on to a pitch Irish Tony and his mates made sure that nobody tried to hustle them off. If the pitch they wanted was occupied the trio would get rid of the occupant by standing around, hustling him and doing all they could to hinder him from trading. It didn't take much of this treatment to discourage the geezer.

Sometimes more drastic measures would be necessary. If the opposition was really heavy there was a trio of blacks on hand led by a vicious character known as Cowboy. They wore denims and the kind of stripey woollen hats worn by many black pop fans. They would press their way through the crowd, out would come the knives and the victim would be left bleeding on the ground while his attackers melted into the hordes around them. It would all be over in seconds and eye witnesses could only describe the assailants as 'three black fellows in stripey hats', which gave the Old Bill the choice of a thousand suspects.

Sometimes there was trouble with mobs from out of town. At a concert at the Hammersmith Odeon a firm came down from the North headed by a villain known as Manchester Freddie. The firm didn't have much of an organisation and even less gear but they began to pitch in spite of being warned off and were in a fair way of ruining Joey's evening. They were dissuaded from further trading and Joey took care of Manchester Freddie personally. He went back North via the casualty ward of a near-by hospital a sadder and a wiser man.

From time to time there were disagreements with

concessionaires who had paid for their pitches inside the building or enclosure and didn't like the way pirated programmes were being sold to the fans. When the Electric Light Orchestra gave a concert at Wembley the chap in charge of concessions, a geezer by the name of Paul Pike, thought he would have a go at gobbling Joey up. He came out of the main entrance of the stadium waving six sets of arms and began to harangue the workers. Apart from being a nuisance he was wasting valuable time, since concerts do not last for ever and lost business cannot be recouped. Billy, Irish Tony and Joey decided to take a hand in the game.

It turned out that Pike was not happy about the quality of the programmes which, according to him were pirated and in breach of copyright, which they definitely were. Still, as both Billy and Joey pointed out, this was hardly the time and place to discuss the laws of copyright. Irish Tony didn't say a word. He merely stood there. In the end, although the workers had been grafting all the time the altercation was taking place, it was agreed that no more progammes would be sold but Billy and Joey stood fast on their right to sell the other gear. By this time all the fans were inside the stadium so there wasn't much point in further argument.

Having been made aware of the facts of life, friend Pike was as good as gold and they had no further aggro with him at Wembley or anywhere else for that matter.

Joey had a rather amusing experience on the Continent. One of the groups was appearing in Rotterdam so a party of workers was sent over with the usual merchandise. At the time Eddie and Pepe were busy and Billy and Joey were setting up for the David Bowie concert at Earl's Court so Billy's son, young Billy, was put in charge of the operation. On the morning before the show young Billy came on the phone. He was having trouble with a local firm who had put the block on.

It was typical of Billy that, instead of telling the boy to pull out, he got on the boat with Joey and Kevin and they arrived at the venue just before the concert was due to start. The Dutch firm was operating while young Billy and his team stood watching. Billy, closely followed by Joey and Kevin, walked over to the geezer who seemed to be in charge and, without beating about the bush, let him know that he was putting his workers in. The fellow understood enough English to realise what Billy was saying. He also knew enough English to tell Billy to fuck off back to England. Billy hooked him one and the fight was on. Joey put a couple on the deck, Billy accounted for two more and Kevin took the tally up to six. After that the Dutch mob gave it up and young Billy and his team moved in.

The funny part was, when the guv'nor of the Dutch mob came to Billy, on his own, to work out some sort of arrangement to get rid of his gear so that the evening wouldn't be a dead loss for him, Billy took the Dutch equivalent of four hundred quid from the fellow. In return for that he was allowed to go to work, but at quite a distance from the busy main entrance. Billy's team did a bomb and the natives didn't do too badly as far as Joey could see.

They stayed overnight in Rotterdam and did a bit of shopping and sightseeing the following morning. Billy's eye was caught by a beautiful pair of flick knives in one of the shops and he promptly bought them, presenting one to Joey, who stowed it away with the mental reservation that it would only be used for cutting bread.

They got back to London in good time to set up for the David Bowie concert. There was no trouble and everything was ticking over like a brand-new Roller as Joey stood with Billy at the entrance to the Underground station where they could keep an eye on what was going on. Suddenly Joey spotted the Dutch firm, mob handed, coming towards them.

'Heads up, Billy,' he said. 'Here comes trouble.'

The guv'nor of the team came up to them, grinning all over his boat-race and sticking out his hand.

'You give us four hundred pound, we let you work here,' he said.

He was laughing fit to bust at what he thought was a great joke. Billy and Joey laughed too, because they were out-numbered four to one and the situation could have been dodgy. They all went in to see the show and had a good drink together afterwards, a sort of Common Market celebration.

By the time Joey had been with the brothers for several months he had sussed out the arithmetic of merchandising at the pop concerts. It was better than a double your money proposition. Laying out ten grand brought back anything between twenty-two and twenty-four, all expenses paid. Joey decided to have some of that, so he counted his pennies, found a backer for the rest and then went to see Eddie and Billy to tell them what he had in mind. They were very good about it and Eddie even offered a loan of a few grand to get started, an offer which was refused with thanks.

Joey went in big at the three-day festival at Reading with a good team of workers and minders. He had bought a coach to transport them and the gear. As they were setting up Joey saw Billy giving them the once-over. His eyes nearly popped out of his head when he saw the size of Joey's operation. Obviously the brothers thought that Joey was going into business with a manky little stall in some out-of-the-way corner, which wasn't the idea at all. To cut a long story short Joey made a killing and finished up with a good few grand.

He did even better at Blackbushe. He acquired a snide pass with which he got his coach and workers into the enclosure reserved for concession holders. When the balloon went up, which it did very quickly, the security sorted Joey out and told him in no uncertain terms to pack up and fuck off. Joey asked them one simple question.

'Who's going to put me out?' he said.

The security took a look at the minders who were standing about with big grins on their faces and had a change of heart or, to put it another way, a sudden loss of bottle. To start off the concert with a fight would have done them no good at all, as they well knew, so Joey stayed. He managed to wangle Pepe and his ice-cream van into the enclosure which was one on the credit side. He came out of that lot well in front.

He did a few more concerts but it wasn't all jam and he had plenty of headaches one way and another. It was a strain on the nerves, dashing about the country, dealing with suppliers of merchandise, keeping his team together and all that. True, the rewards were fine and more than made up for the inconveniences, but the day came when he decided that he had had enough. He disbanded the team, sold off the coach and the stock, paid his debts and called it a day.

As for Billy and Eddie, they ran into a lot of trouble. It started, as so many of these things do, with publicity in the popular press. In May of '78 the *Sun* newspaper had a go at Eddie after one of its reporters had got a job on the team and sussed out the operation. Eddie was referred to as the 'Cornet King' and the article contained some very sensational stuff about the tactics used to scare off the opposition. Then, in July of the following year, the *Daily Mirror* had its turn. 'THE CORNETTO MOB GO TO WAR' was the headline, and there were lurid tales of heavies knocking hell out of the competition as they captured the cream of the tourist trade, pitches outside Harrods, Madame Tussauds, the Victoria and Albert and other museums, the Tower of London, Westminster Abbey and various sites in and around Hyde Park.

Curiously enough there wasn't much mention of the brothers' activities in other directions, such as the pop concert scene, but that came later after the Old Bill had taken a hand in the game. According to reports a number of traders got together and complained to the law that they were being intimidated by the brothers. Now these traders were themselves law-breakers, flaunting traffic regulations when they fly-pitched their vans and often causing considerable obstruction. The Old Bill didn't tell them to piss off. Instead, a special squad of thirty detectives led by two DI's by the names of Lewis and Tucker, set out from Paddington nick on the 29th of October 1980 and rounded up Eddie, Billy, Pepe and a half-dozen others.

The whole story came out when the men appeared at the Old Bailey twelve months later on various charges of conspiracy involving blackmail, criminal damage and assault. The prosecution had built up a perfect case, which wasn't surprising considering that they had had more than a year to do it in, and a troop of witnesses filed in and out of the box to tell the jury how they had been variously assaulted, had stink-bombs thrown into their vans, their tyres slashed, engine oil slipped into their ice-cream containers and so on. The trial started on Tuesday the 10th November 1981 and ended on Wednesday the 23rd December. Eddie, Pepe and Roy Chandler were all found guilty and, by way of wishing them a Merry Christmas, the judge dished out the porridge in what he considered the correct proportions. Eddie got four years and a fine of £2,000, Pepe four years and a fine of £1,000 and Ray Chandler copped for three years. Justice was done, bit was it seen to be done.

The Old Bill's point of view was definite. Said one senior detective, speaking of Eddie, 'he is the nastiest piece of work to hit London since the Kray brothers'. Said another pillar of the law 'It was a classic example of how a ruthless professional criminal could, by persistent extortion and the use of relatively minor overt acts of violence, gain substantial profit by placing people in fear.'

During the six-week trial all sorts of evidence was produced which seemed to Joey to have nothing to do with the charge. For example Eddie was said to have a claim against him by the Inland Revenue for nearly two million quid. Everybody knows that an Inland Revenue assessment bears no relation to the amount actually owing. Also it was said that Eddie was negotiating to buy a house in Cranbourne for a quarter of a million. What these facts had to do with bopping some Italian ice-cream vendor wasn't made clear, but from the prosecution's point of view it was lovely stuff for arousing prejudice among the members of the jury. Joey was aware of that. He'd had some of it.

Listening to the proceedings at the trial, Joey was disturbed by one aspect. The senior detective referred to 'minor overt acts of violence'. This was quite true, but sentences for these offences are normally very light. When conspiracy is added to the charge the situation is changed. Put it this way. If Joey hit somebody on the chin, a minor act of violence, he would be charged with assault, dealt with in a lower court and probably be fined or, at the worst, get three months. If however it can be alleged that he committed the offence in company with another person then up comes a charge of conspiracy, it's a job for the Sessions or the Central Criminal Court and the sentence can be very heavy indeed. This was the flanker that was worked on Eddie and the others.

Another shady aspect of the trial was the spectacle of the law taking sides in a disagreement between two gangs of lawbreakers. This sort of action has been the subject of criticism by many eminent jurists. What it boiled down to was this, that the Old Bill guaranteed immunity to one lot if they gave evidence against the other lot, so there was a very expensive trial, the lawyers paid their fat fees into the bank and Eddie, Pepe and Roy Chandler were removed from circulation for some time.

So the tourists were protected – or were they. Outside a museum in Exhibition Road Joey watched one of the Eyeties grafting. He was ripping off the customers to the tune of a couple of quid per ice-cream cornet. Joey took his place in the queue and came to the counter.

'Cornet, pleace,' said Joey. He tendered a fiver. He was handed the cornet and three pounds in change.

'Bit heavy isn't it, mate,' Joey said. 'Where's your price list?'

The vendor gave Joey a big smile and another pound.

'Sorry, a little mistake,' he said. 'Next please.'

16. Mercenaries

Come the summer of 1980 Joey had retired to his country seat. It wasn't a Georgian mansion set in rolling pastures, merely a flat on a council estate in Northolt, but it was a welcome change from Notting Dale where, as a known face, he was always under the threat of getting his collar felt for something he hadn't done. He had a good few quid tucked away so they didn't go short but he wasn't content to sit around and let his reserves dribble away so he looked about for some sort of straight job which would at least pay the rent and groceries.

He heard a whisper that there were jobs going at Heathrow with one of the maintenance sub-contractors so he went along and applied. He was asked a few questions and, when it came to the criminal record bit, he didn't actually say no but shook his head, which was good enough for them and satisfied Joey's conscience. Anyway he got the job, which was shift work in the cargo terminal, and started the following day.

The cargo terminal was a fascinating place, a massive complex handling thousands of millions in goods a year, a big money box which had been cracked a few times and no wonder for, as far as he could see, security was a joke. He was issued with a pass with photograph which had to be worn on the left breast of his overalls at all times. Armed with this, he had the run of the whole area. One of the places to which he had access was the gold bullion vault section, though he could not enter the vaults themselves.

Joey realised that he was on borrowed time, that sooner

or later someone would put the finger on him, for the Old Bill was forever dodging about. It was a mixture of curiosity and a sense of mischief that led him to conduct the Bello test of security. He got hold of the key to the traffic manager's office and had a duplicate made. Then, at his leisure and over a period of several days, he took copies of documentation relating to consignments of goods, made a detailed plan of the layout of the cargo centre and rounded off the job by taking photographs of the interiors of all the administrative offices.

Joey had been working at the airport for about three weeks when the chopper fell. Curiously enough it was not wielded by the Old Bill but by a reporter on one of the Sundays who had been tipped off that there was an identifiable villain employed in a vulnerable area at Heathrow. When the reporter confronted Joey he was able to tell him as much about his past as Joey knew himself. He had done his homework, and was quite a decent sort of fellow doing his job as well as he could. Naturally, as a result of the exposure Joey was fired on the spot, which didn't particularly worry him because he knew it had to happen.

Joey thought the story would rate a few paragraphs in an obscure part of this Sunday paper. To his surprise it was spread all over the front page. This was not because of Joey's pretty face but by reason of the enormous gaps in security which the reporter discovered when he followed up his original enquiries. One of the blokes he interviewed was quoted as saying 'you could drive a tank in here and no-one would stop you'. This was strong stuff but rather far-fetched. A tank would be an expensive tool to use on a break-in but who knows? One day an enterprising bunch of villains might use one to capture the reward in the bullion vaults.

Joey learned two valuable lessons from this experience.

One was that it was pretty hopeless trying to lie himself into a job since his past was bound to catch up with him. The other was that he learned about the workings of security, which was to come in useful later on when he became involved with the Crime Syndicate.

One conclusion Joey came to as he read the newspaper article was that the whole business of reporting crime is a bundle of contradictions. On the one hand the public is quite rightly concerned to want information about cops and robbers and the tricks they get up to and there is no doubt that this sort of material sells papers and comes in for high ratings on TV programmes.

On the other hand the Old Bill and the Home Office have a vested interest in concealing the truth about levels of crime and prison conditions from the public. The only real information comes from the villains themselves, men who really know the inside stories, and the authorities do everything possible to discredit what they have to say. The latest statistics tell of 45,000 prisoners in jails built for a maximum of 32,000, of men being locked up 23 hours a day, of a huge rise in offences against prison discipline (62,800 in 1981) and of one prison, Brixton, where 320 men share four lavatories.

The same statistics also record that prison staffs number 23,000, roughly a ratio of one staff to two prisoners and that it costs almost £500 million a year to keep miscreants locked away from contact with 'decent' society. If it wasn't so tragic it would be a bloody joke.

Talking about jokes, Joey was watching tele in Parkhurst when the Home Secretary in office at the time appeared on the screen. Waffling Willie was answering questions put to him by a trio of very on-the-ball journalists and it was pitiable to see this unfortunate-looking character ducking and diving and dodging the issues. The usual chorus of boos went up, one wit remarking that Willie had a face like a worn-out dishrag. Somebody replied that the poor fellow couldn't help his looks.

'That's true,' replied the wit, 'but at least he could stay off tele.'

Joey had his own reservations about politicians. So far as he was concerned they were a collection of self-seeking egomaniacs who surfaced at elections, made a lot of promises they had no intention of keeping then disappeared into that exclusive club known as the House of Commons where, according to widespread reports, they spent most of their time pissing it up and using their privileged positions to promote their private interests.

In a way Joey, an honest villain, was sickened by their antics. The party in power had buggered up the economy, created a huge army of unemployed, remained unmoved as riots broke out in the streets and made no secret of their intention to make the rich richer and the poor poorer. It didn't make all that difference to him. He would survive, but he couldn't understand the mentality of an electorate who continued to support the Thatcher regime. Not that he believed another lot could do better, but they would have to try bloody hard to do worse.

Joey was all for male chauvinism. Women had a place in society but it didn't extend to running the country like a grocer's shop in a Grantham back street. The intellectual bankrupts who supported the so-called Iron Lady he regarded as a bunch of wankers. He knew that one day the forty-five thousand inmates in British prisons would break out in open revolt against their appalling conditions. The big stick she used in the Falklands wouldn't be of much use to the Iron Lady in that event.

Joey had come to the conclusion that hunting for a job was a negative occupation, so he put a bit of capital into a little business where he was answerable to nobody but himself and if he got the sack it was down to him. However the past has a habit of bobbing up at the most unexpected times and that was what happened on the 26th February 1982. A note through the letter box was from a Detective Chief Inspector Rattray and it said tersely that the DCI would like to see Joey, gave a phone number where he could be reached and asked that an appointment should be made. By three o'clock that afternoon Joey had spoken to Rattray and it was arranged that the DCI would call on Joey on the Monday, which was the first of March.

It looked very much as though Joey was in danger of being fitted up for something, but the Old Bill wouldn't have it all their own way if Joey could do anything about it. He set up a tape recorder with a hidden microphone and, when the knock came on the door, he switched it on.

The DCI was accompanied by a Detective Sergeant Matteson, and both men were very friendly. The first thing Rattray said was that there was nothing to worry about, so Joey began to worry. It wasn't the first time he had seen the smile on the face of the tiger and this particular tiger was a very big one. Any man who makes DCI in the Met has all his chairs at home, but Joey was reassured by the knowledge that the tape recorder was doing its stuff. If they were going to fit him up he had no intention of going down without a fight.

It transpired that Rattray was from CIB 2, the internal investigation department of the Met, what the Old Bill in conversation among themselves called the 'Rubber Heels', and what he was on about was the three grand that went missing from Val's flat when Chris, Joey and Honeypuff were nicked for the Ilford bank job. Somebody must have had a long memory because that was ten years back. Joey put on a 'don't remember' act which seemed to please Rattray, who went on to say that he had interviewed Chris,

Payne and Ray who had told him that the allegations were a load of old rubbish.

There was a lot more of the question and answer, but it stood out a mile that the DCI didn't really want any information, all he wanted to do was to lose it. He knew that the three grand had been nicked, he knew that Joey knew it but the object of the exercise was very clear. Wherever the money had gone it was down to Mr Nobody. When Rattray saw that Joey was in two minds about making direct accusations he came in with the heavy stuff, like Joey would have to make a statement, be cautioned and give evidence at a resulting enquiry. The last thing Joey wanted was to be mixed up in an investigation of that kind so he took the easy way out and signed a short statement to the effect that he had no knowledge of any money having been kept by the police.

Rattray seemed quite happy with the outcome and, having thanked Joey he took himself off, saying that he wouldn't need to see him again. They both knew that Joey's statement was pure bullshit but, so far as Rattray was concerned it tidied everything up and put a stop to any further investigation. The dossier would be marked 'Case Closed' and disappear into the archives at Scotland Yard along with many others.

Joey had a transcript made of the tape and read it through carefully. Whatever other purpose the transcript might serve, he was sure that he was protected against any backlash. As it happened the transcript did come in useful at a later date when a couple of journalists from the Observer interviewed him in the course of their investigations into police corruption. This led to an exclusive article in that paper on the 25th of April and there were a few red faces at Scotland Yard when a copy of the tape was handed over to them.

Being involved in police corruption taught Joey a few

things he didn't know before, and he began to view the whole dirty business in its proper perspective. After four years and at a cost of four million pounds, Operation Countryman was wrapped up in an atmosphere of slanging matches with the top brass at Scotland Yard, which is not to be wondered at considering the fact that Countryman had named four Commanders, four Chief Superintendents, eight Superintendents, fifteen Chief Inspectors and six Inspectors as being bent. Joey followed the press reports very closely because he had done his share of bunging and he waited for the names to turn up. They didn't, Countryman fizzled out and the whole business passed into the hands of Scotland Yard's own investigation department, CIB 2, which explained why Rattray turned up on Joey's doorstep to look into a ten-year-old incident.

Villains are all kinds of things but they are not children, and nobody but a child would be taken in by the waffle about the probity and integrity of the Met. The crime rate is high because villains know they can either get away with it or bribe their way out of it, and the percentage of crime solved is low largely for the same reason. What is more, this evil cannot be stamped out because the honest cop will protect his bent colleague out of a sense of loyalty, the bent cops close ranks when one of them is threatened with exposure and in all this the villain, who is the only person whose evidence can break the racket, sees that evidence discounted because he is held to be working off a grudge or is a natural-born liar anyway.

The most appalling aspect of the situation was the acceptance of this menace by the very top brass at the Yard. Only an idiot would believe that they were unaware of the canker of corruption. Indeed Sir Robert Mark admitted it and tried to do something about it, but he was on a losing wicket and he didn't last long in any case. After him came a pudding-faced Scot, jeeringly nicknamed the 'Hammer of

Strathclyde', and for all the good he did he might as well have stayed in Glasgow. Now the Commissioner of Police for the Metropolis is a tiny chap with big ideas about quelling riots with plastic bullets but seemingly without a clue as to how to put his own house in order.

As Joey saw it someone had to stand up and he counted. To him it was evident that a decent, law-abiding society couldn't be built by creating an army of unemployed, encouraging them to commit crime out of desperation then employing a highly-paid but suspect legal machine to throw them into jail. Certainly poverty and want are not the sole breeding grounds of crime, but remove from the prisons those who have gone thieving because they're broke and out of a job and the problem of overcrowding is solved. It wouldn't make the misery endured in these insanitary shit-heaps any more bearable but there would be fewer to share it.

Ian Dunbar, who took over as Governor at the Scrubs after John McCarthy had quit, was quoted as saying 'I have to make certain to have the quality of misery spread over the whole establishment'. What a bloody admission! And what kind of a man would make such a statement?

Joey heard an almost unbelievable story which was in common circulation among the prisoners. A Governor at Wakefield jail ordered the construction of cell accommodation for TWO – yes, TWO – dangerous prisoners. Five cells were knocked into one to provide a room for each man with lavatory, shower and wash basin en suite and a central area with angled glass to allow both to watch a common television set. The accommodation was known officially as D suite and the front runners for these desirable residences were Robert Mawdsley who murdered one fellow prisoner at Broadmoor and two at Wakefield, and David Lant, who was also concerned in the Broadmoor murder. TWO MEN OUT OF MORE THAN FORTY-

FIVE THOUSAND! Joey wondered how many cons would be lining up to slaughter each other for the privilege of enjoying similar treatment, and what awaited a con who murdered a Governor. His mind boggled at this supreme example of official idiocy.

Descending from cloud-cuckoo land to the harsh reality of prison life, Joey had red-hot news for the Home Secretary. If something is not done very quickly to ease the intolerable conditions in the jails of this country he will have a series of riots on his hands the like of which have never been seen before. Most prisons are a disgrace to a civilised society, ancient decaying buildings with primitive sanitation crammed with desperate men, many of whom are locked up three to a cell for twenty-three hours out of the twenty-four. These men have lost their liberty and have been robbed of their dignity, they are treated like animals and one day they will react like animals for they have nothing to lose.

During Joey's various spells behind bars he had been on close terms with some remarkable people. One of them was a fellow called John Banks who had been mixed up in recruiting mercenaries for the war in Angola. The stories he told were almost incredible, straight out of the Le Carre-Deighton cloak and dagger fiction school, assassination and invasion plots involving ambassadors, diplomats and presidents, huge sums of money changing hands and all that paraphernalia. Joey actually knew of one of Banks' capers which had come in for a lot of press coverage and earned him a couple of years, during which time he had it away from Coldingley open prison.

One morning in early January '83 this character phoned Joey to arrange a meet. Joey was curious to find out what the man was after so he turned up with an open mind, ready to listen to whatever proposition was put up. It transpired that Banks had been approached by certain elements connected with the Togo government to foil a suspected attempt on the life of the President of Togo, a chap by the name of Eyedema. What Banks proposed was that Joey should go with him to meet the Togo ambassador in Brussels to discuss what could be done. He made it quite clear that there could be a lot of money in it.

This sort of thing wasn't really Joey's scene but he decided to play along with it for the time being. He had no intention of going in blind, however, so he said that he would let Banks have an answer the following day and they parted company. Joey lost no time in shooting round to the public library and filling himself in on all the information he could rake up about the background to Banks' story.

Joey discovered that the Togolese Republic was a small state in West Africa bordering on Ghana with a population of some two-and-half million. There was a long history of trouble there. President Sylvano Olympio had been assassinated in 1963 and this chap Eyedema, an Army type, had taken over in 1967. Olympio's two sons fled the country and set up an opposition in exile, and several attempts had been made to kill Eyedema, the most recent in October 1977. It looked as though Banks was on to something but Joey wasn't sure where he himself would fit in the picture. He decided to give it a go and arranged to meet Banks at Heathrow at 1.30 pm on the 13th of January. Joey proved his usefulness right away by paying for two return flights to Brussels. Banks said the money would be refunded by the Ambassador.

When they arrived they were met by two black fellows in a matching black Mercedes. Joey made a note of the registration number of the vehicle just to be on the safe side. They were whisked off to the Togo embassy where they met up with another bunch of blacks who turned out to be the Ambassador himself, the First Consul, the

Ambassador of Guinea and the Ambassador of Niger. Joey was impressed. In the chat that followed most of the conversation was in French which Banks spoke fluently. Joey filled a vacant hole in the background.

This meeting was merely a preliminary to the main talks and the two men left after the Ambassador had handed Joey a bundle of American Express cheques to the value of four hundred and forty dollars to cover the air fares, so Joey showed a small profit on that transaction. He took the precaution of having the cheques photo-copied before cashing them. In Joey's book it was better to be wise before the event. A further meeting had been fixed for the 19th January, again in Brussels, and during the few days' interval Joey did some serious thinking. Up to now he had done nothing illegal, but what was he letting himself in for?

It was all explained when Banks and Joey went back to Brussels on the 19th. The Ambassador disclosed that the Togo government had uncovered a plot to assassinate President Eyedema and believed that the Olympio brothers were behind it. The long and short of it was that they were willing to hire Banks to get the goods on the brothers. To proved they were not kidding they came up with a preliminary payment of £3,750 to cover expenses. Banks was well pleased and was humming 'we're in the money' all the way back to London. Joey wasn't too sure about things. This sort of intrigue was outside his experience but Banks assured him that all they were doing was to act as well-paid private eyes, and there was nothing criminal in that.

Back in London Joey dug up a few more facts about Togo and the late President Olympio. He was born in Lome in 1902, had studied at the London School of Economics and was for a time district manager in Togo for the United Africa Company. In 1960 he became the first President of Togoland, but he couldn't have been all that popular since, during a nine-month period in 1961, there were three attempts on his life. His short reign came to an end in January 1963 when he was assassinated outside the gates of the US Embassy. His two sons had it away and set up an organisation called the 'Mouvement togolais pour la democratie' which operated from offices in Paris. They were very wealthy. Where the money came from is anybody's guess.

Joey wasn't too happy about the situation. He'd never regarded murder as a solution to a political problem, which seemed to be a habit in the United States where they made no bones about bumping off Presidents who were surplus to requirements and, meaning no disrespect to our black brothers, they seemed to have the same ideas. Joey thought there was a moral in that somewhere.

The next meeting with the Togo lot had been fixed for Saturday the 22nd. Banks had brought in a couple of chaps to help out. One of them, Bobby Sewell, was a very useful boy with plenty of bottle, the other was an ex-soldier by the name of Sean Flanagan. Banks had hired a car and they drove to Dover, crossed to Calais on the ferry and drove on to Paris where they booked in at the Residence Charles Dullin in Montmartre. That afternoon they set out for Lille, a town on the Belgian border, where they were due to have a meet at the Holiday Inn at nine o'clock in the evening.

It was all real spy-drama stuff. The Ambassador was there along with another fellow who had flown over from Togo. Their bodyguards were close at hand, real pros by the look of them, who kept a watchful eye on the proceedings as Banks and his companions were briefed. Their first job was to carry out a surveillance on the 'Mouvement togolais' in Paris and report back on the Tuesday. It looked like money for jam when Banks asked for a further two grand on account of expenses and it was agreed.

They started work on the Monday. Banks had hired a van for the day, a bloody great red thing which made an ugly blotch on the landscape in the fashionable part of Paris where the Movement's offiices were situated. Bobby and Joey did most of the work, running off yards of film as they photographed everybody passing in and out of the building. Banks hovered in the background while Flanagan acted as a sort of messenger, losing whatever bottle he possessed in the process. At one point he hammered on the side of the van and shouted something about a bomb underneath. Joey reckoned he must have watched too many Bond films.

The following day they went to the meet in Lille and handed over the negatives of something like three hundred shots taken outside the Movement's premises. Banks copped for the promised two grand and they left. They had intended to go back to Paris, but they were much nearer Calais so they elected to hop on the ferry and return to England.

During the weekend Joey had been having some thoughts about the caper. He wasn't very pleased about the way the self-styled Major was handling things. Joey knew they were committing an offence under French law by snatching pictures from a concealed position. He also knew that in France the law had a nasty habit of nicking suspects, throwing them into the boob and then forgetting where they had put the key. In France, unlike the UK, you're guilty until you've been proved innocent. Over a meal and a few drinks on the boat Joey tackled Banks about his method of organising the affair. He didn't get an answer that satisfied him.

They arrived in London and split up, Banks saying he would be in touch a soon as he had arranged the next stage of the operation, but Joey had already made up his mind about that. He did not intend to put himself up front to be nicked while Banks stayed in the background and, so far as the Major's organisational abilities were concerned, Joey wouldn't have trusted him to plan a piss-up in a brewery. The upshot was that when Banks phoned Joey cocked a deaf 'un and continued to do so until the fellow got tired and gave up.

That was the end of Joey's involvement with 'Major' John Banks. No doubt Banks carried on with his scheme because he had been promised a quarter of a million dollars if he managed to incriminate the Olympio brothers. Thinking things over and putting himself in Banks' shoes, Joey sussed that Banks had made up a story about being approached by the Olympio's, taken it to the Togos and kidded them it was true, leaked a story to the press that mercenaries were on the way to bump off Eyedema and so constructed a scenario that was nothing more or less than a complicated confidence trick. There was obviously a cloud of suspicion surrounding the Togo camp, with nobody quite sure of what the other fellow was up to. Banks had taken full advantage of the situation.

17. Murder Hunt

True gangsterism in Britain began with the Sabinis. Their business was extortion. They used the crude weapons of their trade, the razor, the knife and the bludgeon. Charles (Darby) Sabini and his brothers Harry and Joseph headed a forty-strong band of brutal thugs. They levied toll on bookmakers at every racecourse in the country. They grew rich.

In 1936 sixteen members of the gang were sentenced to a total of 53 years imprisonment at Lewes Assizes.

In 1939 the brothers were interned as enemy aliens.

In October 1950 Darby Sabini died peacefully at his home in Hove.

The Messina brothers came into prominence in the forties. The sons of an Italian peasant they came to London via Malta. Their names, in order of seniority, were Salvatore, Alfredo, Eugenio, Attilio and Carmelo.

Their trade was vice and prostitution. At one time they controlled the activities of three hundred prostitutes.

In 1950 their activities were exposed by *Sunday People* reporter Duncan Webb, and the police took swift action. In concerted raids throughout the Metropolitan area they uncovered the Messina web of conspiracy. Their reign was over.

The fifties saw the emergence of two powerful gangland figures who were engaged in a bitter struggle for the control of London's underworld.

Jack 'Spot' Comer was a hard man, a ferocious battler from the back streets of Stepney who had clawed his way to the top of the criminal tree with a mixture of guile and brutality. Always impeccably dressed, he was a familiar sight at race meetings all over the country.

The other contender for power was Billy Hill, one of a large family of criminals hailing from Seven Dials. About the same age as Spot (he was born in 1911) he was intelligent, resourceful and a brilliant organiser. He was also utterly ruthless.

The issue between the two men was decided one night in 1956. Spot and his wife, Rita, on the way back home to their flat in Hyde Park Mansions off the Edgeware Road, were attacked by a gang of men wielding knives and iron bars. Spot was beaten within an inch of his life. At the local hospital seventy-eight stitches were put in his face and head.

Billy Hill became undisputed guv'nor of the West End and leader of Britain's gangland.

The sixties saw crime becoming an organised business but the rivalries persisted. The formidable Kray twins established a firm base in the East End then reached out to the west, taking over territory once held by Billy Hill. From Peckham, south of the river, Charlie and Eddie Richardson cast covetous eyes on the rich pickings to be had in that area. Violent affrays broke out in the clubs and restaurants as members of the rival gangs avenged real or fancied insults. George Cornell, a Richardson man, was shot dead in the Blind Beggar public house. It was common knowledge that Ronnie Kray's finger was on the trigger of the gun. Nobody saw anything.

Jack 'The Hat' McVitie was stabbed to death in a basement flat in Stoke Newington. The body went missing. Nobody knew anything.

The law put and end to these capers. In 1967 the Richardsons went away for several years via a lengthy trial at the Old Bailey. The following year the Kray twins suffered a similar fate.

Had organised crime finally been defeated with the removal of these notorious men from society?

Looking back over the past decade, several disquieting facts emerge. Robberies involving vast amounts of money have been carried out. Small fry have been captured and imprisoned. Yet most of the loot has not been recovered and there are men now basking in the sun in Spain who are suspected of being the master minds behind these audacious capers.

Is a new breed of criminal now coming to the fore, the Untouchables who make crime pay and go on to deploy the proceeds of crime into the financing of further crimes? Are they under some protection from those whose business is the upholding of law and order?

Eight men sat round a huge table in the largest room of the villa. The picture windows gave on to a staggering panorama of the Rock of Gibraltar and the blue ocean shimmering in the heat haze. None of them paid much attention to the view. They had seen it before many times.

At the head of the table sat the man from Detroit, impeccable in dress, quiet in manner but with that air of authority which is the prerogative of those possessed of immense wealth and power. On his right sat a coarse-looking individual with a florid face and small deep-set eyes who could have stepped straight out of a gangster movie. He was, in fact, one of Britain's top villains who had driven from his Spanish villa in an opulent white Rolls which was now parked in the driveway of the villa. He was wanted by the British police for a variety of crimes ranging from armed robbery to murder, which did not seem to worry him one iota.

Next to him sat the lawyer, an urbane fellow with a humorous twinkle in his eye as if he regarded the world and its doings as a farce put on for his particular entertainment. One of the most promiment solicitors in Britain he had briefed counsel in the defence of more villains than any other ten members of his profession. Moreover most of them were successful defences in cases where the guilt of the accused was only too apparent.

Across the table and on the left of the man from Detroit sat a handsome, grey-haired character whose age could have been anywhere between forty and sixty. He was soberly dressed and looked as though he might be a senior policeman in mufti. He was, in fact, one of the top men at Scotland Yard, who enjoyed the confidence of his superiors notwithstanding the fact that he lived in a £250,000 mansion, supported an expensive wife and sent his two daughters to an exclusive boarding school which numbered minor royalty on its roll of pupils. Had he been asked to explain the anomaly between his life-style and his income he would have explained that his wife had a private income, as indeed she had. Her husband provided it.

The other four men making up the complement were obviously the junior members. Though smartly dressed and well-behaved there was about them the look of hard men capable of extreme violence. They were the rulers of London's gangland which had been roughly divided by common consent into four areas, North East, North West, South East and South West. All criminal activity of any importance in those areas was under their direct control.

The subject under discussion at this meeting was the setting up of a slush fund for the purpose of bribing jurors in the British Courts of Justice. The man from Detroit was speaking. His manner was that of a judge summing up at the end of a trial which was not surprising for, in addition to being a Mafia leader, he was also a judge of the US Supreme Court.

'We are controlling an operation which is one of the largest of its kind in the world,' he said. 'It is also one of the most profitable. The illegal importation and distribution of cocaine, heroin and cannabis yields large profits. It also entails considerable risks. We have built up an organisation in which every man knows his job and carries it out efficiently. He is a specialist. If in the course of his duties he is arrested and subsequently brought before a court it is in out interests to protect him. Agreed?'

There was a murmur of assent and a nodding of heads.

'In these matters the authorities do not play foolish games,' the man from Detroit went on. 'If one of our men comes to trial they make sure they have a cast-iron case which all the expert pleading in the world will not be able to destroy. Our man will go away for a very long time.'

He looked towards the Lawyer, who nodded his head in agreement.

The man from Detroit continued.

'The result of such a happening breaks a link in our chain of command and ultimately weakens the structure as a whole. The only way to prevent such a circumstance arising, certainly in the British courts, is that the jury return a verdict of not guilty.'

The leader of the South West gang summed up the situation.

'We nobble the jury,' he said.

'Exactly,' said the man from Detroit. 'Not, I would suggest, by terror and threats of violence. Such actions have a habit of attracting unfavourable publicity. We will work on the assumption that every man has his price. It is a price we can well afford to pay. Indeed it is a price that we must pay. Are we agreed?'

There was no dissent. The man from Detroit turned to the Lawyer.

'We may leave the details in your hands?' he said.

'Certainly,' said the Lawyer. 'A sufficient sum will be allocated for this purpose. All applications to me, please. Don't bother to put them in writing.'

There was a burst of laughter round the table.

'Any other business?' enquired the man from Detroit.

It appeared that there was nothing more to discuss. The man from Detroit leading the way, the equivalent of a hundred billion dollars left the room.

Joey was back in business. One day he stumbled across basement premises in Russell Road, Kensington, part of a house once owned by Peter Rachman, a slum landlord who had operated in Notting Hill for several years. Joey got to know him quite well, but their relationship was not to last for the man died that same year. He was mixed up with a couple of birds, Christine Keeler and Mandy Rice-Davies, who later figured in the Profumo scandal. However, that's by the way. Joey rented the basement and opened a drinker which he called the Basement Club.

He did very well and began to scout around for other premises where he could repeat the process. In this type of enterprise it was as well to have several irons in the fire for the drinkers were illegal and could be closed down at a moment's notice by the law. Joey came across many suitable locations in the Notting Hill and Holland Park areas and was soon drawing a handsome income from the operations.

From the point of view of the operator a drinker is a very viable proposition. For a start the costs were almost negligible, because he didn't bother with decoration or any of that nonsense. He knock up a makeshift bar, put in a few chairs and tables and kept the lighting down to hide the holes in the carpets and the tattered wallpaper. As for stock, he was on to a good thing with a wholesaler in Princedale Road who allowed him lengthy credit. Furthermore it was an all-cash affair. Joey had nothing to do with cheques, not even good ones.

During the period when he was knocking around the estate agents looking for premises, Joey came across a bloke called Ken who was working in one of the offices he visited. Later on this merchant approached him with a proposition. He had quit the estate agent and taken a job as resident caretaker of a posh tennis club in Holland Park which was, according to him, an ideal spot for a late-night drinker. As he outlined it, the plan would be to take over the place at eleven and run it until four in the morning as a high-class joint with all mod cons. Realising that the geezer could well be painting a rosy picture of a wooden tennis hut with a counter and sink, Joey said he would like to see the place. Ken took him there that evening.

It was an eye-opener, a large house in its own grounds with lawns and tennis courts and furnished regardless of cost. There were deep carpets, the oak-panelled bar was fully fitted, comfortable leather chairs were scattered around and the full-length curtains were of expensive velvet. Even the toilets were carpeted and the ladies' loo boasted a pair of bidets. Joey couldn't wait to get the joint opened.

The first night went with a bang and after that Joey never looked back. As the word spread the club became the 'in' place to go for a late drink and, as can be imagined, the clients were a very mixed bag. There were brasses and their ponces rubbing shoulders with villains and well-known figures from the worlds of sport and the arts. Joey had recruited a pair of very tasty lads to help him keep order, but the customers were allowed to do pretty much as they liked short of breaking up the furniture or damaging the fixtures and fittings. There was one inflexible rule. At four o'clock in the morning the place was cleared. Then Ken and Joey, with the aid of a gang of helpers, tidied the joint up, replaced the stock they had used and departed.

At odd moments Joey speculated about how the society birds would have felt had they known that the toilets they used were also serving the needs of some painted old slash-pot, probably dosed up to the eyeballs, and that the very carpet on which they stood had been a rumping spot for a brass while her ponce did a piss in the bidet. There were times also when Joey had nightmares in case some old dear, returning from an evening at the theatre, would call to pick up a forgotten article and find her tennis club packed with unauthorised members.

There was also the ever-present threat of a police raid for, though Joey took precautions against excessive noise and always saw that the curtains were tightly drawn, there was considerable coming and going which must have attracted the attention of neighbouring householders. A raid would have put the kybosh on the whole enterprise since the usual practice was that the Old Bill took the names and addresses of the customers, arrested the person in charge of the bar and impounded the stock. Lady Luck must have been on Joey's side on that score. He had no aggravation from the forces of law and order.

One of the regular punters Joey got to know very well was ex-world champion boxer Freddie Mills who would often drop in for a drink in the early hours. Freddie was to die in mysterious circumstances, being found outside his West End club in a car, a .22 rifle by his side and a gunshot wound in his head. The coroner returned a verdict of suicide but Joey's view was that Freddie was a victim of a gangland murder, a view that was shared by Freddie's widow amongst others.

Actor Paul Carpenter was a regular visitor, a jovial boozer who could always be relied upon to be the life and soul of the party, that is until he fell down. One night he passed out on a settee, and a couple of brasses took out his penis and drew a ring round it with lipstick. It was all good clean fun.

In the club business trouble is never farther away than the next row, and most of the rows were caused by the brasses. Joey couldn't bar them for by doing so he would lose the majority of his customers. All he could do was accept them as a necessary evil, and evil was the right word to describe most of them.

Joey was no moralist but he reckoned brasses didn't deserve much consideration. Considering that they were ready to take on ten different men in a night, some of them poxed-up, he wondered what went on in the upstairs department. From the experience Joey had of them they were unscrupulous, unpredictable, unreasonable and without a shred of conscience. Most of them were into petty thieving and in their company trouble was ever present.

The slags at the bottom end of the market charged a few pounds for a knee-trembler against a wall, a blow job in the back of a car or a short time on the grass in a public park. They are a different breed from the high-class whores who chose their clients with care and charged the earth for their services. Joey never needed to use any of them by way of trade. He had no difficulty in getting all the nooky he wanted without paying for it.

The brasses couldn't be kept out of a drinker because they were part of the service so to speak. In the dim lighting even an old slash-pot looked attractive to a bloke with a skinful of booze, and the punters expected to pick up a quick fuck for a few sovs. Joey had often been amazed to see quite respectable geezers nipping off outside for a short time with some raddled old hag to whom they wouldn't normally give the time of day. Joey remembered a sick story about a couple of brasses who were walking down the Bayswater Road. Blimey, says one to the other, my fanny don't 'arf itch. Why don't you scratch it, says her mate. Scratch it? I wouldn't touch it with a barge pole says the complainer.

Joking apart, having these quarrelsome cows in a drinker was like sitting on a keg of dynamite. This was where Johnny came in useful. He was an old pal and had been a schoolmate. He was good fun at a party, laughing and joking and doing his impressions of famous people, especially Schnozzle Durate and Humphrey Bogart, which brought the house down. When Joey had started in the club lark Johnny often dropped in to see him and have a chat. In fact he spent so much time doing this that Joey suggested they put his visits on a permanent and paying basis. It turned out to be a very successful arrangement. Johnny had the knack of being able to turn a tense moment into a laughing matter with a few words at the right time. If, in spite of his amiable approach, there seemed to be no way of avoiding a row people thought twice about tackling this big man with the flattened hooter and the bearing of an ex-prize-fighter. If a full-scale ruck developed Johnny was capable of settling it single-handed.

Normally Johnny drank and joked with the brasses but at times, when he would sort one out for a bit of treatment, he was anything but friendly. It would start off with a few whispered remarks accompanied by some painful pinching. Then he would lead her off into a corner where he would lean against her, fondling her tits and putting his hand up her skirt and not being too gentle about it either. After this he would march her outside and force her to go down to him, holding her by the hair and thrusting his erect penis as far down her throat as it would go. The performance over he would give her a good thumping and tell her to fuck off.

One of the brasses had the sauce to complain to Joey but she didn't get anywhere. If she didn't like the conditions, said Joey, she should stay away from the joint. She then persuaded her ponce to have a pop at Johnny, which was no good to either of them. Johnny beat the ponce to a pulp, kicked the slag senseless and warned them both off the manor. Although it was none of Joey's business how Johnny got his kicks it rather puzzled him when he thought about it. Although he had no criminal record Johnny seemed to relish being mixed up with the shady world of clubs and the people who used them. He took care of his mother, with whom he lived in a flat in Hammersmith.

Joey's thinking led to no real conclusion except that it takes all kinds to make a world and Johnny fitted in somewhere.

A solitary street-walker strolls along a deserted street. A Transit van pulls up alongside her. She goes up to it.

'Doing business, love?' asks the man in the van.

'Cost you twenty quid,' says the girl.

'OK. Get in,' says the man.

The girl gets into the van, which then speeds off into the night.

It was in the nature of things that a brass was responsible for putting an end to the tennis club venture. Her name was Vicky, she was a good-looker but she couldn't hold her drink. She started a fight with one of her mates, but Johnny quickly put a stop to that lark, slung the girl out and told her in no uncertain terms to stay out. In the early morning of the following day, the 8th of April, her nude body was discovered by the river police on the towpath of the Thames not far from a pub called the Windmill.

She was quickly identified as Vicky Russell, a prostitute, and the police lost no time in turning over her drum. Among her belongings they found a card bearing the name Kenny and the telephone number of the tennis club. Now the fat was truly in the fire. Joey closed down the club and made himself unavailable to callers.

A fortnight after the discovery of Vicky Russell's corpse another murder hit the headlines. The nude body of a woman had been found about a mile away from the spot whre Russell had met her end. The papers named her as Irene Lockwood, a prostitute who frequented the West London area, where she was well-known. She was a regular attender at the Jazz Club in Westbourne Road, a gaff which catered for West Indians and was run by a chap called African Peter. Joey had a small stake in the place. He remembered that the Lockwood woman had visited the tennis club on a few occasions. According to reports she was a good performer who made no secret of the fact that she preferred her clients to be black.

The press went to town on this second Jack the Ripper type killing, describing in detail the last night of the victim's life, how she danced and drank at the Jazz Club into the early hours, climbing the steps that led to Westbourne Road and stepping out into the dawn and into a van, never to be seen alive again. This was on the morning of the 20th of April. Medical evidence showed that she had been dead for forty-eight hours when her naked body was found five miles from the scene of her last dance.

Having got nowhere with the Russell case, the Old Bill really put themselves about on this one. They ran a fine dragnet over the manor, pulling in a large proportion of the West Indian population for questioning and poking their noses into every criminal nook and cranny. One night they raided the Basement Club when Joey happened to be there and found a stolen one-armed bandit on the premises. One Old Bill came the heavy and Joey ended up chinning him, with the result that he was nicked for receiving and assault and also lost the club, which was closed down.

It looked as though everything was coming on top, so his feelings could be imagined when he heard that Kenny had walked into the nick and confessed to the murder of Irene Lockwood. The idiot had lost any bottle he ever had and it was odds on that he would cough the lot, in which case Joey and Johnny would be in the frame as suspects. It was obvious that Kenny had made a false confession. The poor sod wasn't capable of killing a fly.

Joey had no option but to get off the manor but he wanted to be near the scene of the action. He holed up at a flat in Soho owned by one of his mates and kept in touch with what was going on in Notting Hill through Johnny, who came and went without attracting any special attention.

Johnny attended the hearing at Acton magistrates court, where Kenny pleaded not guilty to a charge of murder and was committed for trial at the Old Bailey. Johnny brought the news that Kenny had blown the whistle on the set-up at the tennis club and named Joey as the organiser. The Old Bill had got the message and were out looking for Joey. It was all bad news.

There was nothing for it but to sit tight and let things take their course. In the meantime Joey had to earn a living. His friends were by now well established in the West End and were able to put quite a bit of work his way. The Ash brothers, who were minding the Bagatelle in Cork Street, also steered Joey towards a few earners. Very soon he was doing better financially than he had ever done with the drinkers, which was some consolation.

The press had now started to refer to the killings of

Russell and Lockwood as the Nude Murders but they couldn't comment on them in any detail because Kenny was due to appear at the Old Bailey at the end of June. It was a cock-eyed situation. Kenny had pleaded not guilty at the magistrates court even though he had confessed to the killing of the Lockwood woman. Everybody knew that the miserable bastard was as innocent as a new-born babe, but the law had to take its course so Kenny duly appeared up the steps at the Bailey, was duly acquitted and promptly took off for parts unknown.

Three weeks later the nude body of a woman was found on the forecourt of a garage in Berrymeade Road, a cul-de-sac off Acton Lane and three miles away from where the bodies of the other two murdered women had been discovered. In life she had been Mary Fleming, alias Mary Turner, a brass from Notting Hill who had been known as a frequent visitor to both the Jazz Club and the tennis club.

The press had a field day over this new development and the Old Bill had to take quite a bit of stick, which didn't please the top brass at the Yard. At the same time as one of the sensational Sundays implored the killer to give himself up, orders went out to step up the hunt. It was very nearly impossible to move in Notting Hill without bumping into a copper. Joey kept his head down in Soho while the faithful Johnny brought him news of the happenings on his home manor. It was now certain that Joey was in the frame as a prime suspect, for the old Bill had visited his home, questioned his friends and relatives and made it plain that they wanted to get their hands on Joey Bello.

Although he was a only a few miles from Notting Hill he felt reasonable safe. In theory communications between the various divisions of the Met were good but in practice they didn't work out all that well. The newly-organised Regional Crime Squads were having teething troubles in the early stages, a fact well known to all the villains. Joey didn't stick himself up as a target but he did take precautions against having his collar felt, and they worked.

Meanwhile the press had been doing some simple arithmetic after chasing up unsolved murders in the West London districts. Elizabeth Figg was a prostitute. She was found dead on the river bank at Dukes' Meadows near Chiswick Bridge. The partly decomposed body of another brass, Gwyneth Rees, was uncovered by workmen on a patch of waste ground in Mortlake. There was another unsolved case, Hannah Tailford, also found dead beside the Thames. The toll was mounting. Joey decided to have it away from the Metropolitan area.

Johnny drove Joey to Brighton. The evening was fine and they sat in a quiet corner in the bar at Cook's for a drink and a chat. For a while nothing was said. Johnny, who normally rabbited away twenty to the dozen, sat there staring into his glass as though in a hypnotic trance.

'Something the matter, Johnny?' Joey asked.

Johnny was silent for some time then took a hefty swig at his drink.

'They're saying on the manor that you topped those brasses and I helped you,' he said.

'For fuck's sake. You know that's not my line.'

'Sure Joey. I know. So do you. But what about the others? That bloody Kenny . . .'

They both knew what Johnny was talking about. Kenny had dropped Joey right in it. The law was looking for a body and, with his form, there was every possibility that he would be fitted up.

'So, what do we do?' asked Joey.

'There's only one thing for it. You'll have to keep out of the way till the heat's off. I'll go back to London and keep in touch with you on the blower.'

Joey couldn't think of anything else that could be done

so they left it like that. Johnny went on his way and Joey went up to his room with a bottle of Scotch. He had plenty to think about. Was Johnny telling the truth? Or did he know more than he was letting on to him? Joey remembered the look on Johnny's face when he threw the Russell girl out of the tennis club and wondered if the incident had ended there. What did he know of Johnny? Behind the laughter and the joke was a devious mind. There flashed before his eyes some of the news items he had read. The bodies of the women showed signs of having been in contact with rubber flooring and traces of cellulose were found on their skins. Joey had a vivid mental picture of Johnny, the women on her knees before him, caught in a mad spasm of lust, holding her against him while she gagged on a throatful of sperm and choked to death. If it had happened like that what would Johnny have done? He was a cool and resourceful man who knew London intimately. A hiding place for a body would not be hard to find. Joey gave it up. Speculation was not only fruitless but a waste of time.

Two men are sitting in the front seats of a moving Transit van. There is no conversation. They are seen in silhouette against the street lamps and overhead lighting.

The Transit van turns into an alleyway between two towering warehouses. The sound of a ship's foghorn is heard in the distance. The men jump from the van as it comes to a stop. They are wearing overalls and donkey jackets. Their faces are covered by balaclava-type hoods.

They moved quickly to the back of the van, open the rear doors and drag a corpse from beneath a tarpaulin. Then, moving quickly, they carry the body to a pile of packing cases and throw it on the ground. They pull other cases and debris over it so that it is concealed from view.

'How long before they find this one,' said the man in charge. He spoke with an upper-class accent.

'When it's convenient I guess. The other two haven't turned up yet,' said his companion.

'It's rather odd, don't you think?'

'Very.'

They climb into the van and drive away.

Joey wove his way through the stalls and barrows of the Portobello market. It is raining hard, people are ducking in and out of shelter but it is business as usual.

He had returned from Brighton the previous day. There were many things he had to attend to since his finances were at a low ebb. So far as he knew the Old Bill had turned their attentions away from him but he was careful not to make himself too conspicuous.

Old Punchie, one of the stallholders, hailed him.

'Wotcher, Joey. How goes it?'

'Alright Punchie, me old son. How's business?'

'Keeping the wolves away.'

Joey playfully sparred up to the old man. In his day Punchie had been a promising welter. Even now he was very useful.

'What's the word,' said Joey.

'All's quiet on the west eleven front,' said Punchie.

Joey laughed and continued on his way through the market. Turning off Portobello he came to his destination, a shabby building with a sign that said 'Angel Hotel'. The basement housed one of Joey's clubs which he had not visited for some time. He skipped down the stairs, opened the basement door and went in.

The elderly man sweeping the floor of the somewhat bare room looked up.

'Blimey, Joey,' he said, 'where did you spring from? Long time no see.'

'Just been keeping out of sight for a bit,' said Joey. 'How've things been, Gerry?'

'Not bad. I've got quite a bit of cash for you.'

'Good. It'll come in handy.'

Gerry disappeared behind the bar. Joey glanced round the room. The juke box in the corner was playing a recording of Elmore James's 'Dust my Blues'. It was one of Joey's favourite numbers, a haunting tune that brought back memories.

Gerry came out from behind the bar carrying a bulging paper bag which Joey emptied on the counter. He began to count the notes as Gerry watched him in silence.

'Not bad, Gel,' he said.

'Yeah. Not bad at all,' said Gerry.

'We have done better,' said Joey. He separated a thin wad of notes from the bundle and handed them to Gerry, folding the remainder and stuffing them in his back pocket.

'Right. See you soon,' said Joey. 'Keep smiling.'

On the 25th of November the naked body of a woman was found on a patch of waste ground in Hornton Street, Kensington. She had been dead for some time. She was identified as Margaret McGowan, a prostitute from the Bayswater area.

On the 16th of February the naked body of a woman was found in an alley in Acton, West London. She was Bridget O'Hara, a prostitute who had plied her trade in Shepherds Bush, Hammersmith, Notting Hill and Bayswater.

Were these killings the work of one man who followed the same pattern each time? Was he an up-dated version of Jack the Ripper, who stalked the gaslit streets of Edwardian London, leaving behind him a trail of dead whores? Was he, like Peter Sutcliffe known as the Yorkshire Ripper, a man driven by an obsessive urge to slay women of easy virtue.

Or was there more than one killer?

18. Scenario: A Firm Within a Firm

JOEY stands at the bar, a drink at his elbow. He is studing form in the racing pages of the *Standard*. A small group of mates are standing around. BILLY separates himself from the group and joins JOEY.

BILLY

Heard about Cosh boy getting nicked?

JOEY

No. What happened?

BILLY

Dunno the full strength but by all accounts he's in it.

JOEY

Sorry to hear that, Billy.

BILLY

Yeah. It'll be a long 'un this time. Still it's his own fault. He shouldn't have gone out.

JOEY

How's that?

BILLY

Don't you ever read the front of that fuckin' paper?

JOEY
Oh, these brasses being found murdered.

BILLY
Yeah, these brasses being murdered.

JOEY
What's the strength?

BILLY
It's a mystery. Nobody on the manor knows anything.

JOEY
But the bodies end up here.

BILLY
(shouts)
That's what I'm getting at. No good for business.

JOEY
Unless you're a necrophiliac.

BILLY
Eh?

JOEY
Skip it.

The following day. JOEY is sitting behind the bar in the basement club with papers and money spread out in front of him. The club is deserted. There is the sound of footsteps on the stairs. JOEY hurriedly collects the papers and money together and puts them under the bar counter. He picks up a newspaper and pretends to read. ANDY, a uniformed constable, appears in the doorway.

ANDY
Relax, Joey, it's only me.

JOEY
Blimey, Andy, you frit the life out of me.

ANDY
Can't stop. I'm not here officially. Just want to mark your card.

JOEY
What about?

ANDY
Duval.

JOEY
Duval?

ANDY
Yeah. He's looking for you.

JOEY
What's he looking for me for?

ANDY
Dunno. You're in the frame for something.

JOEY
In the frame? Bollocks. I've done nothing wrong.

ANDY
That's what they all say.

JOEY
(sarcastic)
Thanks.

ANDY
I'm doing you a favour, Joey.

JOEY
Sorry, Andy. You know what I mean.

ANDY
Take care, Joey. You're a little bit of priority right now.

Andy moves towards the door. JOEY calls out after him.

JOEY
Hold on, Andy. Have a drink on me.

ANDY
Don't embarrass me, Joey.

JOEY is strolling through the Portobello market when suddenly a police car appears out of nowhere. It screeches to a halt within a few yards of JOEY and four plain-clothes police officers pour out. As JOEY looks up in alarm he is seized by the offices and manhandled into the car.

JOEY
(screaming)
What's the game?

FIRST CID MAN
You're nicked, Bello.

The car roars off. JOEY sits in the back of the car sandwiched between two officers. He is handcuffed to one of them.

FIRST CID MAN
(gazing out of window)
You should be bloody-well hung.

JOEY
(flippant)
Yes, guv'nor.

FIRST CID MAN
(yells)
You heard me, scumbag. H-U-N-G. Hung.

JOEY
They taught you to spell at Hendon then?

SECOND CID MAN
You think this is a joke, Bello?

JOEY
I'm not laughing.

SECOND CID MAN
You'll have nothing to laugh about by the time we've finished with you.

JOEY
I don't know why you've got the hump with me.

FIRST CID MAN
Because you're a bloody murderer, that's why.

JOEY

I'm not a bloody murderer – and I'll prove it.

SECOND CID MAN

Prove it, Chummy? You're done bang to rights. You'll never see dayight again.

JOEY

(very sincere)

Look fellers, you've got the wrong man. While you're messing about with me the real murderer is laughing at you.

FIRST CID MAN

(menacingly)

Nobody laughs at us. Particularly you.

JOEY is being questioned at Scotland Yard by the CID men who arrested him. He has been given a thorough beating. Blood is pouring from his nose, his clothing is in disarray. The FIRST CID MAN holds JOEY pinned against the wall.

FIRST CID MAN

I won't ask you again. Are you going to cough?

At this moment the door of the room opens and DUVAL enters.

DUVAL

What the hell's going on here?

FIRST CID MAN

This man keeps falling over, sir. I've just picked him up.

DUVAL

Get out. Both of you. Get out.

The CID MEN leave hurriedly. DUVAL takes out his handkerchief and passes it to JOEY.

DUVAL

Tidy yourself up and sit down.

JOEY wipes his face with the handkerchief, returns it to DUVAL and sits on one of the chairs. DUVAL draws up another chair and sits facing JOEY.

DUVAL

Do you know who I am?

JOEY

No.

DUVAL

I am Detective Chief Superintendent Duval. I am making enquiries into the deaths of a number of women.

JOEY

What's that got to do with me?

DUVAL

That is why you are here. To help with my enquiries.

JOEY

I don't see how I can help you.

DUVAL

Do you run a late night drinking club?

JOEY

Yes.

DUVAL

Did you ever meet there a prostitute who was known as Vicky?

JOEY

Yes.

DUVAL

Do you know she has been murdered?

JOEY

Yes.

DUVAL

Did you have anything to do with this woman's death.

JOEY

Definitely no.

DUVAL

We have evidence that you were in conversation with this woman shortly before she was murdered.

JOEY

Yes, I did speak to her at the club but that was the last time I saw her.

DUVAL

How well did you know the woman?

JOEY

Only in the course of business. She used the club.

DUVAL

Have you ever had sexual relations with her?

JOEY

No.

DUVAL

Do you know if she had any enemies?

JOEY

None as far as I know.

DUVAL

Did she have any boy-friends? I don't mean clients.

JOEY

No. She was pretty much a loner.

DUVAL

Do you own a video machine?

JOEY

No.

DUVAL

Are you in the habit of reading pornographic literature?

JOEY

No.

DUVAL

Are you a collector of news items referring to crimes of violence, including murder?

JOEY

No. I've got no interest in such things.

DUVAL

Do you own a house in Newton Square, Ashford?

JOEY

Yes.

DUVAL

Would you be surprised to hear that, on searching your house, we found in the loft a large number of video nasties, sadistic porn films and magazines and press cuttings?

JOEY

Yes. It surprises me very much.

DUVAL

And you maintain that these articles are not your property?

JOEY

I do. Definitely.

DUVAL

Can you explain how they got in your house?

JOEY

They must have been planted.

DUVAL

Planted? By whom?

JOEY

I don't know. But I intend to find out.

DUVAL

Do you know a woman called Sally Kellerman?

JOEY

No.

DUVAL

She is a prostitute. She alleges that you were one of her regular clients.

JOEY

Not true.

DUVAL

She alleges that you abused her sexually and treated her in a very sadistic manner.

JOEY

Not true.

DUVAL

She says that you confessed to her that you had murdered a number of prostitutes.

JOEY

She's a liar. Bring her here and I'll tell her to her face.

DUVAL

She's a heroin addict. She is dangerously ill.

JOEY

Look. I've had enough of this pantomime. Are you going to charge me?

DUVAL

My personal view, Bello, is that you committed these murders. I'll be frank with you. I haven't got sufficient evidence to charge you. You can go. But from now on you're under the magnifying glass.

JOEY is with a journalist friend in the cuttings library of a national newspaper. The JOURNALIST hands JOEY a bundle of files.

JOURNALIST

You can use that desk over there, Joey.

JOEY

Thanks, John. I need all the cuttings you have on these murders.

JOURNALIST

You'll find them all there. Take your time.

It is after midnight and JOEY is still hard at work. His coat is draped over the back of his chair and he has loosened his tie. The desk is piled with cuttings arranged in some kind of order. The JOURNALIST comes into the room.

JOURNALIST

(smiling)

Still at it, Joey?

JOEY

Yeah. There's more work than I thought.

JOURNALIST

Got what you wanted?

JOEY

Yes. For the time being.

JOURNALIST

Any time you want to come in again, give me a bell.

JOEY

Thanks. I'll do that.

JOURNALIST

I'm packing up now. Can I give you a lift?

JOEY

No thanks. Got the motor outside.

JOEY collects his notes, puts on his coat and the two men leave. Outside the offices they say their goodnights and go their separate ways.

JOEY is in the Notting Hill area pursuing his enquiries. He emerges from a pub, takes a notebook from his pocket and makes an entry in it. Replacing the notebook he enters a nearby cafe, then comes out almost immediately. He makes another note in the book. As he turns to walk away a woman bumps into him. JOEY recognises her as an ex-prostitute by the name of SHEILA.

JOEY

Hello there. Sheila O'Neill isn't it?

SHEILA

Yeah. I remember you. You're Joey Bello ain'tcha?

JOEY

That's right, love. Where you living now?

SHEILA
No fixed address. Living rough.

JOEY
Sorry to hear that. Here. Cop for this.

JOEY hands SHEILA a ten-pound note.

SHEILA
Ooh, thanks very much, duckie. Very kind of you.

JOEY
If you can give me a bit of info it's worth another tenner.

SHEILA
What you want to know?

JOEY
There's a black fellow mixed up with the murder of Vicky and those other girls. Can you put a name to him?

SHEILA
It's more than me life's worth?

JOEY
You're talking to Joey now, love.

SHEILA
Listen, Joey. This feller's got a lot of money and influence. If it got out that I'd grassed him, I'm dead.

JOEY
Come on, Sheila, no messing. Gimme the name. Nothing'll happen to you.

SHEILA

His name's Leon. King o' the ponces. Got a house just off the Portobello Road.

JOEY

What's the address?

SHEILA

Dunno. His Cadillac's always parked outside.

JOEY

You take me there and I'll double that tenner.

SHEILA

You're on. Come on then.

JOEY and ANDY, the police constable, are standing by JOEY'S car.

JOEY

Thanks for coming, Andy.

ANDY

You're the last person I should be seen talking to. What do you want?

JOEY

A favour.

ANDY

What is it?

JOEY

I want anything you can find out about a chap called Leon. He owns a Cadillac . . .

ANDY
What's the registration number?

JOEY
PMY 114Y.

ANDY notes the number in his pocketbook.

ANDY
I'll do you this favour but in future leave me out, Joey.

JOEY
Sorry you feel like that, Andy.

ANDY
Duval is stepping up the hunt. One of his witnesses died in hospital. You're number one in the frame now.
Better watch your step.

JOEY and ANDY shakes hands and part company.

LEON is a tall, slim, good-looking West Indian. He is sitting in a comfortable armchair, wearing a silk Charvet dressing-gown and smoking a Havana cigar. The room is expensively furnished in very bad taste. JOEY is escorted into the room by two black heavies.

LEON
What do you want with me, man?

JOEY
When these goons got their hands off me I'll tell you.

LEON
(to heavies)
Let him go.

(to Joey)
Right, You've got five minutes.

Very deliberately JOEY walks over to an armchair and sits facing LEON.

LEON
What's your name, mister?

JOEY
Bello. Joey Bello.

LEON
Never heard of you.

JOEY
I've heard of you.

LEON
Everybody's heard of me.

JOEY
You got quite a reputation.

LEON
That's right.

JOEY
Got quite a way with women, havn't you?

LEON
When I tell 'em to jump, they jump.

JOEY
And when you kill 'em, they stay killed.

LEON

Who's talking about killing?

JOEY

I am.

LEON

(menacingly)

You'd better explain yourself, mister. And make it good.

JOEY

Make it good? You fucking mackerel, you know what I'm talking about.

LEON

Watch your mouth. I've been cleared by the police. Who do you think you are?

JOEY

I'm the guy who's in the frame for murders that you've done.

LEON leaps to his feet and stands over JOEY, pointing a finger at him.

LEON

You rassclet. You walked into my kingdom but you'll be carried out of it.

LEON motions to the heavies. Before JOEY can rise they are on him and begin to beat him up.

LEON

Take him outside. I don't want blood on my carpets.

The heavies drag JOEY out of the room.

It is the following day. JOEY hobbles out of the main door of the hospital. He is supported by GERRY. JOEY's face is bruised and swollen, there is a plaster over one eye and his hands are bandaged.

GERRY

Now you gotta take it easy, Joey. The doc told me you gotta couple of busted ribs.

JOEY

Only a couple? Feels like they're all busted.

GERRY

You was lucky, Joey.

JOEY

That kind of luck I can do without.

GERRY

Things are in a bit of a two-and-eight down the club.

JOEY

What d'you mean?

GERRY

Business is bad. People are talking. Your name don't smell too sweet on the manor.

JOEY

Do you think I'm mixed up in this murder lark?

GERRY

Leave it out. Course not. You take it easy. I'll see to the club.

JOEY
Can't take it easy. There's a lot to be done. I'm gonna get to the bottom of this business.

GERRY
Come on. Let's get you home.
(shouts)
Taxi.

19. Scenario: Kill Joey Bello

JOEY stands on the station platform waiting for an eastbound train. Close to him is a man in his mid-twenties, hippy-style dress, long hair, wearing glasses. He has a vacant expression. A train pulls into the station, the doors open and JOEY steps into the carriage. The HIPPY is close behind him. JOEY takes a seat, the HIPPY sits opposite him, staring fixedly at him. JOEY, uneasy, gets up and moves to another seat. He takes a newspaper from his pocket, begins to read it, glancing occasionally at the HIPPY. Suddenly there is a piercing scream. JOEY looks up. The HIPPY is coming at him brandishing a long-handled Bowie knife. JOEY leaps to his feet and swings his briefcase against the HIPPY's head.

JOEY
(screams)
Bastard . . .

HIPPY
(roars)
Aargh . . .

The HIPPY stumbles. JOEY races down the carriage to the communicating door leading to the next carriage. The HIPPY pursues him. JOEY runs down the aisle between the seats. Other passengers cower, alarmed.

JOEY

Stop him . . . Somebody . . . Stop him. He's mad . . .

HIPPY

(screams)

Kill. Kill. Kill.

The train stops at a station. JOEY erupts from the carriage, runs down the platform towards the exit and mounts the stairs two at a time. At the top the HIPPY is close enough to make a lunge with the knife. JOEY swings his briefcase desperately at the HIPPY's head and connects. For a moment the HIPPY totters on the edge of the step then falls back, head over heels. He lands at the bottom of the stairs, out cold.

JOEY is in the flat with ELLEN. His hands are trembling as he pours himself a large whisky. JOEY joins ELLEN on the settee.

JOEY

That guy who attacked me. I can see the strength of it now.

ELLEN

What do you mean?

JOEY

Look, I'm number one in the frame for these murders, right? So I get bumped off. Well then the case is closed because I'm not around any more to deny anything. That's what I mean. There's a logic in it.

ELLEN

You reckon this feller was put up to kill you?

JOEY

Yes.

ELLEN

Who by? Duval?

JOEY

No. Not him. That's not his style.

ELLEN

Who, then?

JOEY

Dunno. Whoever's behind the murders.

ELLEN
(disbelieving)

Yeah.

ELLEN goes to window and peers through the curtains.

ELLEN

I wish that bloody police car would go away.

JOEY

I wish it would all go away.

JOEY is driving a battered Mini, following LEON's gold Cadillac. The Cadillac stops outside an exclusive block of flats in the West End. JOEY slots the Mini into a convenient parking space. LEON and JOEY alight from their respective motors. LEON goes through the entrance doors of the block and JOEY follows him. LEON enters the lift as JOEY, from a place in the lobby, watches the indicator. The lift stops at the sixth floor. JOEY waits.

The lift is descending from the sixth floor. JOEY moves forward and, as the lift doors open disclosing LEON, JOEY rushes him and forces him back into the lift. The doors close. JOEY struggles with LEON who draws a knife and cuts JOEY on the cheek. JOEY disarms LEON, knees him in the groin then batters LEON's head against the wall of the lift.

JOEY

Spill it, you black ponce, or this is your lot.

LEON

Spill what, man. I don't know nothing.

JOEY

You know about them murdered brasses.

LEON

I don't know nothing.

JOEY forces LEON to the floor and begins to beat his face in.

JOEY

Start talking.

LEON

OK man. I'll tell you.

JOEY

(shouts, threatening)

Tell me, you whorseson.

LEON

(terrified)

Yeah. Sure. I knew a couple of 'em. There's this doctor, see. Name's Matthew Gill. He's weird, man. You dig.?

JOEY

I dig. Go on.

LEON

I just supply the girls. I don't know no more. You ain't gonna touch him, man. There's powerful people behind him. He can't be got at. These people can roll over in their sleep and you and me is dead.

An elderly woman stands before the lift doors as they open. She sees JOEY bending over a blood-soaked LEON.

JOEY

My friend's fainted. Could you get him a glass of water?

JOEY, shirtless, is stretched out on an examination table in the consulting rooms of Dr Matthew GILL.

GILL

How long have you had these – er – pains?

JOEY

About a week.

GILL

(probing JOEY's back)

There doesn't seem to be anything seriously wrong.

(touches plaster on cheek)

Have you had a fall recently?

JOEY

No. That was just a little – er – misunderstanding.

GILL

Was this rather extensive bruising part of the – er – misunderstanding.

JOEY

You could say that.

GILL

By the way, what do you do for a living?

JOEY

Bit of this and a bit of that.

GILL

(smiling)

Well, I don't think you have much to worry about. You can get dressed now.

GILL goes to basin and washes his hands. JOEY rises from the table and puts on shirt and tie. He dons his jacket as GILL is wiping his hands on a snowy towel.

GILL

Sit down please, Mr Brown.

GILL moves to a chair behind the desk. JOEY sits facing him.

GILL

There's nothing organically wrong.

JOEY

I'm glad about that.

GILL

I'll prescribe some tablets which will ease the pain. I would recommend a few days bed rest. If that doesn't cure the trouble, come and see me again.

GILL scribbles on the prescription pad, tears off the sheet and hands it to JOEY.

JOEY

Thanks a lot. How much do I owe you?

GILL

Settle with the receptionist on your way out. And steer clear of misunderstandings in the future.

JOEY

I'll do that, doc. Goodbye.

JOEY walks down the Portobello Road. He is wearing a hat and dark glasses cover his eyes. He walks up the steps to the front doot of LEON's house and presses the bell-push. He waits for a while then cautiously pushes the door, which opens at his touch. He goes in and enters the sitting room. It is a horrific sight. LEON and his two minders are lying dead on the floor. The room is in disorder and there are great gouts of blood on the carpets and furniture. A shotgun is lying on the floor.

JOEY

(to himself)

Cor stone the crows. This is a turn-up for the book.

Joey is parked up in the Mini keeping watch on the house in which Gill has his consulting rooms. The front door of the house opens and GILL appears. He walks down the steps and continues down the street to the corner. JOEY gets out of the Mini and follows GILL round the corner and into a mews. GILL enters a mews house outside which is parked a white Jaguar. JOEY steps into a convenient doorway.

GILL merges from the mews house carrying a suitcase. He is accompanied by two attractive girls, one on either side.

GILL opens the rear door of the Jaguar and the girls get in. GILL puts the suitcase into the boot of the car and climbs into the driving seat. JOEY hurries back to the Mini and starts the engine. As he does so the Jaguar comes round the corner. JOEY falls in behind, keeping a reasonable distance. The Jaguar is being driven along the motorway at a moderate speed. JOEY falls in behind, still keeping his distance. The Jaguar leaves the motorway and turns into a narrow lane, then turns into a driveway leading to a large country house. JOEY drives up to the entrance to the drive, takes a good look around at a number of expensive motors parked there then does a U-turn and drives away.

JOEY pays a visit to GILL's mews house. Leaving the Mini parked nearby he makes an entry by means of a piece of celluloid and proceeds to search the place. He switches on the lights in the bedroom. The curtains are drawn. JOEY ferrets through the drawers of the dressing table, inspects the interior of the wardrobe. A heating vent over the bed catches his eye. He levers away the grill to uncover a cavity in which are a number of objects. He takes them out and puts them on the bed. There are jewellery cases, bundles of Treasury notes and a brown carrier bag. There are six video cassettes. JOEY looks at the titles and his eyes open in amazement.

JOEY
(a low whistle)
Right, Doctor Gill. I've got you now.

PUNCHIE's one room flat is no palace. There is a table, a couple of chairs and a bed in one corner of the main room. The central feature is a large colour television set. JOEY is sitting in one of the chairs. The door opens and PUNCHIE enters carrying a video player.

PUNCHIE

This bleeding thing weighs a ton. Come on. Get your arse off that chair and give us a hand.

JOEY jumps to his feet, takes the player from PUNCHIE and puts it on the table.

JOEY

Got the leads?

PUNCHIE

Give us a minute for Gawd's sake.

PUNCHIE takes a tangled mass of wires from his pocket.

PUNCHIE

Corblimey, boy. There must be a million Old Bill round the Angel club. They swagged Gerry away and closed the place down. They're mob-handed round your pad as well.

JOEY

What's the bad news?

PUNCHIE

There ain't none.

JOEY

I'm glad about that.

PUNCHIE

Never mind son. You're welcome here for as long as you like. Keep your head down. I'll look after you.

JOEY takes a roll of notes from his pocket, peels off a tenner and hands it to PUNCHIE.

JOEY

Here you are, Punchie. Have a drink on me.

PUNCHIE

You don't have to do that, boy.

JOEY

Take it.

PUNCHIE

Bless you, son.

JOEY plugs in the player to the TV set and takes cassettes from carrier bag.

JOEY is in a phone box. He is wearing a beret, dark glasses and a scarf over his mouth. He dials a number.

JOEY

Duval (pause) Joey Bello (pause) I've got some video tapes you ought to see.

There is a long tirade from the other end of the phone. JOEY listens patiently.

JOEY

No I won't bring them to you. I want a meet. Just you and me. Nobody else (pause) Right. Outside the Goat and Boots. Half an hour. See you.

JOEY hangs up, leaves the phone box.

JOE enters PUNCHIE'S flat followed by DUVAL.

DUVAL

If this doesn't check out I'm going to take you in. You know that?

JOEY

I'll take that risk, guv'nor. Sit down.

DUVAL sits in one of the chairs. JOEY switches on the video player. The tape runs for a while. Gradually an expression of horrified amazement comes over DUVAL's face. He grips the arms of his chair.

DUVAL

Alright. I've seen enough. Turn it off.

JOEY gets up, switches the set off.

JOEY

Turns your stomach, don't it?

DUVAL

It's unbelievable.

JOEY

You should see the rest of 'em. They make this one look like Blue Peter.

DUVAL

There are some well-known faces there. How the devil did they get on tape?

JOEY

Perhaps they didn't know. Perhaps Doctor bloody Gill likes slow-motion replays – or maybe he might need to put a bit of pressure on his important friends. You tell me. What do you know about this Doctor Gill?

DUVAL

I've heard the name. There's some MI5 connection. I

don't know why. I don't know who he works for.

JOEY

I don't give a bugger who he works for. You've got the evidence. Now use it.

DUVAL

I've got to get on to the Commander about this. I can't handle it my level.

JOEY

Look, I've lost me clubs, I've been beaten up, I've lost all me money, somebody tried to have me killed. I don't give a monkey's who you get on to so long as I get out of this bloody mess.

DUVAL

Get the tapes together, Joey. I'll phone the Commander now.

JOEY and DUVAL are standing beside DUVAL's car. JOEY carries the brown carrier bag.

JOEY

What kind of a feller is this Commander?

DUVAL

Well – he's a Commander in the Met. That speaks for itself.

JOEY

Bit unusual meeting him in the street like this, ain't it.

DUVAL

He's a very unusual fellow.

JOEY

Takes his bloody time, doesn't he?

DUVAL looks over to the other side of the street where a black cab is drawing up.

DUVAL

There he is now.

The COMMANDER, in plain clothes, gets out of the rear of the cab, followed by another man. They are joined on the pavement by the cab driver. JOEY and DUVAL cross the road to meet them.

COMMANDER

(to Duval)

Where are the tapes?

DUVAL turns to JOEY and holds out his hand. JOEY gives him the carrier, which DUVAL passes immediately to the COMMANDER.

COMMANDER

Are there any copies?

DUVAL give JOEY a questioning look.

DUVAL

Did you have them duped, Joey?

JOEY

Yes.

COMMANDER

(to Joey)

Where are the copies?

JOEY

In my lock-up.

COMMANDER

Where is that?

JOEY

Royal Docks.

COMMANDER

(turns to the two men)

Right. You two go with them. I'll follow.

DUVAL

(to Commander, quietly)

Can I have a word, sir?

COMMANDER

Well, what is it?

DUVAL

Isn't this slightly irregular, sir? Shouldn't we go back to the Yard?

COMMANDER

Don't argue, Duval. Just do what you're told.

DUVAL returns to his car, gets into the driver's seat. JOEY sits in the rear with the two men, one on either side of him.

DUVAL

Are you two on the Commander's staff?

There is no reply.

DUVAL

Funny. I haven't seen either of you before.

There is still silence.

JOEY

I think they're mutton, guv'nor.

DUVAL

Mute of malice probably.

The COMMANDER is speaking into a radiophone in the moving cab.

COMMANDER

I've told you. Repeat. The Royal Docks (pause) That's right (pause) Get them there right away. I don't want any slip-ups this time. Over and out.

DUVAL's car comes to a halt in front of the warehouse in which JOEY has left his Mercedes. DUVAL, JOEY and the two MEN get out of the car and almost immediately the black cab driven by the COMMANDER draws up alongside them. The COMMANDER leans out of the cab window.

COMMANDER

Duval. Over here.

(to the two men)

You two. Take Bello and get the tapes.

DUVAL

(quietly to Joey)

Something's wrong here, son. Be careful.

COMMANDER
(shouts)

Duval.

DUVAL

Coming sir.

JOEY is at the door of the warehouse. The two MEN stand close to him. JOEY takes out his keys, unlocks the padlock and pulls open one of the double doors. The three enter the warehouse. One of the MEN turns to JOEY enquiringly.

JOEY

You'll find what you're looking for at the bottom of that big box over there.

JOEY points to the rear of the warehouse and the two MEN begin to make their way there. JOEY picks up a heavy tyre lever and follows them. The first MAN to get to the box throws back the lid to get a look inside. The other man stands by. JOEY swings the tyre lever and connects with the head of the standing MAN. The other MAN hears the thud and looks up with an amazed expression as JOEY once more swings the tyrelever. The two MEN are out cold. JOEY goes to the door of the warehouse and looks out on to the wharf.

The area is completely deserted. DUVAL's car and the cab have disappeared. All is silent. JOEY comes away from the door of the warehouse and goes towards the Mercedes. Suddenly a length of heavy chain crashes to the floor in front of him, missing his head by inches.

JOEY looks round. Within a few yards are three men with evil grins on their faces. One of them is the HIPPY who attacked JOEY on the Underground. He is waving a knife. The others are swinging lengths of heavy chain. As they advance JOEY lets out a fearful scream.

JOEY

Aa-rrgh . . .

The attackers halt momentarily. JOEY makes a dash for the Mercedes, opens the door and leaps into the driving seat. The key is in the ignition. JOEY starts the engine, engages gear and the car moves forward. The attackers flail their chains against the body and windows of the car. JOEY puts his foot down, the car erupts through the partly-open doors and on to the wharf. Behind the warehouse a Jaguar comes into view and sets off in pursuit.

PUNCHIE reels out of the pub door. He is very drunk. He stands on the pavement looking around him.

PUNCHIE

(mumbling to himself)

The bastards. The bastards. The bastards.

PUNCHIE faces an imaginary opponent, shooting out lefts and rights.

PUNCHIE

Must get to Joey. Must get to him. Don't worry old pal. Punchie's coming.

PUNCHIE goes along the street, staggering and weaving from side to side. Occasionally he does a little skip, shooting out a left, crossing with a right. He literally runs into Gerry.

GERRY

Hold up, Punchie. You alright?

PUNCHIE

Alright? Alright? Don't worry about me. Course I'm alright. It's our pal Joey you should be worrying about.

GERRY

What do you expect me to do?

PUNCHIE

Help him out – like he's helped you out many a time. He was always ready to put his hand in his pocket for people round here. Now he's in trouble nobody wants to know. My life, Joey Bello's no killer.

GERRY

You can't do nothing for him, Punchie. Come on. Let's get you home.

PUNCHIE

Bugger getting me home. I'm going to find Joey.

The Mercedes is speeding along the dockside. The pursuing Jaguar is not far behind. Suddenly, out of nowhere, PUNCHIE reels into the road. The Mercedes swerves to avoid him but the Jaguar hits him fair and square, catapulting him into the air. His lifeless body crashes to the ground. The Jaguar carries on.

GILL and the COMMANDER sit in a quiet corner of the lounge of a gentleman's club. Brandy goblets are on the occasional table in front of them.

COMMANDER

Gill, you're a stupid man. Whatever possessed you to make those tapes?

GILL

Never mind about that. We've got them back, haven't we?

COMMANDER

There might be copies. You know what that means.

GILL

I know what it means. So do you.

COMMANDER

I do indeed. That's why we've got to get Bello.

GILL

Who is this Bello?

COMMANDER

He's the man who stole the tapes from you. A man with a long criminal record. Has a fresh knife-wound on his cheek. He's just the body we need to carry the can.

GILL

Fresh knife wound on his cheek? The fellow consulted me a few days ago.

COMMANDER

Ah. He's more enterprising than I thought.

GILL

So what's being done about him?

COMMANDER

Steps are being taken. It's only a matter of time. Unfortunately one of my Chief Superintendents is involved.

GILL

I've no doubt you can take care of that situation.

COMMANDER

It's already been attended to. DCS Duval has been transferred to the Robbery Squad – and Bello is as good as dead.

GILL

Fine. Now could I have my tapes back please.

COMMANDER

I think not.

GILL

Bello is not the only person to have access to copying facilities. Now may I please have the tapes.

The COMMANDER brings up the brown carrier bag from beside his chair and passes it to GILL.

GILL

Thank you very much.

COMMANDER

I trust they won't go astray again.

GILL

They won't. Now, if you'll excuse me I have an appointment. You'll keep me posted.

COMMANDER

I will.

The Mercedes is travelling at full speed along the by-pass, the Jaguar still in pursuit. A hand holding a gun protrudes from an open window in the Jaguar. half a dozen shots are fired in quick succession. JOEY's face is set in fierce concentration as he pilots the Mercedes into the back streets of Rainham, taking corners at high speed and keeping an eye on the driving mirror. He comes out on the open road once more. A look in the mirror shows no sign of his pursuers.

JOEY
(to himself)

Lost the bastards.

The Mercedes is travelling east. Behind the wheel JOEY relaxes. Looking in the mirror he sees a Daimler limousine pulling out to overtake. As the Daimler draws level JOEY glances at the uniformed chauffeur who appears to be alone in the vehicle. He is about to turn away when a movement in the rear of the Daimler catches his eye. A shotgun is being aimed at him from the back window. JOEY slams on the brakes and the Mercedes stops dead. The Daimler skids and slides off the road. JOEY treads on the gas and rapidly gets away from the scene.

The Mercedes, still travelling at high speed, is on the way to the Dartford Tunnel. It goes straight through the toll barriers and into the eerily-illuminated tunnel under the Thames then out at the other end heading for the Kent countryside. JOEY is pushing the car to its limit. From time to time his head nods and his attention wanders. Suddenly a front tyre bursts, the car swerves wildly from one side of the road to the other, then crashes through a fence and plunges into a valley. As the car rolls over and over JOEY is thrown out. The car ends up in flames.

A well-dressed, bearded man looks back at the terminal

building as he mounts the steps of the aircraft. The beard covers a livid scar on his cheek. To the sound of Elmore James' 'DUST MY BLUES' the airport recedes into the distance.

20. Costa Del Crime

Joey stretched out on the padded sun-lounger at the edge of the pool. Over at the bar Micky and a couple of chums were talking in low voices. There was a clink of ice against glass and an occasional burst of laughter. The white walls of the villa in the background reflected the glare of the Spanish sun on to the still surface of the pool.

The well-stacked blonde on the neighbouring lounger put out a hand and gently stroked the hairs on Joey's chest. He turned on his side and looked at her. She was certainly a dish, topless and with a tiny triangle of material that tantalisingly revealed almost everything – but not quite. She had an all-over tan which had certainly not been acquired in a few days.

Micky had introduced them the previous evening in a club in Marbella where a few faces had gathered for what they called 'a good drink'. The good drink turned into a riotous party, an anything goes affair in which everything went, including most of the girls' scanty clothing. The girl who was Joey's companion was taken back to the villa where she ended up in Joey's bedroom and where Joey gave her, in his own words, a good seeing-to. They were now recuperating in the mid-morning sunshine with large and well-iced gin and tonics within arm's reach.

Joey had arrived at Malaga airport the previous day. Micky, driving an ostentatious white Rolls, had whisked him off to the villa overlooking Puerto Banus. The welcoming committee included Danny and Peter whom he had last seen in Parkhurst. At the well-stocked poolside bar the drinks came fast and furious and there was much talk of the old days as Micky ensured that no glass remained empty for long. They ate at a magnificent buffet table laden with the best that the Costal del Sol had to offer in the shape of huge gambas, cold meats, a staggering variety of fish and a profusion of fruits. Bottles of Dom Perignon in ice-filled coolers were range at intervals on the snow-white tablecloth.

'Blimey,' said Joey to Micky. 'It's like something out of Dynasty.'

'Something out of Dynasty?' Micky hooted with laughter. 'My son, you ain't seen nothing yet.'

The afternoon was spent lolling round the pool. Iced tea was served by a Spanish maid. Ronnie and George turned up in a shining Mercedes and greeted Joey warmly.

'Always glad to see an old mate from the smoke,' said Ronnie. 'I think you'll like it out here.'

'Have much bother getting out?' asked George.

'No trouble,' said Joey. 'Got fitted out with a moody passport. Booked on a charter flight from Luton to Malaga. Micky picked me up at the airport and here I am.'

The talk turned on old times and old friends as the afternoon and early evening passed. Finally Micky hoisted himself from the lounger.

'Time to make a move,' he said.

'What's on?' enquired Joey.

'Little trip into town,' said Micky. 'Put your glad rags on, son.'

They were six-handed as they walked into the bar in Marbella. Micky led the way, followed by George, Ronnie, Peter and Danny. Joey brought up the rear. The Spanish proprietor moved quickly to greet his guests.

'Senor Micky. So nice to see you. Where you like to sit?'

Micky waved a hand towards a table in a discreet corner. A brace of waiters materialised, ushering their distinguished customers to their seats. At this comparatively early hour the bar was not crowded but it was immediately evident that this group of well-dressed patrons would be given preferential treatment.

'The usual, Pedro,' said Micky to the hovering proprietor.

'At once, senor,' said Pedro and in almost no time at all a half-dozen bottles of Dom Perignon appeared, each in its cooler. The entire waiting staff busied themselves opening the bottles and filling the sparkling glasses. Joey watched the performance.

'You got these monkeys well trained,' he said to Micky.

'I told you, son. You ain't seen nothing yet,' Micky replied.

The party went with a swing. As each bottle was finished another took its place, while Pedro danced attendance, supervising a constant flow of tapas.

It was Ronnie who proposed the next move.

'Fancy a bit of Indian?' he shouted above the general hubbub.

There was a chorus of assent.

'Right then. Off to my place.'

My place was a classy joint along the coast. George and Ronnie led the way in the Mercedes, Micky drove the Rolls with Joey in the front passenger seat and Danny and Peter in the rear. Headlights blazing, the two cars tore along the road with scant regard for any pedestrians who happened to get in the way.

'Don't you worry about the law?' asked Joey as the Rolls clipped the pavement and swerved towards an approaching vehicle.

'The law. Why should we worry. We pay their bleedin' wages,' said Micky.

There was no answer to that. Joey held on to the grab-handle on the dash and relapsed into silence.

The 'bit of Indian' was a revelation to Joey, accustomed as he was to the pseudoethnic flock papered establishments around the Portobello Road. Ronnie owned the joint, and no expense had been spared in its construction. Excellent decor, soft lights and muted music providing a setting in which very wealthy people ate the finest Indian cuisine and paid very handsomely for it.

Ronnie led the way into the restaurant, which was his right as the owner of the place. From that moment on everything went like clockwork. The service was impeccable, the food as near perfection as made no matter and the only discordant note in the proceedings was struck by Danny, who was by now rather under the influence. Taking exception to the manner of one of the waiters, he gave the offender a slap. Now a slap from Danny, a powerful man, was tantamount to a kick from a mule and the waiter went out for the count. The manager rushed to the scene, the unconscious man was fired before being carried out by two of his colleagues and the incident was closed.

Ronnie leaned over to Danny, his tone mildly remonstrative.

'You shouldn't have hit him in here, Danny,' he said. 'You should've taken him outside and given him a real belting.'

The next move was proposed by George, who suggested that they visit a club in Puerto Banus which was renowned for the quality and quantity of its high-class English birds. Micky put Joey in the picture.

'They're real classy bits of stuff,' he explained. 'Mummy and Daddy think they've got good jobs out here. What they're doing is opening their legs for the Arabs and anybody else with money. Some of 'em are making fortunes.'

'Lead me to it,' said Joey. 'I could do with a bit of the other.'

The club provided action in no uncertain manner. Champagne flowed like water, the music was loud and erotic, and groping on the dance floor appeared to be compulsory. Micky brought a cracking blonde over to the table and introduced her to Joey, accompanying the introduction with a wink that spoke volumes. It was in the early hours of the morning that the party broke up. Micky drove Joey and the blonde back to the villa and, after a nightcap, left them to their own devices.

That was Joey's introduction to the Costa del Crime. He loved every minute of it.

Joey opened his eyes as a shadow came between him and the sun. Micky was standing over him.

'Wake up, Joey,' he said. 'Business.'

'Right, Micky.'

Micky jerked a thumb at the blonde.

'Finished with her?' he asked.

'For the time being,' Joey replied.

Micky reached into the back pocket of his gaudy shorts. His hand emerged clutching a roll of notes from which he peeled several. Bending down, he tweaked the blonde's nipple at the same time thrusting the notes down the front of the scanty scrap of cloth covering her pubes.

'There y'are, love,' he said. 'Buy yourself something nice. Paco'll drive you back to town.'

The blonde got up from the lounger and sauntered towards the Rolls standing in the driveway. Over her shoulder she tossed a nonchalent 'so long, fellers'.

'Good sport, that kid,' said Micky. 'Give you a good time, did she?'

'Very tasty,' said Joey.

'Right. Come over to the bar. Bit of business.'

The two men strolled over to the bar, which was now deserted. Micky mixed a couple of stiff gin and tonics.

'Now then, Joey,' he said. 'You're on the firm.' He produced his roll of notes, peeled off half without counting and handed them to Joey, who made a quick mental calculation and concluded that he had copped for a couple of grand at least.

'You won't go short of money,' Micky went on. 'There's plenty of it about. A couple of dozen of us got out here before the extradition and we pretty well run this part of Spain. We've got the law straightened. It costs but it's worth it. All you have to do is settle down, work with me and in six months you'll have your own villa. How's that for starters?'

'Sounds fine,' said Joey.

'Right. We'll have a bit of lunch and then I'll take you down to the harbour and show you my little boat. We won't be late up tonight. Early tomorrow we go fishing.'

Joey looked puzzled. 'What's wrong with buying fish?' he said.

Micky laughed. 'Wait till you see what we catch,' he said.

After lunch the two of them drove down to the harbour at Puerto Banus. The little boat turned out to be a fifty-foot ocean-going yacht with all the comforts of home, a spacious saloon, luxurious sleeping quarters and a well-equipped galley. Joey met the skipper, a bearded Scot with a limited vocabulary and a smell of Barlinnie jail about him.

'All ready for tomorrow, Jock?' asked Micky.

Jock nodded and grunted something that sounded like 'aye'.

'See you then. Seven o'clock,' said Micky. 'Come on, Joey.'

The following morning they drove to the harbour in Micky's second car, a gleaming black Porsche. The engine of the yacht were already turning over as they went aboard. The deck-hand, a young Spaniard burnt almost black by the sun, cast off the moorings and the vessel headed out into the Mediterranean. Micky and Joey stood by the skipper on the bridge. Pedro, the deck-hand, served them with steaming mugs of coffee.

They had been underway for an hour when Jock looked at the chronometer mounted above the compass, then checked his position on the chart beside him.

'We're here,' he grunted.

Micky took the binoculars from the case slung round his neck and scanned the expanse of ocean ahead. After a few moments he removed the glasses from his eyes.

'Over there,' he said, pointing to port.

Jock reduced speed and turned the wheel. Joey could now see quite clearly a thin plume of smoke rising from the water some two hundred yards away. As Jock brought the yacht alongside the source of the smoke Joey could see the canister floating on the waves.

Pedro stood by with a boathook and deftly hoisted the canister aboard. Attached to the canister was a thin wire hawser which he pulled in hand over hand. A bulky oilskin-wrapped package broke the surface. Pedro hauled it on to the deck. He disconnected the canister, shut off the smoke signal and looked up at the bridge.

'Got it,' said Micky.

The skipper shut down the engines and the yacht drifted lazily in the slight swell. Pedro went aft and rummaged in a locker from which he produced a number of fishing lines.

He busied himself baiting them before throwing them over the stern.

Joey and Micky stepped down from the bridge on to the deck, where Micky gave the package a close inspection. He called to the skipper.

'All in order, Jock', he yelled.

He turned to Joey, who was now in no doubt about the nature of the fishing trip.

'Let's go below and have a drink,' said Micky.

They came on deck an hour later. The package had been stowed away in the bottom of a gunny sack and covered with a load of wriggling fish. Pedro returned the fishing lines to the locker, Jock started the engines and the yacht headed back to Puerto Banus.

They came ashore, Pedro carrying the gunny sack. The uniformed man on the dock gate saluted.

'Buenos dias, senors,' he said. 'Good fishing?'

Micky laughed and waved a hand towards the sack.

'Mucho good,' he said.

Back at the villa Micky tipped out the fish on the floor of the kitchen, extracted the package and put it on a table. Unwrapping several layers of oilskin, he finally came to the inside contents, a number of transparent plastic packets filled with a white powder.

'There we are,' he said. 'Take a look at that, Joey. Coke. Ninety per cent pure. When it's cut on the street – how much?'

Joey hazarded a guess. 'Half a million?'

Multiply that by six, my son, and you're right,' said Micky. 'Three million quid. That's what this little lot's worth.'

'How many trips do you make a month?' Joey asked.

'Average, two,' said Micky.

'Blimey,' said Joey.

*

After the initial experience, life for Joey fell into a routine. Days of over-eating and over-drinking, nights spent bonking the nubile young ladies of Marbella, long periods of lazing in the sun round the pool and the occasional trip out to sea on the yacht. Despite a daily work-out in the villa's gym he began to put on weight, and he derived little satisfaction from the fact that his bank balance increased in direct proportion to the size of his belly. Waking one morning he decided that he had had enough of the good life. He knew there were more than thirty men in Spain who were on the British wanted list. Not one of them had any financial worries but each and every one of them would welcome a chance to return to England. They were only deterred by the prospect of doing quite a lot of bird.

At the poolside bar he had a chat with Micky.

'I'm going back to London,' he said.

'Don't be a fool,' said Micky. 'Over here you're protected, you're in the organisation. Back in London you're on your own. You've upset the wrong people and they'll move heaven and earth to put you out of the way.'

'I'll take my chance,' Joey replied. 'I've got enough cash to hire the best, and I've still got a few tricks up my sleeve. I've made up my mind. I'll be on the side of law and order. If those people want a fight, then that's what they'll get.'

Micky shook his hand.

'If that's what you want, OK,' he said. 'We don't like to lose a good man, but that's the way things go. Good luck to you, Joey.'

Joey couldn't wait to get back to the Old Smoke. He was well aware of the fact that trouble was waiting, but he looked forward to the coming fight with relish. He was not afraid.

England. Autumn. Season of mists and mellow fruitfulness, as the poet said.

London, here I come.

JUDGE ME NOT

JOE CANNON

In this book, the final volume of the trilogy following BORN ROTTEN and ENGLAND'S TOUGHEST VILLAIN, the saga of Joey Bello continues.

Here the author draws on his considerable knowledge of sophisticated crime to give a picture of computer frauds carried out by Bello and his confederates. While not being a guide to the essential elements of this type of crime, the fiction presented here has a basis in fact, as any computer hacker will know.

A chapter of this book is devoted to a fictionalised account of the probable circumstances surrounding the murder on the Costa del Sol of Great Train Robber Charlie Wilson. Amid a welter of speculation, the author's informed opinion is as good as any and better than most. He opens a window on criminal activity which has hitherto been securely locked and bolted.

Price £4.50

Yellow Brick Publishers
2 Lonsdale Road
Queens Park
London NW6 6RD

ENGLAND'S TOUGHEST VILLAIN

JOE CANNON

Gripping, exciting, and often horrifying, this is the story of Joey Bello, an ex-criminal, who wages his own personal war against corruption in the highest places: the untouchable echelons of our own police force and especially the Mafia.

Joey Bello fights on his own terms. He meets violence with violence, brutality with brutality.

ENGLAND'S TOUGHEST VILLAIN opens a window into the sub-culture of the underworld, introducing the reader to a side of life which he would ordinarily and otherwise not see: a world of thieves jargon and evil deeds, where danger lurks in dark corners and where the threat of death is ever present: a world in which a sawn-off shotgun is no respecter of persons: where a .45 automatic is a great leveller.

Price £4.50

Yellow Brick Publishers
2 Lonsdale Road
Queens Park
London NW6 6RD